AN IMMORTAL'S PAIN

AN IMMORTAL'S PAIN

CHRONICLES OF AN URBAN DRUID BOOK 7

AUBURN TEMPEST
MICHAEL ANDERLE

This book is a work of fiction. All of the characters, organizations, and events portrayed in this novel are either products of the author's imagination or are used fictitiously. Sometimes both.

Cover by Fantasy Book Design

A Michael Anderle Production

LMBPN Publishing
PMB 196, 2540 South Maryland Pkwy
Las Vegas, NV 89109

First edition, April 2021
Version 1.04, April 2022
eBook ISBN: 978-1-64971-695-8
Print ISBN: 978-1-64971-696-5

THE AN IMMORTAL'S PAIN TEAM

Thanks to our JIT Team:

Dave Hicks
James Caplan
Diane L. Smith
Dorothy Lloyd
Micky Cocker
John Ashmore
Deb Mader
Debi Sateren
Jeff Goode
Kelly O'Donnell
Rachel Beckford
Larry Omans
Paul Westman

Editor
SkyHunter Editing Team

Beart de reir ar mbriathar. Glaine ar gcroi. Neart ar ngeag.

CHAPTER ONE

"Happy Bone-iversary, boys." I swipe the hotel keycard through the slot and lead the way inside. The room is elegant with ten-foot ceilings and decorated in a classic French chateau-style. It's fancy with gold-gilded mirrors, crystal chandeliers, and vintage furnishings. It's everything I paid extra for. "King-size canopy bed, double Jacuzzi tub, raindrop shower, complimentary canapes, and an in-room fireplace. This weekend, we're living it up."

Calum and Kevin follow me inside and grin at the velvety rose petals scattered on the bed and the chocolate-dipped strawberries awaiting them on the nightstand. "Wow, you went all out, Fi. This is awesome."

"You two deserve it. What good is being a Governor of the Lakeshore Guild if I don't take advantage of the perks and treat the people I love?" I leave them looking around to go check out the view from their window. "Look, we can see the Rideau Canal and Confederation Park from your room."

Calum's smile grows even wider when he joins me and spots the people milling around at the Winterlude events below. "I'm so freaking excited about the ice sculptures. I've always wanted to come to see them."

The incessant *creak, creak, creak* of a squeaky wheel announces Sloan's arrival in the hall. The elevator was too small for all of us and the luggage trolley, so my valentine waited for the next lift.

"You found us." I abandon the sight-seeing view of Ottawa's yearly winter carnival and rush to help him with the bags. "Did you have any trouble? I was worried that bell captain might be looking at us a little too closely."

He shakes his head, moves a throw blanket off the top of the luggage pile, and points at our animal carrier duffle. "The man is simply intense about his concierge duties. Daisy was perfect, and no one is any the wiser that Calum's girl is in the hotel."

"Of course, she was perfect." I hand him the keycards for our room across the hall, take Daisy's duffle into the room, and set her on the bed.

Calum gets things unzipped and lifts out his fluffy black and white skunk companion. "Look how nice our room is, baby girl." He cradles her against his chest and takes her for a tour. "Are you excited about your first vacation?"

Kevin collects the rest of their bags from the cart and unpacks Daisy's bowls. He sets them on the floor at the end of the dresser and takes her little litterbox into the bathroom. "You're all set, sweetie."

"Don't forget her pill," I say. The wee woodland stinker has epilepsy and inadvertently sprays if she has a convulsion. Thankfully, Gran has the remedy, and there's no issue as long as she gets her medication. "Let's try not to have any aroma accidents in the historic luxury hotel, 'kay?"

Calum kisses his girl and sets her on the sofa by the window. "I'll put out the Do Not Disturb sign now, so no unwanted visitors startle her. Other than that, what could possibly go wrong?"

"Funny guy." My brothers have all taken to saying that around me. They think it's hilarious that I now attract danger and disaster like killer bees to a honey farm.

It's slightly less hilarious for me.

I set their keycards on the dresser by the TV and blow them a kiss. "We have an hour and a half until our dinner reservation downstairs, so settle in and enjoy. We'll meet up in the hall and go down together."

"Sounds good." Calum sends Kevin a searing look and starts unbuttoning his shirt. "Are we coming back up between dinner and going out to the sculptures?"

"Yeah, then we don't have to take our coats and everything to dinner." I laugh as Kevin pushes his jeans down his thighs. "Seriously, guys. You live together. Can't you wait the two minutes until I'm out of the room?"

"It's our bone-iversary, sista." Calum waggles his ebony brows at me. "There's no slowing this love train."

I turn on my heel and hurry for the door. "For the rest of the world, it's known as Valentine's Day. You could call it that, you know?"

"Where's the fun in that?" Calum finishes unbuttoning his shirt and shucks it off his shoulders as he waves me out. "Don't let the door hit you in the ass."

I'm still chuckling as I grab the last bag off the luggage trolley and join Sloan across the hall in our room. Our accommodations are the same as theirs but decorated in cornflower blues instead of golds. "Not too shabby, eh?"

I booked us the same "Romantic Getaway Package" as I booked for Kev and Calum. It's amazing, and yet I still wonder if the impact hits him. It's tough to impress a rich boy who grew up in a castle.

"It's lovely." Sloan exits the bathroom. "I unpacked our toiletries and hung up the things that should hang. I found these on the counter too."

He hands me a super soft and fluffy bathrobe with the hotel

insignia embroidered on the shoulder in navy blue silk. "Noice. I look forward to putting it on. Speaking of being nakey, are we breaking in the room before dinner?"

"Definitely. Let me take the cart down and return it to the bell desk taskmaster first. I'm quite certain he's timin' me and will track me down if I don't return it to him directly."

"Have a lot of trolley thefts, do they?"

"Crime is risin' everywhere in the big city. First, it's trolleys, the next thing ye know people will be stealin' planters from the lobby."

"Well, better you deal with him now than having him up here in twenty minutes knocking at our door."

He bites his bottom lip and grins. "Very true."

I meander over to check out our view. Kevin and Calum's is better, but I don't care. I'm not here to look out the window. "All right. I vote we enjoy the Jacuzzi and the fluffy robes first, then test the mattress."

Sloan grins. "I like the way ye think, Cumhaill. I'll be right back. Don't start anything interestin' without me."

I laugh and hand him one of the door cards. "No promises, Mackenzie. I'm an independent girl."

Our hour and a half together fly by and though everything in me wants to lounge around naked with the fireplace turned on while eating chocolate-dipped strawberries, I relent and get dressed for dinner.

"This is a working holiday," Sloan says as the four of us slide into the elevator and push the button for ground level. "Leviathans to track down and murderers to catch."

Calum chuckles. "Tomorrow starts a working holiday. Tonight it's still our bone-iversary."

Sloan laughs. "Ye really like sayin' that word, don't ye?"

"You mean the word that describes the tenth anniversary of the first time we boned? Yes, I do." Calum grins and swoops his hand through the air before us. "Picture this. Two awkward and shy sixteen-year-old boys—"

Kevin snorts. "Neither of us was awkward, and you've never been shy a day in your life."

Calum sends him a look and starts again. "Two tortured souls yearning for more—"

Kevin laughs again. "Start with two drunk and horny teenaged boys and go from there."

"Tough crowd. Fine. Two drunk and horny boys get roped into a double date with two girls from school."

"Our dates were the girls, not each other," Kevin adds. "And we weren't drunk when we got roped into taking them to the party."

"But we were horny."

"We were sixteen. Of course, we were horny."

Calum laughs and flashes Kev a grin. "Do you want to tell the story?"

"Honestly, yes. I think that's best." Kevin sweeps his hand through the air as Calum did. "Two horny, sixteen-year-old boys get roped into a Valentine's Day party at Johnny McMarten's place. We were the catches of grade ten, and all bets were on us making Kimmie and Michelle two very happy girls that night."

"Until the drunk part of the night," Calum interjects. "Then it was the old bait-and-switch."

Kevin nods. "It was. The two of us wandered away from the girls to discuss our plan for getting laid."

"We were both still figuring ourselves out and kinda freaked out about getting too close and personal with girls. Because, ew, not our thing."

"No offense," Kevin says to Sloan.

Sloan laughs. "None taken."

Kevin grins and gets back to his story. "So, two angsty

teenagers head down to the basement and end up having a private party in Mr. McMarten's carpenter's workshop."

Calum smiles. "To this day, the smell of wood shavings still makes me randy."

Now it's my turn to laugh. "I've had the bedroom next to yours for our entire lives. You don't need pine shavings to make you randy. You two have always had great chemistry."

"That's why it's so important to celebrate the important moments." Kevin winks at my brother.

"Like the bone-iversary," he says.

"Exactly."

The elevator doors open, and I laugh at Sloan's face. "Sorry you asked, aren't you?"

"A little. Only someone in your family would celebrate something called a bone-iversary."

"I know. Great, isn't it?"

Dinner in the hotel restaurant is way too good, and I eat way too much for a night of romance. I'm glad I said we'd go back up to our rooms before we go out to see the ice sculptures because I need to change out of my dressy pants and into my stretchy pants. "We need to walk for a few hours and burn off dinner, or I'll fail our first Valentine's Day."

Sloan chuckles and pulls on his jacket. "Not possible. Even if yer too bloated to do anything but flop on our bed, this is already the best Valentine's Day I've ever had."

"Excellent. So the bar is already met. That takes the pressure off."

I finish folding my slacks over the hanger as my phone rings. Pulling it out, I frown at the unknown caller on the screen. It's a 353 exchange code, the same as Gran's and Granda's so I accept the call. "Hello?"

"Hello. Is this Fiona?"

"It is."

"Grand. I'm ringin' ye to wish ye a Happy Valentine's Day, luv. Yer man Sloan said ye'd get a kick out of a call."

I arch a brow at Sloan and chuckle. "He did, did he? Who am I speaking to?"

"It's Niall Horan. Sloan says yer a bit of a fan."

All blood drops from my head and the room spins. "No way. You can't... Are you serious? Niall Horan." My voice cracks pitchy at the end as my heart stumbles in my chest.

His deep chuckle on the other end of the line makes all the butterflies in my very full belly flutter at once. "I *am* serious, yeah. Now, I won't keep ye because I know ye've got yer romantic weekend away, but I wanted to wish the two of ye well. Sloan's aces. I look forward to singin' at the weddin'. He says that's been yer plan fer a few years."

My jaw drops. "Seriously? Ohmygawd, I don't even care if you're teasing me." I brush a trembling hand over my forehead. "Thank you for taking the time. Yes, I'm a huge fan."

"My pleasure. Give my regards to yer man, and I'll talk to ye again another time."

"I will. Thank you. Seriously, you made my decade."

That deep chuckle sounds again, and I can imagine his smile on the other end. "Well, good, then. *Slán leat.*"

"*Slán leat,*" I echo, wishing him good health.

When the call ends, I stare at the phone for a moment. Then my wits return, and I save that number into my contacts. "Ohmy-gawd, I have Niall Horan's number on my phone." I blink up at Sloan holding my coat and chuckling, and launch. "Best boyfriend, evah! Mind blown, Mackenzie."

His chest bounces against mine as he winks. "I'm glad ye liked yer surprise."

"We said no gifts, though. This weekend is supposed to be our gift to each other."

"A few calls made is all it was. It didn't cost me anything, and it was as much fer my pleasure as it was fer yers."

"Your pleasure for sure. Let's bag the ice sculptures and stay in."

Sloan laughs and helps me into my coat. "As tempting as that sounds, no. Yer brother and I are quite excited about seein' the exhibits. The room awaits us upon our return. Until then, educate me on yet another Canadian wonder."

I slide my feet into my boots. "Okay, yeah, Winterlude is a big thing. I think the highest attendance topped one and a half million visitors."

"That's a lot of people looking at ice."

I free my hair from the collar of my coat and tuck my scarf around my neck. "There's more than that. There are three sites running events over three weeks. Most stuff happens on the weekends, but there are skating races up the Rideau, snow sculptures and ice parks for kids, triathlon races, snowshoeing excursions, fat bike rides. Anything and everything to celebrate the season."

Checking that I have a keycard, I slide it into my wallet and loop my purse's strap over my head.

The boys have their door propped open and are ready to roll. "What took you guys so long?"

My cheeks ache from smiling too wide. "I got a Happy Valentine's Day call from Niall Horan."

The two of them chuckle and grab their gloves.

"You knew?"

Calum shrugs. "I'm glad it worked out for you, Fi. Irish went to a lot of trouble arranging it."

I eye Sloan. "A few quick calls, eh? You're not supposed to lie to your valentine."

His grin is unrepentant. "It was worth every bit of stress to see the look on yer face."

I laugh. "You mean when I almost passed out."

"It was a bit dodgy there for a moment, wasn't it?"

"We gotta take care of our girls," Calum says.

"Is Daisy all good?" I peer into their room.

"She's in her glory." Calum grips the door and nudges away the book they were using as a door stop. Kev joins us in the hall, and we wait until it clicks shut. "She's nibbling away on our left-overs and plans to curl up in her bed by the fire for a quiet night."

"Excellent. Then we're all set."

Chatter and excitement for our night out consume the four of us. We leave the hotel and cross the street to join the crowds at Confederation Park. The night isn't warm by any stretch of the imagination, but we were told by the lady at the check-in desk that this is ideal weather for the artists to produce inspiring work.

"Where do we want to start?" Kevin asks.

I scan the closest competition entries and point at one that catches my eye. The first one we come to is a life-sized grouping of a native man with a hide drum, a polar bear reared up on his hind paws, and a child playing on the ice next to a harp seal. It's lit from below and glows white against the backdrop of the night sky.

"It's stunning," Sloan says.

"This one is called Spirit of the North." I read the particulars from the competition sheet the volunteer handed to me. "The artist is from Nunavut and declares this a celebration of the land and animals of Mother Earth."

Sloan circles the platform, looking at it from another angle. "I understand the excitement now. This is unbelievable."

"Right?" Calum is grinning like a kid on Christmas morning. "These are entries into the national competition. I'm glad I don't have to judge them."

When everyone has finished admiring the Spirit of the North, we move on, and I read the next description. "This one is by a guy from Whistler, BC. It's called Shredding the Slopes."

Calum and Kev move in to check out the snowboarder kicking up curls of snow. He's got his legs kicked back and is grabbing his board behind his back, suspended in the air.

"It makes me wish I got into snowboarding," Calum says.

I laugh. "I suppose that's the sign of a well-crafted piece. It's inspiring you."

Sloan and I linger a little longer at the snowboarding sculpture while the boys move on to a pair of reindeer about to engage their antlers in a headbutt.

"Hey, check out her rack," Kevin says.

I snort and roll my eyes. "I can't take them anywhere."

Sloan slides in behind me and sets his chin on the top of my head. "Happy Valentine's Day, *a ghra*."

"Happy Valentine's Day, hotness." I hug his arms where they cross my chest. "I'm glad you stuck around long enough to adapt to my kind of crazy."

"I love yer kind of crazy. Every day is an adventure, Fi."

I chuckle. "Not always good ones."

"Maybe not, but I wouldn't trade them fer anything." He slides his hand back and turns it palm up, showing me a black velvet ring box. "Don't panic. I'm not askin' ye to marry me."

I choke and suck in a breath. "Thank you for saying that. I was about to have a heart attack and freak out."

His deep chuckle behind me helps me steady. "It's a Valentine's gesture fer both of us. Nothing worth cardiac arrest."

Thank you, baby Yoda. "All righty, then. I'm excited." He opens the ring box and holds it in front of me for me to admire. Two platinum bands nestle in the padded slots.

I'm back to panicking. "Those look like wedding bands."

"Well, they're not. Claddagh bands *can* be for marriage, or dating or the closest of friends."

All right, I knew that.

Auntie Shannon and her best girlfriend have matching

Claddagh rings. I pull off my glove and take out the smaller one. It has the traditional crown for loyalty, heart for love, and hands for friendship, as well as two words engraved into the design, *A GHRA*.

"They're beautiful, and it's a lovely gift. Thank you."

"Yer welcome. They're not just decorative. I had Dora spell them with a locator so the next time ye disappear, we'll have a way to find ye."

Smart man. "All righty, then, I'll never take it off."

He circles me so we're standing face-to-face. "Now, the question is, what finger and what direction?"

Claddagh rings have been a Celtic tradition since the seventeenth century. It's said if you wear it on the right hand with the heart facing out, you're single, and facing in, you're dating. If you wear it on the left hand with the heart facing out, you're engaged, and facing in, you're married.

"Well, we're not single, and we're not married." I narrow the choices in half and start us off.

"True. My query comes from the two choices left. We live together and share a house, so we're more than dating, and yet we're not engaged."

"And it's much too soon, and too much pressure to say the word engaged when we're still learning about ourselves." My words come out with more force than I meant, but he doesn't seem offended.

Calum snorts while looking over my shoulder. "Hilarious. Say what you want, but the two of you are practically married. You live together in the house he bought for you when he moved across the ocean to be with you. Left hand out."

I frown at my brother. "He bought the house for many reasons, not only to make me happy...and we're not engaged."

He shrugs and wraps his arm across Kevin's shoulder. "Don't be defined, baby girl. Make your rings mean what *you* want them to mean."

I check with Sloan, and he seems to read my panic. "It's all right, *a ghra.* Right hand in."

Now I feel bad. "Is it all right? I agree we're more than dating, but I'm not ready to give it a name."

"There is no right or wrong, Fi, only what is or isn't."

Kevin snorts. "Thanks, Yoda."

Sloan ignores the snickering of the peanut gallery and offers me a smooth smile. "I'm in no rush to be anywhere beyond right where we are." He takes the band from my hand and slides it on my finger. Then, he takes out the companion band and slides it on his. "I thought about a diamond or an emerald fer yer gemstone but figured the band works better when wielding Birga."

Kevin traps my fingers and tugs my hand to get a closer look. "Not every girl has to worry about the sensibility of her jewelry based on spear battles."

I giggle. "I'm cut from a different cloth."

"Definitely." Kevin releases my fingers and smiles. When he straightens, he looks at Calum and asks him an unspoken question.

Calum rolls his eyes. "Fine. You'll never last until we're home anyway. Go ahead."

Kevin turns back to us and grins. "Unlike the two of you, we *are* engaged. Calum asked me before dinner."

I squeal and launch into Kevin's arms. "Congrats, Kev. I'm so happy for you. It's about time."

When Kevin sets me back on my feet, I repeat the congratulatory embrace with my big brother. "You're a smart man, making it official. Kev's a keeper."

"Yeah. He is."

Give them my congratulations, Red. Bruin says to me.

"Bruin wishes you both congratulations." I rub the flutter in my chest. "When we get back to our rooms, we'll have a celebratory drink before parting for the night."

Calum wraps his arm around the back of my neck and kisses my temple. "Don't tell anyone. We want to announce it on Wednesday night when everyone's gathered at the house for game night."

I twist my fingers over my lips and throw away the key. "All right. We've been standing in one spot too long. My toes are numb. Let's see the rest of the sculptures, then go thaw out in front of our fireplaces."

"A great plan." Sloan drops the empty ring box back into his jacket pocket.

I pull my glove back on and sigh. It's a shame to cover up my new ring, but it would be worse if I got frostbite and my fingers fell off. All kidding aside, with my talent for drawing chaos, it could happen.

CHAPTER TWO

Morning comes, and I blink through the gray haze at the ceiling. Why am I wide awake? What time is it? I lift my arm and check the time. Damn. I'm up earlier than Sloan. I close my eyes. It sets the world on unsteady footing for me to wake up before him. I should go back to sleep.

However, *deciding* I should go back to sleep doesn't mean I *do* go back to sleep. I lie there and listen to the steady in-and-out breaths of Bruin sleeping on the rug by the window. Sloan's breathing is soft and shallow on the pillow beside me.

I keep my eyes closed, listening to the clicks and ticks and distant hollow noises that plague hotels.

It's funny how you learn the little house sounds of home and hotel sounds are never quite the same. Is that why I'm up? I don't think so.

My Spidey senses are tingling, but I have no idea why.

Giving up on sleep for the moment, I roll out of bed and shrug into the hotel robe. I pad over to the window, sidestep around my bear, and pull back the curtain to look outside.

Nothing out of the ordinary...other than me looking out the window at five in the morning.

My shield isn't weighing in on anything, so I don't think there's anything to be alarmed about, but over the past eight months, I've learned to trust my instincts.

I let the curtain fall back into place, head to the other end of the room, and look out the door's peephole. The warped and wonky view of the hallway and Calum's and Kevin's door tells me nothing.

"What is it, *a ghra?*" Sloan's voice is rough and graveled with sleep. "Are ye all right?"

I abandon my five a.m. tour of our hotel room and head back to bed. Unwilling to give up the comfort and protection of the robe, I climb back under the covers as-is.

Sloan pulls me close, and I snuggle in. "It's nothing, I'm sure. Likely a bad dream or something woke me up."

My words don't sound convincing even to me, but I'm stumped. With no idea why things feel off, I push the sensation away and close my eyes. Maybe I can get another hour or two before we get up and start our murder investigation.

That would be nice. I hate tracking down murderers when I'm overtired.

Morning comes too soon, and before I know it, the four of us are headed toward P1 to get my truck and hit the road. "All right, folks, here's what we know. Arthur Lloyd Montclair was a highly-respected private solicitor here in Ottawa. He was a long-time star of Emeril, Schmitt, and Cline until he suddenly quit and moved to Toronto."

"That didn't work out well for him," Calum says.

"No, it did not." I think about the violent leviathan attack at Kevin's art gallery and my heart hurts. Kev did great, but we all hate that he got caught in the crosshairs of an empowered conflict. "As much as I like that Toronto doesn't have a population of leviathan, we need to figure out why they followed Montclair to our home turf and beat the snot out of him."

"If they only wanted to kill him, they could've done that with quick efficiency. Instead, they drew it out."

"They wanted him to suffer," Kevin says.

"Or they wanted him to talk," Sloan adds.

Calum nods. "I've gone over the autopsy report Garnet provided us from the Guild lab. They didn't find anything remarkable about the injuries or the man to raise any flags."

"Other than the fact that leviathans tracked him down and pulped him in my place of employment," Kevin adds.

"Yeah, other than that. He was a human who, despite having high cholesterol and psoriasis, would have lived another forty years if he hadn't gotten dead."

After we hit Tim Horton's and get our breakfast sandwiches and coffee, we get back on the road.

I point at the ten-story steel-and-glass building out the front windshield of my SUV once we get to where we're going. "That's us. According to Google street view, there's a parking lot entrance on the west side."

Sloan follows my instructions and hits the indicator to take us there. When we're parked and ready to roll, the four of us step out of the truck and brave the elements at once.

"Man, I hate winter." Kevin snaps the furred collar of his black bomber jacket up to block the buffeting wind. His perfect, blond hair flips in the gusts and falls back into place as if it's been trained and knows what to do. "It's a cold one."

Calum slips in beside him and takes his hand. A moment later, the tension in Kevin's frame dissolves.

"*Inner warmth*?" I ask.

My brother smiles. "One of my favorites."

"True story."

The foyer of the office building is the same as any other. It's a vast open space with shiny floors, window walls facing a busy street, and the sound of clacking heels and male voices echoing off all the hard surfaces.

After a brief look around, we strike off toward the long reception desk facing the glass, double-door entry. It takes a moment for the man behind the desk to finish what he's working on, then he looks up. "What can I help you with?"

Calum flashes his shield. "Can you direct us to Emeril, Schmitt, and Cline?"

"Toronto PD," he says, checking out his badge. "You're a long way from home."

True story. Door-to-door from our place to the hotel took us five and a half hours. It's why we decided to come on Friday and leave Monday. That way we don't forfeit any of our weekend while traveling.

"Unfortunately, this is an official visit. So, Emeril, Schmitt, and Cline?"

He tilts his head to his left. "Sign here."

Calum grabs the pen and fills in the boxes.

The security guy checks the sign-in sheet and nods. "Eighth floor. Left out of the elevator. You can't miss it."

We back away and get our groove on.

"Hold up." He waves us back. "*He* showed me a badge and signed in. We don't have an open door here. Who are you three?"

I grin and turn back to address the man's concerns. Inwardly, the kid in me is jumping up and down clapping. Outwardly, I play it cool.

I pull my shiny new badge and flash it.

He frowns and curls his finger in the air, beckoning me closer. I hand over my Team Trouble ID and meet his gaze. Maybe it's silly, but everyone else in my family has a badge. I like having one too.

"What's SITFO? Never heard of it."

"It stands for Special Investigations Task Force of Ontario. It's a hand-picked unit that looks into cases like this."

"Like what?"

"Like the one we're investigating." I snatch back my badge and tuck it in my pocket. After grabbing the sign-in sheet, I fill it in for me, Sloan, and Kevin. "Eighth floor and left. Thanks for your help."

The four of us say nothing while we wait for the elevator. The building is bustling with workers, and though we're not dressed slovenly, we certainly won't be mistaken for anyone who belongs here. The *hiss* and rumble of metal doors sliding in their tracks invites us inside the elevator car. I thumb the button for the eighth floor, and the doors rumble shut.

When the pull of the elevator bumps us into motion, Sloan opens the file on his phone. "Emeril, Schmitt, and Cline handle big-ticket clients and their millions. According to what Maxwell could find, the company is legitimate and has never given anyone reason to believe otherwise."

"How long have they been in business?" Calum asks.

"Eighteen years."

I nod. "According to what Garnet could find, it's a human company with no ties to the empowered world."

"Not even Montclair?" Calum asks. "With the number of leviathans sent to kill him, I would've thought at least *he* was involved with a badass race of fae or a demon or something."

"That's what we're here to figure out. Right now, he's a dead human who was paranoid about going to the gallery during public showroom hours." I yawn and shake myself.

"Are we keeping you up, sista? Did you two forget we have a full day and enjoy your suite too much last night?"

Sloan raises his palms. After two months of living with Calum, Kevin, and Emmet, he's used to being razzed by them.

"Yer sister's lack of sleep is all her doing. I caught her up and wandering around at five this morning."

I shrug. "Not my bed. King Henry has spoiled me. When we sleep at home, there's no light or sound. He's like a deprivation pod."

"Does that make you a pod person?" Calum asks.

Kevin nods. "I'm pretty sure it does."

"That explains so much."

I flash them a middle finger salute. "Har har. You two are hilarious."

The elevator bumps again, and the panels open. Calum leads the way and hangs a left. The doors for Emeril, Schmitt, and Cline are opaque, frosted glass, so we don't know what we're in for until it's too late.

"What the hell is this? Did we just step in it?" I stop inside the main entrance and take it in. People are rushing around, carrying files, and looking like they're experiencing some kind of shared psychotic break. "Is it something in the air ducts?"

"I hope not. Otherwise, we're done for," Calum says.

A girl shuffles past as fast as her pencil skirt will allow. Sloan reaches out and taps her shoulder. "Excuse me—"

The high-pitched scream she lets out as she turns and throws the files in the air makes us all jump back.

"What the hell, lady?" Calum slaps his chest. "Was that necessary?"

She doesn't stop to answer. She scrambles to collect the files she dropped and rushes off the way she was going.

"Are we being punked?" Calum asks. "Did Garnet set this up to test us?"

A man in slacks and a snazzy silk vest strides our way. I throw my hat in the ring and step in front of him. Holding up my badge,

I drop the leather cover and wait until I have his full attention. "Two minutes of your time, sir. Who's in charge here?"

He sidesteps me and answers on the fly. "No idea. It depends on who's still alive."

I meet the confused gazes of my team and shrug. "Was anyone expecting that answer?"

"More are dead?" Calum asks. "Who? How? Why?"

"All good questions, bro." I chuckle as I take a moment to absorb the chaos. "I guess we're investigators, so we should investigate. Spread out and find the biggest offices. That should lead us to the biggest players, amirite?"

"Sound logic. I'll go this way." Calum strides off down the cubicle corridor to the right.

"I'll watch the door," Sloan says. "They're afraid of something. It can't hurt to lock things down."

"Good point, hotness. Holler if you need us." Kevin and I strike off to the left of reception. "This building is square. There has to be a corner office."

"Or four." Kevin laughs. "Geometry never was one of your best events."

"Smartass. Go find a corner and sit in it."

He laughs harder and heads off. I'm walking along, looking every which way for people in the empty cubicles when I have to throw myself flat against the wall to avoid getting run over. A woman pushing a mail cart blasts past with no concern about whether or not I'm standing in her way.

I'm still shaking my head about nearly getting run down when I follow Trolley Girl's trajectory as she gets to the end of the hall and ducks into a corner office.

She's not in there long. It's a case of push the cart inside and back out the door as if her Jimmy Choos are on fire. "I think I've found Ground Zero, Bear."

Hurrying to close the distance before the tides in this workplace craziness turn, I get to the office in seconds. I knock on the solid maple slab and wait. When nothing comes back to me, I try the door. It's locked.

"Hello? I'm Agent Cumhaill, and I'm here regarding the murder of one of your staff members."

The white noise of the stir and shuffle of panic comes to a sudden and alarming halt. Turning on my heel, I stare out at the four people who have now prairie-dogged up from their cubicles.

The guy blinks, all color washed from his face. "You can't be here."

"I need to be here. I need to speak to someone about Arthur Montclair and why some very bad men might've targeted him."

"Artie's dead too?" Trolley Girl shrieks. "Ohgodohgodohgod…"

As her mental meltdown spins out of control, I take advantage of having their attention. I pull my badge and let them see how official I am. Not really, but it's fun to think so.

"What's going on? Who else is dead?"

The guy with the silk vest jogs around to comfort the woman babbling. "Who's not dead?"

"All right… how many are dead?"

The guy looks at the others. "At least three but the day is young, and apparently there's no place to hide."

"Poor Artie," another woman says.

"Poor Mr. Cline, now that she knocked. They'll think we called the cops."

I hold up my finger. "Who are *they* and where is Mr. Cline?"

The four of them look ill, but I'm starting to put the pieces together. I turn and point at the locked door behind me. "Is this Mr. Cline's office?"

They nod.

"Who else is in there with him?"

By the fear in their eyes and their headshakes, I've got the last of their help I'm getting. I press my fingers to the base of my tongue and let out a piercing whistle.

With the cavalry called, I press my hand on the lock plate, and I reach out with my gift. "*Open Sesame.*"

I enter without permission and curse at two thugs shoving a man in a fancy suit out the window. "*Whirlwind Force.*" I call on the blustering cold outside and pull it to me with all my might. The frigid air responds immediately and hits Mr. Cline with tremendous impact.

It blows the thugs back as Mr. Cline is thrown ten feet into the room. He lands on his ass with a *thud* and rolls like a high-powered tumbleweed until he crashes to a stop against the wet bar.

"What the hell?" Thug One recovers from my blowback. "What are you?"

Sloan hip-slams into the door, rushing into the office. He searches the group and checks me out. "Yer all right?"

"So far so good. Close the door and make sure I didn't kill Mr. Cline by saving him with too much enthusiasm."

Sloan moves to check on the unconscious businessman, and I release Bruin. "Before you boys get any big ideas, close the window and let me introduce my battle bear companion."

Bruin takes form between them and me and stands up on his hind legs looking pee-your-pants intimidating.

"This is Killer Clawbearer, mythical battle bear, and avid bloodshed enthusiast. I am Fiona, Governor of the Lakeshore Guild of Empowered Ones, Head of the Toronto Druids, and agent of the SITFO task force." I forgo pulling my ID because these two don't seem the type to be impressed by a badge.

"You're dead, bitch," Thug Two snaps. "When we get through with you, you'll wish you were never born."

Cliché. He loses intimidation points for that. I shake my head. "Remember, Bear. Decapitation is the way to go if they step out of line."

The two narrow their gaze on me. "Yeah, we know what you are and how to kill you. What we don't know is why your buddies came to Toronto and killed Arthur Montclair."

"So, he is dead," Thug One says. "They weren't supposed to kill him, only rough him up and make him talk."

Thug Two frowns. "That's why they haven't checked in. They're afraid to face the boss."

Calum and Kevin slide in to join us and close the door behind them to keep this a private party.

"No. Your boys didn't check in because we killed them. You should've said hello to the local authorities before you sent a death squad into our city."

They take a step forward, tip their heads back, and flash me six rows of long, serrated teeth. My reaction is the same as the first time I came up against their kind.

Gross.

I call Birga and my armor forward. "Now, now, boys. Don't do anything you'll regret. I just finished telling you we killed your fellow freaks in Toronto. That's why we're here. We want to know what it's about and ensure you don't come back and kill more people in our city."

"He's coming around, Fi," Sloan says.

I release Birga and my armor and pat my chest for Bruin to resume his place. When everything is back to normal, I meet their stormy gazes. "Now that we know who and what we're dealing with, catch us up. What's going on and why were you pushing poor Mr. Cline out the window?"

Sloan helps the man up off the floor and settles him onto one of the visitor's chairs. "Are ye all right, sir?"

The man blinks up at us with equal parts confusion and fear. "Who are you? What are you doing here? Now's not a good time for you to be here."

"It's too late for that, I'm afraid," Sloan says. "We're here, and we aren't going anywhere."

"You've got a death wish," Thug Two snaps. "When the boss finds out you're all dead."

I make a tsking noise with my tongue. "Can't we all get along? You killed people. Then we killed people, and you killed people… do you really want us to take our next turn?"

Calum pushes off the back of the door and moves in to join the conversation. "How about you tell us who your boss is and what he's trying to find out by torturing and killing the employees of this legal firm? We found the bodies of the other two partners and dudes… You two have serious issues."

Mr. Cline's pallor turns a putrid shade of green. When he heaves forward, I barely have time to scootch my feet across the floor and out of the way before he hurls. He groans, his head hanging over the side of his chair. "So Jim and Mark are both dead? You're sure?"

Calum sighs and hands him a golf towel off the bag of clubs in the corner. "I'm sure. I found them in their offices and checked for vitals."

Mr. Cline cups a trembling hand over his mouth. "Christ. What am I going to tell their spouses?"

Sloan moves in and places a supportive hand on the man's back. I feel his power in the air as he offers the man some aid—his soothing touch maybe or it could be a bit of an emotional mind wipe to lessen his panic.

"You won't be alive to tell them anything if we don't get back to the point," Thug One says. "The files, asshole. We need those files. You still have staff you can lose, and we've made it clear there's no limit to the lengths we'll go to get what we want."

Calum's brows crease hard. "What files?"

Mr. Cline looks like another wave of "breakfast show-and-tell" is about to begin but gets hold of himself. "They want the files from all the cases handled by a former executive."

"Arthur Montclair," Calum says.

Mr. Cline's gaze is clouded and confused. "How did you know

that?"

Calum pulls out his badge and introduces himself. "Because Arthur Montclair was murdered in Toronto earlier in the week. It's why we came. To find out who had the motive to kill him and if it could be related to his job."

I run my fingers through my hair and study the two leviathans biding their time before they pounce. "I think it's safe to say it's related."

Calum turns his attention back to Mr. Cline. "What kind of work did Mr. Montclair do here?"

"Private adoptions."

"And the files they want are what?"

"They want everything Arthur worked on from December of last year up until the first of February."

Calum looks at the two thugs. "That's a very specific window of time. What are you looking for?"

"None of your fucking business."

My brother chuckles. "All right, this is what we're going to do. You two are going to tell us which file your boss needs. You can't have all of them—that's greedy, and it's a hard no—but if he can convince us he has the right to the information in the file he needs, we'll consider helping."

"If he promises to stop leaving a trail of bodies," I add.

Having seen the mess that was once Arthur Montclair after the leviathans finished with him, I don't doubt the partners in the corner offices did not pass peacefully into the next life. There's no need for the rest of the office staff to suffer the same fate.

The leviathans don't seem convinced of Calum's plan. They stand there giving us the stink eye.

I hold out my palm. "Dial your big bossman and let me speak with him. This is now beyond your pay grade, and we'll deal with him directly."

Thug Two's frown turns upside down, and he pulls out his phone. "It's your funeral, bitch."

CHAPTER THREE

By the time Calum and I end the call, we know three important facts. One, the big bossman is a woman. Two, she claims her child was taken and sold by a member of her household staff. And three, she will raze the Earth to get her baby boy back. I am also positive she will make good on her threat to rip out our throats if we fuck up her chances of getting her son back.

Once I relay that information to the room, everyone seems a little calmer. At least we know who and why. Now we need to figure out where Baby Boy Leviathan is and confirm her story about being the boy's mother.

The new information seems to convince Mr. Cline to be a little more helpful as well. Although he doesn't know the leviathan part of things, he knows these people are highly motivated, and his company may have facilitated the illegal sale of a kidnapped child.

Instead of breaking privilege with fifteen or twenty rich and powerful clients, we'll try to whittle it down to only one. If the woman's claim is true, the criminal offense of stealing the baby boy invalidated the right of privilege.

We move as a group into the boardroom, and I cast a reassuring gaze to the support staff when their heads pop up over the cubicle walls. "We're making progress. Deep breaths. This is almost over for you, folks."

One of the women whimpers.

"Sorry. Over for you in a good way, I mean. Bad choice of words."

Now that we know what we're looking for, we make progress quickly. The boy was born in mid-December and was noticed missing in the wee hours of New Year's Day. The alleged mother had a quiet gathering of friends over for the celebration, and she asked the nanny to stay the night so she could have a few drinks and an adult evening.

It was close to four in the morning when she checked on her child before she went to bed and found him missing.

Mr. Cline won't allow us to open the files, so he checks each one himself.

Calum is the real cop, so I sit back and let him do his thing. "The first thing to do is separate boys and girls and see how many we're left with."

That narrows it down to fourteen.

"The child was only two weeks old. Check the ages. We're looking for a newborn."

That brings us down to six.

"Next, we look at physical characteristics."

I point at Thug Two. "If you were tracking down her baby, I assume you have a picture of the little guy to go on? Let's see it."

He doesn't seem to appreciate the shift of authority but does as he's asked. Aww...how cute. "The baby has jet black hair and alabaster white skin."

I lean forward and set the phone in front of Mr. Cline. He studies the photo and goes back to the files. "Blond...Asian...oh, this little fellow has a cleft." He shifts those three file folders over, and we're down to three.

Mr. Cline straightens and presses his fingers on the three files still in contention. "How can we be certain the adoption went through this office? This woman is understandably distraught. Perhaps she got it wrong. Perhaps she's been misled."

I shrug. "Anything is possible, but she said her people tracked the finances of her staff and found that the nanny's mother, who resides in a palliative care facility, received seven hundred and fifty thousand dollars into her account from this law firm. It was reported as income in trust after the sale of a home, but when they checked, there was no home."

"Just a law firm giving an old woman a chunk of cash," Thug One says. "There's no mistake, asshole. We did our homework."

Calum nods and reaches to take the files out from under Mr. Cline's hold. "Now, we'll do ours. Give us some time to make a few calls and look into these three adoptions. If it checks out and your young prince is one of these babies, we'll make sure he's returned."

"Or we could go there and look at the kids and kill the people who bought him."

I blink. Oh, Thug Two. Such a dark sense of humor.

While Calum calls Garnet and is looking into the first file, I take the second and call Nikon.

"Hey, Red. How's the romantic weekend going?"

"Not so romantic at the moment. We're looking into the dead guy at the art gallery, and I need someone to be my computer guy in the Batcave."

"Sure. Give me… Okay, I'm here. Give me a sec to scan in and get set up. What do you need?"

The fact that he can flash anywhere in the world in the blink of an eye will never stop amazing me. "We think we have a handle on what happened and our next steps to make the carnage stop. First, we need to verify our intel."

"Computer spinning up, ass in seat, fingers on the keys. Ready when you are."

We spend the next twenty minutes going over the details in my file. Then he hands me over to his sister. "Hey, Andromeda. How's things?"

"I got a text from Garnet a moment ago. He wants me wherever you are. He doesn't like the sound of you and your brother reading through the nuances of adoption papers to reclaim an empowered child sold into the human population. I'll come to ensure none of you get into a legal bind."

"Sure. I'll text your brother the address. We're on the eighth floor at Emeril, Schmitt, and Cline. Although I guess it's just Cline now. The two partners are dead in their offices."

"Now? While you're all there looking through files?" Andromeda's tone raises the hair on the nape of my neck.

"I take it that's a bad thing?"

"Well, it's not good, Fi. Okay. Give me two minutes to grab my briefcase and my coat. We'll be right there."

I hang up and text Nikon the address of the building. "Nikon and Andromeda are coming."

Cline frowns at me.

"Andromeda Tsambikos is the SITFO lead counsel. Our boss wants our attorney here to oversee what's happening to mitigate the fallout and to make sure this is handled properly."

"Only you, Red." Nikon is standing in the public hallway by the elevators when I exit the ladies' room ten minutes later. "You never cease to amaze me."

Between the stress of the morning and sitting around reading through adoption paperwork, I needed a break. "Everyone goes pee. It's hardly worthy of amazing an immortal Greek god."

He wrinkles his nose and grins at me. "Not a god and you know it, smartass."

Behind the guyliner, ripped jeans, and goth persona hides a

man of legend. He has that amazing Mediterranean skin tone, the tall, chiseled frame of a warrior, and a hint of an accent that sneaks out after a night of drinking. He's kept himself locked away for too many centuries, but thanks to his engagement with my family, he's come to life again.

"I wasn't talking about your visit to the facilities, and you know it. I meant, your romantic getaway turning into two dead lawyers and a leviathan showdown in front of a bunch of clueless humans."

I chuckle. "Oh, that. Yeah, I do have a knack for keeping things interesting. Sloan says it's one of the things he loves most about me."

"Luckily for you."

"True story. If he wasn't odd like that, he'd have run for the hills months ago."

"Speaking of running for the hills. Irish said you guys missed lunch and you're likely getting hungry. Cline mentioned a deli on the main floor. I've been tasked to escort you down and get you fed."

I shake my head. "I'm fine. We can all grab something when we wrap up here."

He gestures at the elevators and holds up a piece of paper with lunch orders on it. "Make no mistake, we're ordering for everyone. They're all hungry, and they're looking at another hour or two of fact-checking before we move out."

I press my hand on my tummy. A couple of hours? Relenting, I push the button to take us down. "A deli, eh? I can work with that. If it were just about me, I'd suck it up. I'm not going to fall over if my tummy is rumbly."

"What can I say? The man is in love. I don't fault him for wanting to take care of you."

The elevator doors open on the lobby floor, and we make our way out into the building's traffic flow. It takes a moment to orient ourselves toward the deli, and we're off.

Rueben's isn't overly busy, but since it's almost two o'clock, the lunch crowd has died. I stop at the back of the line and tilt my gaze up to read what I want off the menu boards. "It certainly smells good."

"This is new." Nikon lifts my hand and tugs my fingers close to examine my silver band. "A Claddagh from Irish?"

"Yep. It's nice, isn't it?"

"Elegant and understated, like the woman who wears it on her finger."

We both hold a straight face for all of three seconds before we burst out in a fit of giggles.

"Hey." I sober as we move farther up in line. "I've grown a lot more congenial in the past year. I think before I say things much more than I used to."

Nikon grins. "Don't change perfection. I prefer when you let your thoughts fly. You say some crazy shit. It's hilarious."

"So, you only love me for the chaos I cause?"

He swings his arm up beside me and hangs it heavily across my shoulder. "Oh, I love you for a lot more than that."

He kisses my temple, and for the second time today, my Spidey senses fire to life. I stiffen and look around. "Do you feel that?"

"Feel what?"

I reach out with my senses but get nothing back. Maybe I'm tired. Or perhaps I'm hungrier than I thought. "It's likely nothing...just a weird feeling."

Nikon shrugs. "Is your shield going off?"

"Nope."

"Then maybe your months of being kidnapped, stabbed, beaten, and targeted have left you a little jumpy."

I don't think that's it, but I have no other explanation.

"Next in line." I turn my attention back to the menu board and focus. We're two customers away from ordering, and I haven't a clue what I want.

By the time we get back upstairs, the others have things well in hand, and I don't want to break their flow by getting into the mix. Nikon and I set up the orders on the opposite end of the table, and Kevin joins the two of us for lunch.

"How's it going with the baby hunt?" I lift my top bun and take my pickle out to eat first.

"Good. They narrowed it down to one and are double-checking the info before we set off to do a home visit."

"There's still a chance it's not him," Nikon says. "They narrowed it down to one based on the information they have here, but we're still only making assumptions."

Kev nods. "That's why they're keeping Beavis and Butt-Head over there at arm's length. They don't want them to rush off to massacre a happy couple who think they adopted a baby and can live happily ever after."

Nikon shakes his head. "Do you think the adoptive parents are innocent?"

"You don't?" I finish my pickle and wipe my fingers.

Nikon frowns. "If they went this route, they're more the 'get me a baby at any cost' kind of people. I wouldn't be surprised if they know things aren't on the up and up and don't care. They got a baby, so they're happy."

Kevin shrugs. "The way the paperwork reads, the adoptive parents arranged a private adoption for that baby. It wasn't a random stork dropping off a bundle of joy."

"How could they have arranged for that baby specifically like a private adoption when the mother had no intention of giving her baby up?"

"It must've been a planned event."

I sit deeper in my chair and chew my turkey club. "I don't understand how people can be so desperate for a child they would go that route. There are so many kids around the world who need someone to love them. Why not foster or adopt through the right channels?"

Nikon pauses with his sandwich, his expression solemn. "The ache to procreate is a powerful thing, Fi. To know your legacy will continue for the next generation. To watch your heirs grow and pick out which characteristics come from you and which come from your lover." He takes another bite of his sandwich and nods while he chews. "I get it."

There is a haunting echo in the way Nikon speaks, and I remember a convo with Dora a couple of months ago where we were speculating he'd have many kids. "Do you have kids, Greek?"

He drops his gaze and adjusts the foil wrapper on his sandwich. "No."

"Why not? It sounds like it's something you've thought about in great detail."

"Never got around to it, I suppose."

I chuff. "In two millennia? That's some case of procrastination."

"Calum and I are going to foster." Kevin finishes sipping through his straw and sets down his drink. "It's a little scarier because of forming attachments with the risk of them returning to their biological parents, but we figure if it's meant to be, we'll find the children who need our help most."

I reach for one of his fries and grin. "I didn't know that's what you guys were thinking. That's awesome. Why go that route instead of adoption?"

"Have you ever talked to Kinu about some of the baby repo's she's done?"

I laugh and cover my mouth with my hand while I swallow. "I don't think they're called baby repo's, but yeah, I have. There are cases when taking a child out of its home is a kindness. She's working up the courage to talk to Garnet about building a children's protection agency within the empowered community for that reason."

"That's awesome," Kevin says. "Maybe Calum and I should start there. With the tenets of secrecy, fostering empowered kids must be tricky."

"You two will be amazing. I can hardly wait for your family to grow."

Nikon wraps the second half of his sandwich and stands up. "I think I'll head back. Sloan, can you make sure my sister gets home when you're finished with her expertise?"

Sloan looks up from where he and Andromeda are scrolling through screens on her laptop. "Of course."

"'Kay, thanks."

"Why the sudden rush for the door, Greek?" Kevin asks. "Was it something we said?"

Nikon waves that off, but I see the lie in his denial. "Nah, I'm good. I have things to take care of. Call me if you need me, and I'll be back in a flash."

I set my sandwich on the table and jog after him to catch him in the hall. "Hey, Greek. What's going on?"

He turns and feigns ignorance. "Nothing. I'm good."

"My bullshit meter is redlining."

He stares off at the wall behind me and grits his teeth. "Leave it alone, Fi. I know you like to talk things to death, but this is none of your business. Drop it."

I hold up my hands and step back. "Consider it dropped."

His gaze narrows. With a sigh and a curse, he stomps into the copy room and flashes out.

Damn. What lit a fire under him?

Feeling bad that I struck a nerve, I head back inside. Andromeda is standing back from her laptop with her soup, so I figure it's safe to disturb her. "Hey, Andy?"

I tilt my head to the open space by the bookshelf, and she

follows my lead. "Can I ask you something personal about your brother?"

"You can ask." Her tone is guarded. "That doesn't mean I'll answer."

"Fair enough. Nikon, Kevin, and I talked about babies, and why people would be so desperate they would steal another person's child, and he bolted. When I tried to talk to him, he shut me down hard."

Andromeda has her lawyer face on and is giving nothing away. "What's your question?"

"He said he has no children. In twelve centuries, he's never had a baby? If he weren't interested, I'd get that, but he obviously is. What's that about?"

"That's Nikon's story to tell, Fi. When you live as long as we have, you learn to cherish your privacy. If he wants to share with you, he will. Otherwise, as his friend, you should respect him enough to leave him alone."

Her tone isn't precisely clipped, but it certainly isn't warm.

I dip my chin and offer her an apologetic smile. "Right. Sorry. I'll mind my own."

Andy lets out a long breath and touches my arm. "I'm sorry too, Fi. Being immortal looks amazing from the outside, but there are drawbacks. When life is great, it's great, but when there are pains to endure, those pains never end."

She steps back and returns to help Sloan at the table.

"Everything okay, baby girl?" Calum asks when I return to my seat and steal another of Kevin's fries.

"No. I don't think it is." I pick up my bottle of water and take a drink. "I think we inadvertently snapped one of Nikon's heart-strings by bringing up him not having kids...or repossessed kids...or something about kids. I'm not sure where his pain-point is, but we hit it."

Calum frowns. "Honestly, I never really thought about it. I

forget sometimes he's lived as long as he has. When we hang out, he's our twenty-something buddy."

"The reality is, though, he's much more than that." I plunk back into my seat and pull out my phone. Calling up Nikon's contact, I start moving my thumbs.

Hey. Obvi our convo hurt you. I'm so sorry.
Don't know what you're talking about. S'all good.
Liar. We don't need to revisit, but you have an apology hug coming your way.
I'll never turn down one of your hugs.
K. Take care of you, Greek.
Take care of you, too.

I slide my phone into my pocket. "We've agreed not to discuss it and hug it out."

"In true manly form," Calum says. "Avoid the emotional baggage and move straight to the physical affection."

Kevin waggles his brow. "I guess I owe him some physical affection too. I was one of the offending parties."

Calum laughs. "You sound broken up about making things right."

We're still chuckling about that when Sloan straightens. "All right. We confirmed all we can from here. It's time to visit this couple and see if their child is the boy we're looking for."

CHAPTER FOUR

The couple who adopted Baby Boy Leviathan lives in a mansion within a gated community. Being Canada's capital city, Ottawa has many expensive areas where powerful politicians and dignitaries live. The Brently Estates is one of them.

"Schmancy." Kevin looks out our window at the sprawling mansions. "How much do you think these go for?"

I'm already on that, my search bringing back two houses that were up for sale late last year. "About twelve million."

Kevin whistles between his teeth. "I guess that knocks us off the list of potential home buyers, babe."

Calum chuckles. "Damn, and I already had my grand piano on order."

Sloan pulls to a stop behind an eight-foot wrought iron gate, hits the button to lower his window, and holds up his SITFO badge to the guard hanging out the window of the gatehouse. "Good morning. We're here on official business and need to visit one of your residents."

"To see who?" The man adjusts his glasses to see the badge better.

"Mr. and Mrs. James Denton, Ninety-six Laurier Court."

"Are they expecting you?"

"No. The matter is sensitive, and it's better if they aren't aware we're coming."

"Then I'll have to have someone escort you."

"That's fine. There's room in the truck behind us."

The gatekeeper hands Sloan a clipboard and ducks back inside the little house. A moment later a forty-something guy in a gray and blue uniform comes out and slides into the back seat of the leviathan's truck behind us.

When Sloan finishes signing us in, the gate master checks the entry log and points past the gate. "To get to Laurier, go straight at the first roundabout and take the first right at the second. You can't miss it."

A moment after he ducks back inside and closes his window, the iron gate hums to life to allow us entrance. Sloan presses on the gas and my Hellcat SUV pulls us toward what I hope is the end of this cross-province crime spree. "I feel bad about leaving Andromeda behind to take care of the police side of things."

"You shouldn't," Calum says in the back seat. "She works in our system and knows what to say and not say. She'll be fine. Besides, Anyx is there with her."

Yeah, that's good. When we updated Garnet on our progress, he sent Anyx to watch over Andromeda, and he'll take her home when everything there is sorted out with the two dead partners.

"Here we are." Sloan pulls into the driveway of Ninety-six Laurier Court and the leviathans pull their Suburban up tight behind us.

"Do you think they just blocked us in on purpose?" I frown into my side-view mirror.

Calum snorts behind me. "The driveway holds three cars side-by-side and they chose to pull up tight enough to our ass they should get a slap in the face. Hard to mistake that as a coincidence."

"You'd think they would block the Dentons car," Kevin says. "There's a better chance they make a run for it than us."

Sloan pulls the keys from the ignition. "Unless they don't anticipate the Dentons getting that far."

"Well, that's a dark thought, hotness."

"Simply exploring possible motivations."

The leviathan thugs are out of their truck, so I grab the door handle. "Hustle boys, or we're going to be left behind and following a trail of blood."

The four of us get out and manage to keep ahead of our leviathan escorts. The guard pushes through the bodies on the front porch and rings the bell. The chiming rhythm of the song rings inside, and I laugh. "*La Cucaracha* in a house like this? Hilarious."

When the door opens, the man of the house looks over our group and bristles. "What is it? Who are you people?"

"I'm sorry to disturb you, sir," the gate guard says. "They are the police. They need to speak with you and your wife."

"What about?"

Calum shows the man his badge and gestures inside. "It's a private matter. I'm sure you'd rather discuss it inside than have your neighbors watching the show."

He straightens and tightens his grip on the door. "I don't give a flying fuck what the neighbors see. What's this about?"

"We have reason to believe your son's adoption was through illegal means and the boy was kidnapped on New Year's Eve and taken from his birth mother."

I'm watching Mr. Denton's expression as Calum lays things out and there's no surprise or look of fear there. If anything, the man's position hardens.

Sloan sucks in a breath behind us and reaches forward to take mine and Calum's hands at our sides. The moment we make contact, the enhanced sight from Sloan's bone ring takes hold. Well, crappers.

Calum forces the guard away from the door, his gaze locked on the vampire ahead of us. "Kevin, escort the guard back to the truck and wait inside the vehicle."

The tone of Calum's voice leaves no room for second-guessing. Kevin grips the man's elbow, and they retreat from the front verandah.

"What is it?" Thug One asks.

"I don't want the two civilians caught in the crossfire and exposed to what happens next."

I wish I didn't know what happens next, but I do.

"What are you talking about, druid?"

"Mr. Denton is a vampire."

The moment Sloan says the word vampire, Mr. Denton raises his clawed fingers, and his eyes flip red. He opens his mouth and his incisors drop, exposing a row of sharp and pointies a saber-toothed tiger would be proud of.

I realize I've had limited experience fighting vampires—the ensorcelled jailor when Barghest and Moose kidnapped me down in the subway tunnels with the hobgoblins—but neither time did their eyes go all hellfire freaky.

It's terrifying, and at the same time, it makes things feel more like we're part of an episode of *Supernatural.*

I activate my body armor and call Birga forward. "Find and secure the baby, Bruin." I release my bear and the pressure building in my lungs eases with a gentle *pop.* There's no breeze this time.

He launches out of me and is off with gale force.

The unfortunate thing about us standing on the front step when hostility hits the fan is that it bottlenecks us from getting inside. The vampire is blocking our path and—

I'm knocked hard to the side as Thug Two plows me over and

smashes me into the porch furniture beneath the living room window. The world tilts, and when Calum reaches to catch my arm, there's enough of an opening for the leviathan to barrel through.

I'm quick to regain my footing and collect Birga, and we push inside to join the chaos in progress.

"I've got upstairs," I shout, me and Thug One taking the stairs at a run.

There's a massive leviathan versus vampire throwdown in progress on the polished floor of the front foyer. I don't know enough about the strengths and vulnerabilities of the two races to have any idea about how that will end—other than the part where the only way to kill them is decapitation.

"Bruin, have you got the baby?" I shout when I'm almost at the top of the stairs.

I'm here, Red. The nursery is off the master suite. "Master bedroom," I shout to Thug One.

I'm three steps behind the leviathan when we break into the master suite. Bruin has materialized and is fighting with a female vampire. Another female has donned a cloak and is scrambling out the window.

She has a baby carrier against her chest and is scrambling across the shingles on the garage below like a crab across the sand.

The leviathan goes after her, and as I reach the window to follow, my shield flares hot. I scan for danger at the same moment he throws his hand back. A ball of thick, black tar catapults at me at an alarming rate.

I curse and duck away from the open window.

The *splat* is loud and sizzles when it hits. I face the damage to continue and stop dead. Whatever he threw at me sealed the window and made it impassable.

There's no getting past it, so I turn on my heel. "You good, Bear?"

Gettin' my groove on.

I chuckle, return Birga to her resting place on my forearm, and race out of the room. "We have a runner jumping off the garage roof."

Running straight at the second-floor railing, I up-and-over it, casting *Diminish Descent* as I fall toward the marble floor below. Air pulls at my hair during the freefall, and I focus on a spot for my landing that doesn't involve me joining the deathmatch between Thug Two and the male vampire.

I land gracefully in a crouch, my knees bending to absorb the momentum. When gravity finishes with me, I straighten and propel myself toward the open door.

Bolting out of the house, I crank my head around, searching for—

"That way, Fi." Kevin points. "They ran between that blue car and the house next door."

"Thanks, Kev." After rounding the trucks in the driveway, I focus on where Kevin said they went.

"*Fleet Feet.*" The spell takes hold and gives me the extra oomph I need to regain visual. Arms pumping, adrenaline pulsing, heart pounding, I beat feet across the road. Sadly, vampires are way too fast for me to catch on foot.

"*Sleet Storm.*" I raise my hands as I run, lifting the snow from the ground to combine with the moisture in the air to hit the fleeing female with a wall of hostile weather.

The rush of air brushing past me makes me smile. "What, you think you get to battle both females, Bear?"

To the victor goes the spoils, Red.

"No fair. I can't fly."

Excuses are beneath ye, Red.

I laugh, feeling much better knowing Bruin will be able to catch up and navigate the situation.

Each house on this block seems to have a few acres of land, and behind the houses, there's a treed area that runs the length of the development. It's no Don River Valley System, but it's dense enough that whatever goes down with us apprehending the vampire should be out of sight from civilians.

I arrive at the standoff, white puffs of breath condensing in clouds before me. The icy windstorm I called up is blowing like a cyclone. I release *Sleet Storm*, thankful for its help.

"Now we can talk without being whipped with ice."

The leviathan and the female vampire are crouched and standing off. Bruin is holding the two in check. I'm hauling thin air into heaving lungs. Yeah, I may be the only one winded, but I'm also the only human.

"It's over," I pant. "Give us the baby. No one wants him to get hurt."

The female has one arm clutched against the carrier slung against her chest and the other out for defense. "We deserve him. The bitch queen cheated us."

"Lies," Thug One says. "Filthy, stinking lies."

The vampire's eyes narrow. "Their queen refused to fulfill her side of an arrangement. She won't give us the money she owes, so we took something we wanted even more."

"I hear what you're saying, but you can't steal her child."

"He's not hers anymore. Demitri is ours now."

Thug One growls, and the sound is wet and phlegmy. "His name is Jos, and he will always belong with his mother. Give me the child now."

The woman is crouched to fight, and as much as I understand her intention to defend herself, something is missing.

My instincts fire and I pause to study her stance. It takes a few, fleeting moments but then it clicks. She's defending herself, not the baby. The look in her eyes registers next. There's no fear there… it's determination.

A sickening rush washes over me, and at that instant, I'm almost sure I'm right. "You don't have the baby in that carrier, do you? You're a decoy."

Now there's fear in her eyes.

She frowns, cradling the bulge in the sling with a mother's care. "Of course our baby is here. You'll never take him."

"Yeah no, I don't think so. Bruin, this is a goose chase. Head back and help the others."

"No!" she shouts, searching the trees with a frantic gaze. "If you move, I'll snap his neck. Then no one will have him."

Crappers. I'm ninety-nine percent sure I'm right but won't risk being the cause of the baby's murder. My hamster is racing in my mental wheel trying to figure out how to prove my theory when Thug One presses the matter.

I shout as he lunges forward and takes the female to the ground. Rushing in to—I'm not sure what I expect to do—Help? Fight? Stop them? I grab the sling as they face off. The moment I feel the density of the 'child' filling out the sling, I know I'm right.

"It's a doll. Back to the house, Bruin." The two of us head back at a run and leave the two of them to sort things out.

I'm almost back to the driveway when Sloan and Calum walk up the street from a different direction. Calum has a wrapped bundle in his arms and is grinning like he's the man of men.

"You got him?"

"Yeah, baby." Calum smiles down at the baby in his arms. "That's you, baby."

I meet them at the curb and smile at the prize of the fight. "Hello, baby Jos. You've stirred up quite a bit of trouble. You know that?"

Sloan checks me over as we head back to the house and I do the same with him and Calum.

We're all whole. Yay Team!

"So, what happened?" I ask.

Calum adjusts the blanket around him and smiles. "Sloan and I flushed another female out of hiding at the back of the house. We took chase and cornered her in a community maintenance shed over that way. While I talked sense into her, Sloan *poofed* back to get the leviathan. Once she saw it was three against one and the boy was caught in the middle, she gave him up without a fight."

"Rather than risk him getting hurt. A real-life Judgement of Solomon moment."

Kevin gets out of my truck and comes to see baby Jos. "Hey, baby."

"He's a cute little bugger, eh?" Calum brushes a tuft of black hair across the baby's forehead as Kevin leans in for a closer look.

"Okay, what now?" I ask.

Calum shrugs. "This isn't our playground. I guess we let the leviathans take care of the vampires. Then they'll take their baby back to their queen. Sloan, you might have to do a little memory magic on the guard, but other than that, this was empowered on empowered, so no one needs to involve the public world."

I gesture at the house and tug my brother into motion. "We should take him in and make sure he's fed and warm. When Thug One and Thug Two finish dispatching the kidnappers, I'm sure they'll want to leave right away."

We head back into the house, the guard meeting us on the way. The guy looks down at the boy and back at us. "That's what this is about? Their baby?"

"Not *their* baby though," I say. "He was taken and has a mother anxiously awaiting his return."

CHAPTER FIVE

By the time we get back to our hotel, I'm ready for a long, hot soak in the Jacuzzi tub, followed by an hour or two of languid lounging by the fireplace in my puffy robe while receiving a foot massage. Does it get any better? We deserve it. What was supposed to be a luxurious and romantic weekend has turned into another adventure in the days of urban druids.

We step out of the elevator and trudge up the hall, the adrenaline of the baby hunt fading fast. At least it is for me.

Then again, I've been up since five o'clock.

"I vote we part for a couple of hours of private time, then go downstairs for a late dinner. Sloan can call down and see if we can get a table."

"Perfect." Calum checks with Kev that he's good with that plan. "That'll give us some Daisy time too. Our poor, wee girl has been alone all day and deserves some loving."

When he swipes his keycard through the door scanner, I catch sight of what's been happening inside his suite. "Or maybe she hasn't. Maybe she had friends over while her dads were out."

Calum follows my gaze to where Nikon is lounging across their bed snuggling Daisy and feeding her treats.

"Hey, Greek. What's up?"

Nikon scrubs the skunk's head and rolls off the bed. "I came to apologize to Kevin and Fi...well, to all of you. I shouldn't have bailed and flashed off. You were in the middle of a case, and I could've stayed and helped. Instead, I buggered off like a jackass."

"No harm done." I meet his gaze and try to gauge how annoyed he is at me. "I upset you and compounded that by pushing. I'm sorry. Now that I know kids are a sore spot for you, I'll be more careful about what I say."

He shakes his head. "No, please don't. One of the things I love most about you, Fi, is that you say what's on your mind unfiltered. Having the ability to hear the thoughts around me, you can't imagine how refreshing that is."

"Refreshing, you say." Calum chuckles. "That's a nice way to put it. You're too generous, Greek."

He's not wrong. "Honestly. You're not the first person I've pissed off by letting my tongue wag. Why do you think all my friends are guys? Women get so touchy about things."

"True story," Calum says.

Kevin snorts. "Have a lot of experience with disgruntled women, do you?"

Calum arches a brow. "You don't know everything about me. I have women in my purview."

I roll my eyes and get back to Nikon. "I'm saying it's easier for me to communicate with you guys because men don't trigger as easily."

"Until we do," Nikon says.

"Until you do."

Nikon steps aside to let Calum and Kevin into their room and gestures to the hall. "Irish, do you mind if I steal your girlfriend for a minute for a private chat?"

Sloan shrugs. "Ye don't have to ask my permission. Fi's her own person. She decides fer herself."

I reach up on my toes and kiss his cheek. "Point for you,

hotness. Good one."

He chuckles and heads across the hall to our suite. "I'll get yer robe ready and run yer bath, *a ghra*. Take yer time."

When the two doors close, Nikon gestures at the antique *chaise longue* at the far end of the hall. As we close the distance to the seating area, the upcoming convo's pressure grows in my chest.

"I *am* sorry I hurt you, Nikon. I would never intentionally do that."

"I know that, Fi."

I bump his shoulder with mine as we walk and chuckle. "You'd think that after killing you, I'd be a bit more careful. It's a wonder you even like me."

Nikon takes my hand and pulls me to sit beside him. "Fi, I love you. You know that. Sure, you stabbed me and pilfered a bottle of my favorite scotch, but you're my girl."

I chuckle. "You spent too much time isolated from the world, Greek. You've skewed your expectations of the women in your life if I'm coming out on top."

Leaning back, he stretches his arm across the back of the couch and shifts sideways to face me. "Why do you think I steer clear of women? Too much trouble."

"Agreed. We're the worst."

"Absolutely." We chuckle together for a moment, and his expression turns serious. "So, about the kid thing."

I wave my hand between us and shake my head. "Not my monkeys. Not my circus. You don't have to be an open book. I take you as you are, Greek. I don't need to read ahead."

Nikon became part of our found family almost immediately after he followed me home from the first guild meeting and we got into trouble hexing the altar stone in the druid circle. What can I say? Some people just fit.

Nikon is one of them.

The relief in his expression tells me that I said the right thing for once. "Do you mean it, Fi? We're good even without dragging everything into the light?"

"Of course. We're better than good—we're awesome." Everyone has their things, and I have more than most. I don't need the details of his innermost pain to know who he is. "Sorry I didn't take more time getting to know your heart. If I had, maybe I wouldn't have stomped on it."

He shakes his head. "You didn't stomp on it. The three of us were having a perfectly reasonable conversation, and I let things get personal and went off. Forgive me."

I open my arms and smile. "There's nothing to forgive. It's over. We're good. And I believe I owe you a hug."

He hugs me tight, and when he eases back, he waggles his brow. "So, where are we on makeup sex?"

I bark a laugh and get off the couch. "Nice try."

As the two of us head back toward my room, our privacy is broken. A door up the hall opens, and a couple steps out.

A weird sensation fogs my mind, and I spin, scanning the corridor to figure out where it's coming from. "There it is again...that feeling I had earlier in the deli."

My skin tingles as panic tickles my instincts. It's nothing so blatant that it's tripping my shield, but it's something.

Nikon straightens and looks around, his smile fading. "I *do* feel that now that I'm reaching for it. It's magic, Fi—and by the resistance I'm getting while scanning its source, it's a lot of magic."

A cold chill runs the length of my spine. It's invasive, and everything in me wants to screech and jump around shaking my arms. "What the hell was that?"

"*That* was a ghost." Nikon's head cranes around, and he glares at the couple down the hall. They seem oblivious to what's happening, but you never can tell. "I don't like this. We need to get back to the others."

With a firm hand at the small of my back, we pick up the pace, hurrying to return to the rooms.

Red? Bruin asks on our channel of internal communication. *What is it? Your heart rate is climbing. Do you need me?*

"I'm not sure yet, buddy. Something wicked this way comes. Stay tuned."

In all the time I've known Nikon, I've never seen him scared. Worried, sure. Angry, yes. But the expression marring his teen heartthrob beauty is flat-out terror.

"Nikon, talk to me. What is it?"

The doors to our two rooms fly open, and Calum and Sloan rush out from opposite sides of the hall.

"What's wrong?" Sloan snaps. "Do ye feel it?"

Nikon's jaw drops, and he's about to answer when my ears pop and the world around us stops—it literally locks in time. Goosebumps break out over my skin as I stare at the couple rounding the corner toward the elevator.

I point. "They're frozen mid-step."

The woman's silk scarf stands straight out from her neck, pointing behind her instead of fluttering to fall against her shoulder. The man dropped his glove, the leather accessory stuck in time, suspended in the air over his shoe.

"What. The. Fuckety-fuck?" Kevin says.

"That's disturbing on so many levels," Calum says.

A sickening thought strikes and my gaze spins toward Nikon. No. It's okay. He's blinking and breathing. He's merely gone mute. My heart starts up again. "You're all still with me, right? You guys see this?"

Calum is curling Daisy to his chest. "It's hard to miss."

"Have we been sucked into an episode of the *Twilight Zone?*" Kevin asks.

Sloan has an arm around me and grips Nikon's shoulder. "Greek, what's happening? Do you know what this is?"

He's not listening.

On a typical day, no one seeing Nikon on the street would

consider him dangerous. He looks like a teenaged surfer with long blond hair, guyliner, and a perfect smile.

Usually.

At the moment, he looks wildly homicidal.

I shift to stand in front of him and cup his face in my hands. "Greek, what's happening? You're scaring me. You gotta talk to me."

He breaks away from my hold, his eyes wild as he searches up and down the hallway. "Catey, where are you?"

A melodic laugh fills the air around us as a long-legged woman appears out of thin air. Her image comes into focus in undulating waves as if approaching a mirage from across the hot desert sands.

Her hips sway as she walks out of the illusion, the slit of her gown opening high enough and wide enough to see the round of her toned and tanned ass.

Nikon shifts in front of us, raising his arms to become our shield. "It's been a long time, Catey."

Raven-black hair cascades down overly generous boobs to hang loose at her pinched waist. Her lascivious gaze is locked on Nikon before she's even fully visible.

"Without hesitation, you know I am near, *agape mou*. Am I so prevalent in heart and mind my name yet lives upon your tongue?" Her words dance in the air like the sweetest seduction, the cadence educated, her voice deeply accented.

"Why are you here, Catey? What do you want?"

She stiffens, lifting her chin. "You forget yourself, lover. Speak with courtesy or lose the ability to speak at all."

Nikon dips his chin. "The years have been long and many since our parting, Hecate. Apologies. I've grown accustomed to speaking informally and with common tongue. My manners fail me."

Hecate? Seriously?

When we fought the dark witches back in October, Nikon

commented on not being fond of Hecate. I didn't know they used to be an item. I understand his panic now. If they had a bad break, she's not the kind of ex you want poking around.

Hecate holds her hands out from her sides and offers him a ruby-lipped smile. Man, I thought Andromeda was the most beautiful woman imaginable.

I was wrong.

This woman is a goddess. I mean…yeah, she's actually a goddess. "Speak the truth, *agape mou*. Have the years diminished my beauty in thine eyes?"

Nikon hasn't moved an inch. He's standing directly between his goddess ex-girlfriend and the four of us—well, five if you count Daisy.

He straightens to his full height, his frame rigid. "You are resplendent, as always. Your radiance bursts forth like the golden glow of sun through clouds. The brilliance of your beauty blinds me after being shunned to darkness for eternity."

"Wow, Nikon has poetic game," Kevin says.

Hecate seems to appreciate the stroke to her vanity. She tugs on an obsidian curl, then releases the lock of hair, and it springs up and back into place. She sends him a coy smile. "My heart's sorrow of centuries lost sings to learn I am not forgotten by you, *agape mou*."

"Not a day passed in two thousand years when I have not thought of you, Catey. Hear the truth of my words."

Either Nikon is a better liar than I thought or that is one hundy percent true. Huh, I didn't know he was hung up on an old love. It would explain why he's an impossible flirt and yet never seems to be dating anyone.

Hecate's smile shifts from him to land on me. "Yet, in the same breath that sets your affections free, you stand with another. One to whom only moments ago, you professed your loving affection."

Hubba-wha? Um, no, crazy lady.

"Fiona is a dear friend. We are not here together."

"Fiona is here with me." Sloan sidesteps and gathers me to his side. "Nikon is our friend."

Hecate eyes Sloan up and down and frowns. "She beds the Moor, I witnessed as much, yet spoke hearts' truths a moment ago with Nikon."

There's so much wrong with that sentence. "First off, he's not a Moor. He's a Celt. Second. There were no hearts' truths spoken. I apologized for upsetting him, and he said we're all good."

"He said he loves you."

I roll my eyes and meet Sloan's gaze. "Out of context and not like that. He said, you know I love you, Fi."

"As I said."

As the goddess shifts to see me, Nikon moves to block her view. "Get that thought out of your head right now. Fiona is not *my* female, Catey. You are mistaken. I love her as a sister and dear companion, not a lover."

Hecate eyes me up and down and frowns. "She is wholly unworthy of you, *agape mou*. A common whore would be better than a Celt."

"All right, quit with the Fi bashing," Calum snaps. "Like Nikon said, there's nothing between them except friendship. How about we move this along? Those people down the hall are likely getting tired of being living sculptures."

Hecate studies Calum and her mouth narrows to a fine line. "I see the truth of your protestation, boy. The two of you have carnal knowledge of my love and think me unaware." She lifts an elegant hand and points at my brother and Kevin.

Nikon curses. "No. Don't do this again, Catey. Listen to me. You are wrong. I know better than to love again. I live by your rules."

What the hell does that mean? "What rules, Greek? Don't do what again? What is she holding over you that has you so freaked out?"

Hecate pegs me with a glare, and my heart squeezes in my chest. The more intense her gaze becomes, the tighter the constriction grows. "Our business is none of yours, female."

I press my hand to my chest.

"Let her go," Sloan shouts, holding me up.

"Don't," Nikon snaps, turning toward me, his eyes wide. "Please, Catey, release her. Fi meant no offense. It's her way. She speaks her truths. You used to appreciate that."

My eyes are watering. It feels like they have a pulse all their own, throbbing deep in my skull.

Nikon drops to his knees before her. "I beg you, Catey. Not again. I can't go through this again."

Hecate's perfect pouty lips purse and the restriction on my lungs releases. I gasp for breath and collapse against Sloan's chest while I suck in a few lungfuls of oxygen.

Calum and Kev each place a hand on my shoulder, and I nod to tell them I'm all right.

Nikon doesn't check on me, but I get it. If he shows me any affection, he's afraid Hecate will kill me.

"Now then," Hecate says. "The next time one of you dare address me unbidden, I shall cut your tongues out at the root."

Quite a charmer. Maybe Nikon's fondness of me even after I killed him is telling. Perhaps his taste in women hasn't improved much over the centuries. Maybe he's a masochist.

Nikon rakes his fingers through his hair and draws a deep breath. "Catey, why don't we let Fiona and the others go inside, and you and I can go somewhere private to talk."

A cool smile graces Hecate's lips. "Privacy is a wonderful idea, *agape mou*. Let us take our leave."

I'm about to protest him leaving with a psycho-stalker ex when her power flares and realize, despite Nikon's suggestion, it's not only him being taken along for the ride.

Awesomesauce.

CHAPTER SIX

It takes a moment to orient to my surroundings. We've gone from the corridor of an Ottawa luxury hotel to standing in the center of a Greek pergola set high on the summit of a hill. The overlook gives us a stunning view of the tropical blue and turquoise waters of the sea on one side and the rolling, green velvet countryside on the others.

Once the change of venue takes hold, I realize the warm, Mediterranean breeze is kissing entirely too much of my skin.

"Oh, for fuck's sake." Nikon averts his gaze, and I give him my back. Shit. Kevin and Calum are naked too.

"Return their clothes, Catey."

"Why feign modesty, *agape mou*? I seek only to learn what sparks interest for you. Why are the two of them covered in all those hideous inkings? Were they marked as someone's slave?"

Nikon storms across the open-air temple to the elaborately set table. When he grips the edge of the tablecloth, he doesn't so much do the magician thing where they yank it from beneath the plates as turn, and it's in his hands.

With a speed and skill that leaves me dizzy, he folds and tucks and fashions a toga to cover all my girl bits. When he's finished, he squeezes my wrist. "I'm so sorry, Fi. You can't know how mortified I am right now."

I can't meet his gaze. Or Calum's. Or Kevin's.

Smoothing the fabric against my body, I blink against the sting of my eyes, my cheeks flaming hot. "Not your fault."

"Intriguing. The two of you act as though embarrassed."

"We *are* embarrassed," Nikon snaps. "I told you Fiona is *not* my female. She and Sloan are my friends."

Sloan. I turn, searching the interior of the pergola. "Where is he? What have you done with him?"

Hecate frowns and I remember my last lesson about speaking out in class.

I turn and plead with Nikon, my pulse thundering in my ears. "What did she do to Sloan?"

"And Daisy," Calum says.

Nikon turns to ask, but Hecate beats him to it. "I did nothing to them. Your Moor and your pet remain undisturbed at the inn. They held no interest. It is the three of you with Nikon I wish to observe."

"Then observe us with clothes on, Catey. You've had your look and checked out the goods. If you keep us naked much longer, people might think you're starting a harem."

"Nonsense," she huffs. With a wave of her hand, Calum and Kevin are in ivory togas. "I hold no designs on the common. I merely want the truth of your affections."

"I've told you. These are my friends."

"You said you love her and embraced only moments before I appeared in the corridor. You said it earlier when you purchased victuals in that strange restaurant."

I think back, wondering what the hell she's talking—right, on the couch, he said he loved me even though I stabbed him. When we were in the deli, he said he loved me for the chaos I cause and a lot more.

Nikon must be replaying the same highlight reel in his head

because he sighs and groans. "Yes, I said I love her, but it's not an intimate love, Catey. Fiona's family has become *my* family of late. Her father is a strong man I admire, and her brothers are my closest friends. Fiona is the keystone to all that. You're reading too much into this."

Hecate scowls at Nikon and flings her fingers at him in a dismissive gesture.

In the span of a racing heartbeat, Nikon transforms into a true Greek Adonis. He straightens wearing a traditional gold chiton with his arms and chest clean of all tattoos and his face clean of guyliner.

"Why do the people of your culture mark yourselves? It's profane and ugly."

Calum curses. His inked spells are all gone.

I glance down at myself and mine are gone too.

When I see him flexing his right arm and frowning it dawns on me. Birga. Her image is no longer inked on my forearm. I curse and try to call her forward.

Nothing.

I realize Hecate was speaking to me when the heat of her displeasure sizzles against my skin. Perfect. I anger her if I talk *and* when I don't. What did she want to know? Right.

Why get tattoos?

"I...uh, we've never discussed why Nikon got his tattoos, but mine and Calum's are tied to our druid powers."

"Powers?" she says, her gaze narrowing. "What sort of powers do you possess?"

Nikon answers that one. "Fiona and her brother are druids. They hold a connection to nature and possess fae gifts that allow them to command weather and commune with flora and fauna."

"Like Rhea and Persephone?"

Nikon dips his chin. "Similar, yes, but they are not gods. They are human and mortal."

Hecate glances over and offers us a pitying look. "How awful for you."

Nikon sends us an apologetic smile and straightens. "I implore you, Catey. My friends need to return to the hotel. Sloan will be frantic, as will the rest of their family."

"And if I refuse?"

Nikon sweeps his hand and bows his head. "You are, of course, the power here, but I promise this. I shall never forgive you if you allow them to come to harm."

Hecate tugs an ebony lock of her hair and frowns. "Your life is what *I* decide, Nikon of Rhodes. That fact escapes you yet, after all these years. I should think that after the last time, that lesson would be emblazoned in you."

Nikon's entire body becomes deathly still. "Do not speak to me of Kallista and the lesson I learned."

"Still sore about that are you?"

Sore? Is she blind? One look at the man and you can see he's homicidal about that.

Hecate steps forward and plucks at the fabric of his chiton. "Why must we speak of such tedious matters? The Fates shine on us this day. We are reunited. Are you not pleased to be here with me even a little?"

He withdraws and strides barefooted to one of the arched openings between ivory Corinthian columns. His longing seems almost palpable as he stares out over the countryside of his origin. "Of course. It's my home and my soul. I never thought I would see this place again."

A warm sea breeze catches my hair, and I block it from flying in my face. While the two of them are busy, I ease a couple of steps closer to Calum and Kev.

Seeing the two of them standing against the backdrop of the Mediterranean is like viewing a hauntingly beautiful work of art. I feel like we're intruding simply by bearing witness to their dysfunctional reunion.

I turn and assess our position on the summit. There's

nowhere for us to go. The overlook is situated high above any navigable land—likely with the gods in mind. I can't imagine humans being able to scale the terrain to get up here.

I study the blank skin on my upper arm and miss my spear. My dragon band is gone. I'm pretty sure that means it overwrote the portal, but I'll try it out when we have a chance to get away. I flex my palm once again to call Birga forward, but nothing happens.

Bruin? Tell me you're here with me.

I'm here, Red. What's happening? Are ye in danger?

Hearing his gruff and grumbly voice in my head is more comforting than anything I can remember. *I'm not sure. The goddess Hecate brought us to Greece because she's jealous and wanted to put us on notice. I think we've set her straight. Now, we have to wait and see what that means.*

Can we get away from a jealous goddess?

I have no idea.

"Come." Hecate gestures at the table. "Let us break bread and reacquaint ourselves instead of picking at old and festered wounds."

It's a statement, not a question, so there's no arguing the point. We arrive at the table, and I take in the spread. Yes, I'm wearing the tablecloth, but that doesn't take away from the splendor.

The wooden table set in the middle of a marble pergola is laden with golden platters, colored glass flutes, and golden cutlery. Each surface reflects prisms of light in a magical glittering dance. Add that to the vista of the sea, the smell of salt air when the warm breeze hits and I'm breathless.

Nikon makes a point of seating Hecate first and rounds the table to seat me. I'm cool with that.

No need to piss off the jealous goddess.

"Thank you," I whisper under my breath.

Nikon brushes my arm with his fingers. It could've been inadvertent, but I don't think so. He is trying to offer me comfort in an uncomfortable situation.

The three of them each take a seat, and I meet Calum's and Kevin's gazes and smile. This is their first abduction. Being the pro, I figure it's my job to set the tone.

Hecate waves her hand, and a meal appears, filling in the spaces on the table. It's enough food to feed a dozen people and boasts a broad selection of delicacies.

Five small, fire-roasted hens sit next to a platter of fish grilled in a creamy white sauce next to apple-glazed pork rolled in herbs. Steam rises from wide-brimmed bowls of vibrantly colored vegetables. By the aroma coming off them, some are topped with vinegar, and others are roasted in butter and garlic.

"Shall I pour?" Nikon gestures at the crystal decanter filled with rich, burgundy wine.

I wait until Hecate nods for me to answer before I reply. "Yes, thank you."

"Yeah, thanks, Greek," Calum says.

Hecate's chin lifts as she studies us with narrowed eyes. "If what Nikon says is true, and you and he are merely friends, why do you all hold yourself in such reserve?"

I swallow and lay my napkin over my lap. "To be frank, we're smart enough to realize you have designs on Nikon and don't want to offend you."

She seems to appreciate that and looks at Calum. "You're protecting yourself from what you anticipate I will do if you displease me?"

"Absolutely. I have no interest in being obliterated by an angry goddess because she believes we've overstepped."

She looks at me next.

"Also, we don't want to make things difficult for Nikon. We respect him and enjoy his company. It hurts us to know he's hurting and we don't want to add to that by causing trouble between you two."

Hecate flicks her hand, and each of us now has one of the small hens on our plate with a varied array of vegetables and other food. "Your concern for his situation is of primary importance to you. Why?" She pegs Kevin with a glare.

"His happiness is important to us, and he's upset."

When Nikon finishes pouring the wine, I take advantage of the libation to steady my nerves. The wine is better than any I have ever tasted, and I close my eyes as the robust fruitiness bursts to life in my mouth. I take another long sip and remind myself that getting drunk right now would be a bad idea.

Hecate sips from her glass and turns her full attention to Nikon. "Is that true? Are you upset, *agape mou?*"

"You know I am, Catey. The last time I saw you, things were said and done that I've had to live with for millennia. Yes, seeing you upsets me. Having you bring me here upsets me. The fact that you're imposing our dysfunctional past on my friends upsets me."

She doesn't respond. After picking up her cutlery, she begins to eat. When it becomes apparent the discussion has been paused for our visit's eating portion, the four of us pick up our cutlery and join the feast.

Say what you will about a possessive ex-girlfriend goddess kidnapping you. Hecate knows her way around manifesting a feast. The meal is delicious. I find having warm and buttery food in my belly soothes some of the rough edges of being targeted as the interloper in a relationship that failed to work out years ago.

We eat in silence, and I can't tell if Nikon is playing a game of waiting Hecate out or if he knows better than to speak out of turn.

Either way, we follow his lead.

Behind him, the view of the sea grows more spectacular by the minute. The slow sink of the tangerine sun washes the pink sky with a soft glow while streaks of oranges and reds make dramatic swipes across the horizon as if a painter is adding to the sunset.

When dinner is over, the meal disappears although grapes and the like remain, and Nikon tops up our glasses. I smile at him, thankful to see eating and some time to think has fortified him as well.

I don't know the story behind any of this or what kind of trouble we're in, but if Nikon isn't panicking, I take it as a good sign.

"When are we, Catey?" He sits back and sips his wine. "This summit was destroyed centuries ago. What time are we in?"

Hubba-wha? My head pivots and I project my thoughts toward Nikon. *When are we?*

Nikon can speak telepathically. I haven't said anything this way yet because Hecate might be able to as well, but seriously... We're in another time?

Whatever happens, I'll make this right for you guys, Fi. I'll get you back to Sloan and your family.

I don't like the sound of that. *You'll get* us *back, right?*

That's my fervent wish, yes.

Good. That's good.

Hecate seems oblivious to our telepathic conversation, so I take it that intercepting thoughts isn't one of her abilities. "I brought you back to when you made your mistake. A second chance is given. Advise yourself to choose wiser this time."

Nikon stills. "You brought me back to talk myself out of choosing my family instead of a life as your consort?"

She lifts her chin. "I did."

"Catey, when you didn't like my decision, you sentenced me to be alone and killed my wife and unborn child the one time I dared to live a full life. Do you honestly believe I can forgive you—that I would choose that for myself?"

Her gaze narrows, and she seems genuinely confused. "I hoped the error would be clear to you by now. In light of your hostility, this is the best solution. Convince your younger self to choose life on Olympus, and you won't have to suffer as you have. I won't be forced to harm—"

"—*Harm?*" he shouts, his voice booming. "You murdered my pregnant wife."

She grips her knife and Calum, Kevin, and I freeze. "I had *no* knowledge the female was with child. It never would've happened if you adhered to our terms."

"*Your* terms—" Nikon snaps, mottled color creeping up his neck and jaw. "I had no voice in any of it. You gave me an ultimatum, and I refused it. Then you sentenced me to pay the price for eternity."

The two of them fall still, glaring at one another.

I studiously focus on what's in front of me and keep my eyes on my glass.

Nothing happens for a long time. Then Hecate dabs her napkin against her lips and stands. As angry as he is, Nikon still rises, and it's a gentleman move straight out of an old-fashioned movie.

"More's the pity you learned nothing in all this time," she says, her voice quiet. "You remain as irrational and spiteful as ever. Either speak to your younger self and set things on a different course or remain here and rot."

When she disappears, Nikon holds his finger in the air.

We all wait without uttering a sound.

After another moment he nods. "Motherfucking hell. Such a bitch. Such a colossal, self-entitled, fucking bitch."

From there, Nikon launches away from the table and into a colorful tirade of cursing like I've never heard—and considering I grew up in a house of six Irish men, that's a high bar to beat.

While he vents a lifetime of pent-up hatred, Kev, Calum, and I sink heavily into our chairs and give him the floor. I, for one, am stuck on her parting threat. Either he convinces himself to choose Hecate, or we rot in the past.

Not only is he Hecate's ex-lover but he's the one that got away, and she hasn't forgotten.

When Nikon runs out of expletives, he falls back to his seat, exhales, and refills his glass. Lifting it to his lips, he sucks it back without breath or pause. His Adam's apple bobs until his goblet is empty. Wine isn't the booze I think of when I think of chugging, but I guess when the occasion calls for it...

Calum breaks the silence first. "If you're trying to drown your sorrows, Greek, I should tell you—sorrow knows how to swim."

Nikon arches a brow and tops up his glass again. This time, he holds the crystal up in salute. "When in Greece do as the Greek does."

All righty then. We lift our glasses to match his toast and take a couple of healthy swallows to join him.

When I've emptied my glass, I set it down and draw a deep breath while Kevin refills it. "Tell me you can flash us home and that part about stay here to rot stuff was bluster."

He shakes his head. "Sorry, Red. Timeshift is not among my talents. One of my cousins, Alec, can do it, but he won't be born for three hundred years, so we can't expect much help from him, I'm afraid. I can flash us a thousand places in this world, but that doesn't get us home."

Calum takes his glass for a tour around the pergola. "All right, so we're here. It's not time to freak out yet. Fi's been kidnapped into different times and realms before, and she always manages to get back. Let's operate under the assumption that this will end in our favor."

Kevin nods. "Okay, let's take a moment to soak it in and be thankful we're alive and sharing a moment."

Nikon looks at the two of them and me. "Speaking of sharing a moment. Fuck, Fi. I'm sorry. I don't want you to get the wrong idea...it isn't a regular thing...Kev and Calum are as much the super couple as ever. It's just...."

I laugh and raise a hand to stop the tailspin. "Please. I've known from the beginning."

Calum blinks. "What? How?"

"The night Nikon showed up to shut down the demon rift from Hell he was wearing the pizza cat sheet I bought Kev for his birthday. *And* I shared the bedroom wall with you guys. *And* during the night of hide-and-seek, I caught the extra tackle and flirt sexiness while in my hidey-hole. You guys aren't nearly as covert as you think you are."

Calum and Kev look so guilty it's hilarious.

"Don't give me that look. I genuinely don't care. As long as you two are still solidly in love and you three are good and don't let it screw up a great thing, it's none of my business or concern. You do you—or each other, as the case may be."

Calum side hugs me and kisses the side of my head. "Okay, awkward but I'm glad you're cool. Now can we change the subject?"

"Yes, please." I point out at the sea and smile. "Can I say how spectacular this is? Wow, Greek. Nice life."

There's no missing the pride that lights up Nikon's gaze.

He strides over to stand beside us and look out at the water. "You know that fierce passion you all feel for Toronto, the landscape, and the culture? Well, this is my Toronto. This is the land of my heart."

The four of us stand shoulder-to-shoulder and watch the sun go down over the sea. I want to get lost in the moment but mental images of Da, my brothers, Liam, and Sloan spin in my mind. "How much trouble are we in, Greek?"

He sighs. "I honestly don't know. Something made her track me down, and now that I'm here, I'm not giving her what she wants. In a lot of ways, she's a superpower. In other ways, she's a petulant child."

"She's still in love with you," Kevin says.

He shakes his head. "She chose me from the beginning because I was immortal and she fancied having a partner who was inferior to her who could also live with her indefinitely. She's in love with the idea of permanent arm candy, but the truth is I turned down life with her, and she never forgave me. She lives to make me regret it, and I've done everything in my power to ensure I never do."

I hear the anger and resentment in his voice and realize what he meant earlier. "So, when you said you thought of her every day for two thousand years…."

He meets my gaze, and my pulse quickens. "Oh, that was true. Every fucking day I live a half-life because of her. I can never love. I can never marry. I can never have children. When I turned her down and said I couldn't stay with her for eternity, she swore I'd never be happy without her. I learned the truth of that threat the hard way."

I take his hand and squeeze his fingers. "I'm sorry about your wife and baby. It breaks my heart you lost them because of Hecate's jealousy. The woman you two argued about at the hotel —Kallista—that was her?"

Nikon winces at the sound of her name. Whatever Hecate's lesson entailed, it left a welted scar on his heart.

"Yeah, that was her."

"I'm so sorry, Greek," Calum says.

He shakes his head and drifts off, padding bare-footed across the marble floor. "Don't be. Your family made the past months the closest to happy I've been in millennia."

"Do you think that's why she's circling?" Calum asks. "You're not suffering enough?"

He turns and throws his wine glass, shattering it on one of the columns on the other side of the pergola. The burgundy stain drips down the pristine marble to pool on the floor.

"I'm so sick of this," he shouts. "I'm sick of living a hollow life. I'm sick of the threat she holds over me. Most of all, I'm sick of looking in the mirror every fucking day and seeing this child's face."

He turns away, lets out a long groan, and grips his long blond hair with rough fingers. When he turns back, he gestures up and down his body with a frantic motion of trembling hands. "I look exactly the way I did the day I told her I was too young to leave my family and stay with her for eternity. If I cut my hair, the next day it's back. When I mar my face, the next day it's healed. I'm trapped in this one moment in time, and it's horrid."

He wrings his hands together, pacing our open-air prison. I capture him on one of his frenzied passes and hold his face between my hands. "I'm sorry, Greek. I may not be able to fix it, but whatever it takes, I promise you, I *will* help."

The look of despair he pegs me with steals my breath. "How, Fi? How does dragging you into my misery do either of us any good?"

"We'll figure it out. Hecate is the goddess the witches worship, right? So maybe it's a hex or a curse. Maybe we can learn the origin of your sentence and break it."

Nikon's shoulders slump as he exhales a heavy breath. "Fi, you know I believe in you, but I have spent centuries trying. How do you think I know magic? Because I learned everything I could about Wiccan practices. Hecate is the goddess of magic, witchcraft, the night, moon, ghosts, the crossroads, and necromancy. I studied every facet of her domain to try to break her hold on my life. Nothing worked. Hecate did this, and she's the only one who can undo it."

My heart breaks for him. I wish something I could say would give him hope. I don't know what. He's immortal. If he says he tried everything, I believe him.

"How did she do it? Was it a hex, a potion, a curse?

He shrugs. "It was stupid actually. I told her as amazing as it was to be with her, I was too young to give up my life on the mortal plane to live with her on Olympus. My mother and grandmother were mortal, and I wasn't willing to forfeit the finite years of their lives being the plaything of a goddess."

"Obviously that went over well," Kev interjects.

"She glared at me with a look very similar to the one tonight and said, *'Too young, say you, then too young you shall remain.'* And *bam,* my future was cast."

The four of us talk a little longer, drink a bit more wine, and watch the landscape until the dark of night swallows it. When the breeze cools, and it becomes obvious Hecate isn't returning, Nikon says we should make our exit.

"Will she be pissed if we leave?" Calum asks.

He picks a giant pink bloom off one of the vines that wrap the columns and inhales. "No. She told me what she expects, and she's too conceited to think I won't do it. She won't come back here."

I pick up a couple of grapes off the table and pop one into my mouth. "All right, where do we go? What's our play?"

Nikon shrugs. "The same play I always fall back on. There's one person I always count on for advice and support, no matter how twisted up life gets."

"Andromeda?"

He shakes his head. "My grandfather."

Calum and Kevin close the ranks, and my brother steals a grape. "Do you think you can find him? If we're in the days of you turning Hecate down, do you know where he will be?"

He holds out his hand and grins. "Papu has owned our family lands since the beginning, his father before him, and his grandfather before that. He is the compass of our family. Come. I'll introduce you and Fi can exchange her tablecloth for a real dress."

I smile down at my makeshift attire and shrug. "No complaints. I think you did a great job on my DIY toga."

Setting my hand in his, I draw a deep breath and smile as Kevin squeezes my palm, and Calum joins the chain. For the first time in almost two hours, I think maybe things aren't so bad. They're not good—I'm not kidding myself—but perhaps they're not *so* bad.

CHAPTER SEVEN

Where Sloan's wayfarer gift feels like a *poof* of power and you're there, Nikon's power of transportation is more like a snap. It's like the shock you get from dragging fuzzy socks across the carpet in wintertime. You touch something metal and *snap*. The energy lets loose.

It doesn't hurt. Traveling with Nikon's raw fae prana power merely holds a wallop.

"Home sweet home," Nikon says.

The Tsambikos family villa sprawls across the grassy crest of sheer rock cliffs overlooking the sea. White marble terraces, tiered and supported by a span of symmetrically spaced columns and archways, run the length of the façade.

I have no doubt it will be spectacular in daylight because, at night, the rising moon casting a silver band across the terracotta rooftops is dramatic and daunting.

The grounds stretch off endlessly into the darkness. The boundary lined by a high iron fence holds lit torches at measured intervals. The regularity of the golden flames serves to reinforce the air of intimidation.

"Holy shit," Calum says. "This is a massive property."

The comment pulls Nikon from his thoughts, and he nods. "It's larger still. What you see here is the main house. Papu divided the property for my father and his two younger brothers. The house where I grew up is a five-minute walk down the slope."

"You grew up here?" I ask.

He nods. "A blessing and a curse."

"How so?"

"Because nowhere and in no time will I ever find a place more perfect to call my own."

"Then why not stay here?"

He smiles down at me. "You forget, I come from a family of immortals, Fi."

"And?"

"So, every child Papu and my father and my uncles and their children give birth to *all* belong to this property. There are too many of us to stay."

"I never thought about that."

He nods. "There are drawbacks to immortality."

"Andromeda said something similar earlier today. Was that today? Damn. It feels like a week ago since we were tracking down baby Jos."

Calum nods. "Hells yeah, it does."

Kev shrugs a shoulder and shakes his head. "I guess I only considered the bonus of you not dying when Fiona accidentally skewered you as her fae trickster."

Nikon catches his flyaway hair and combs it back from his face with his fingers. "That goes in the pro column."

Calum chuckles. "Fo shizzle."

"Shall we?" Nikon tilts his head toward the iron gates surrounding the grounds and waits until we're connected and give him the nod.

He flashes us inside the private property, and we approach the house. The feathery fronds of the palms wave in a steady dance above us as the cool moisture of sea spray misting the air kisses our hot skin.

I hear his deep exhale of breath and cast a sideways glance. He's grinning at the house with more joy than I've ever seen in him. "What now?"

He tilts his head. "Now we talk to Papu."

Calum makes a face. "What if you're already here? You said you spent a lot of time here, right? What if it's one of those sci-fi moments of the same person not being able to occupy the same space?"

Nikon scowls at the house for a moment, then shrugs. "That will be weird and maybe disastrous, but it changes nothing. At some point, we gotta announce ourselves."

As we approach the front door, two massive black beasts barrel around the corner of the house, snapping and snarling.

"Demon dogs!" Calum shouts while grabbing Kev.

Nikon grabs us, and suddenly, we're standing on the open verandah of the second story.

A muscled and wiry man in his mid-thirties rushes out the front door. He's carrying an ax and searching the grounds for what set off his guard dogs.

"What are you going to do with that, old man?"

The man turns to find us on the verandah behind him. "I'm going to split you down the middle and feed you to my dogs for calling me an old man."

That is funny because his grandfather doesn't look much older than Aiden. He's also the opposite of Nikon in almost every feature. Where Nikon is tall, lean, and blond, this man is five-foot-ten, muscled, and has dark brown hair and eyes.

Nikon chuckles. "That would be a shame, Papu, because of all the grandchildren you ever sire in your endless life, I'm your favorite."

His brow arches. "Is that a fact?"

"First-born son of your first-born son. I'm the one named after you, aren't I?"

He chuckles. "What has you acting so queer, *agori mou*? Why did the dogs chase after you?"

"I'd blame it on these losers, but it's more likely because I'm not the Nikon they know. We're in a bit of trouble and need to talk about it with you and Yaya."

"Trouble? Your father is in Sparta. Shall I send a slave to fetch your uncles?"

He shakes his head. "No. Let me explain first."

Movement behind us brings a sparsely dressed man through the patio door. He charges us like a gladiator, his muscled chest and arms bulging in the flicker of firelight.

Nikon flashes back down onto the lawn.

His grandfather spins, his eyes widening when he finds us down on the ground with him once more. "What kind of magic is this?"

"You know what kind, Papu. I carry your gift in my blood. Your visit to the Cistern of The Source gave you immortality, which then passed through your bloodline. Father got precognitive sight. Andromeda got fae glamor, and I got teleportation."

His gaze narrows on us. "There's a fault in your story, boy. Neither you nor Andromeda have come into powers yet."

"We will. That's part of the trouble I mentioned. I've been drawn back in time by an angry goddess. I'm actually from over two millennia into the future."

He shakes his head. "I've often wondered… So, we truly are immortal?"

Nikon nods. "We are. No disease or illness will take us down. Not even a spear through the chest will end our lives. When the end takes us, we regenerate back here and within days are as healthy and strong as ever before."

"Then how is it you haven't aged a day from the boy I spoke to this morning? Your father and uncles all ceased to age at thirty-four as I did when I entered the cistern."

Nikon rubs a hand over his face and exhales. "Please, Papu. Put the ax down and send Atlas and Chaos on their way. I'll explain everything. We need your help, and Fiona could use one of Yaya's dresses."

With a bark of command and a hand gesture, Nikon senior sends the dogs on their way. "Very well. Come here, boy. Let me look at you."

Nikon flashes us closer.

"The future, you say."

He nods. "On my honor."

"There are gods and creatures who could take your likeness and pose as you."

"Then you should test me. I'll answer anything you ask."

He nods. "Very well, tell me of my wife."

Nikon grins. "Helene Bakirtzis of Messenia is the third daughter to an owner of bakeries. When she was thirteen, he arranged for her to go to Athens to make a life with her uncle's adopted son. On her travels, she met a dashing soldier fresh home from invading Melitene. The two of you fell in love while sharing a carriage toward the city, and despite the disapproval she would face, she accompanied you to Rhodes to be your wife. You were wed the first night you arrived, and since you hadn't received your stipend for service yet, she paid the town magistrate with the only thing of value she had, her mother's gold bracelet."

The man's gaze softens as his mouth curls into a soft smile. "How is it you come to be here?"

"That's a long and harrowing story. Might we go inside?"

He studies us for a long moment and gestures to the door. "Very well. You mentioned trouble?"

Nikon nods. "Woman trouble."

"Ugh, the worst kind."

Nikon's grandfather ushers us into the symposia, a Greek room for social gatherings. It's a large, rectangular space with lit torch stands in the corners and an open wall that leads out to a central courtyard. Wood-framed couches with puffy cushions face each other in the center of the room, and Nikon and I take our seats.

Papu sends one of the house servants to invite his wife in for drinks with guests while he sets out glasses for wine and begins to pour. "Women problems, you say."

Nikon nods, but before he gets a chance to respond, a silver-haired woman in her mid-sixties strides in. In a peacock green dress that flows over the floor like she's floating, Helene Tsambikos seems to suck the air out of the room.

The moment Nikon sees her, his eyes glass up. "Yaya."

"Yes, my darling?"

He strides across the room to meet her and grips her hand to pull it to his lips. "The reality of you outshines even my brightest memory."

She presses an elegant hand to Nikon's cheek, and he closes his eyes. "My darling boy. What stirs you to tears? What's happened?"

I blink back the tears blurring my vision, and honestly, Calum and Kev look a little shaken too.

Nikon senior eyes us like we're all crazy. He clears his throat and hands his wife and me each a glass of wine. "Sit, my love, before emotion takes hold and they've lost all sense of decorum."

I accept my glass and rein it in.

Nikon releases his grandmother's hand and wipes his eyes. "Apologies. As I explained to Papu, I am not the Nikon the two of you know from this time. I have lived so long without seeing you and so long without hearing your voice… I'm simply overwhelmed."

Helene accepts her glass of wine and sits on the next sofa over from me with her husband. Nikon sits to my right and opposite his grandparents. Kev and Calum sit opposite me. "How long has it been since last we parted, my darling?"

"Over a thousand years, Yaya. I've missed you terribly."

Her face falls. "A thousand years? I... Oh...and are your Papu, Helios, and your uncles still with you?"

Nikon nods. "Yes, but you and Matera are gone."

The two of them look like he's shattered their world.

"Forgive me." Nikon swirls the wine in the bowl of his glass. "Let me start from the beginning."

The six of us drink wine while Nikon brings his grandparents up to speed on our situation. As reserved as Papu is, Yaya recovers from the news of her husband's longevity and appears to sit at the opposite end of the spectrum.

She's thrilled to have us tell her a little about life in the years to come and dotes on us as I'm sure she did on Nikon when he was a boy.

While they speak, I look around the room and let it sink in. This is ancient Greece. Nikon's family are wealthy at this time and are wealthier still in my time.

The six of us lounge on the couches picking at fruits, cheeses, and olives on the low table between us while their house servants buzz around, refilling the wine decanters and trays of food.

Part of me knows the servants are slaves and not staff, but it's a different time, and I try not to judge. After all, his grandparents speak to their help with more kindness and respect than Sloan's mother uses with Dalton.

That has to say something, doesn't it?

It's surreal, sitting here with the warm sea air and the togas and the rooms painted in frescos and lit with lanterns. Even more compelling is watching Nikon's grandparents interact with one another. Helene is an aged woman for ancient Greek society while her husband looks as young and full of vitality as ever.

Another con for immortality—growing old while your

partner remains locked in the prime of his life. Or worse, being the one who doesn't age and losing the people you love over and over again.

I see the depth of that sadness in Nikon's eyes.

He hasn't taken his gaze off Helene since she first walked into the room. While the immortality of the bloodline is an amazing byproduct of his grandfather's time at the Cistern of The Source, it doesn't extend to the family's spouses.

"Are you certain you wish for nothing more to eat?" Helene smiles at us. "It would be my greatest pleasure to fill your bellies."

"My belly is as full as my heart, Yaya," Nikon says. "If I ate even one more morsel, I fear I might burst."

"What about you boys? Or you, Fiona? Have you needs yet to be met?"

I look to Nikon, almost afraid to ask. "Are there bathrooms in ancient Greece?"

He chuckles. "Yes, Fi. Do you think us Neanderthals?"

"No. I didn't know how you handled things."

Calum and Kevin chuckle and I fight the urge to give them the finger. I'm trying to make a good impression.

Nikon and Nikon senior both stand when I stand.

My Nikon gestures toward the hall. "Second door on the left. There's a tapestry hung across the doorway for privacy and a lantern hook inside the door to your right. Take the lantern from the little table inside with you. Everything else is self-explanatory. Not much has changed."

I leave them to their reminiscing and make my way down the hall. At the second doorway on my left, I see a heavy tapestry of woodland animals and a lantern on a small side table.

After hanging the lantern on the hook inside, my anxieties ease. The washroom is like an indoor outhouse. There's a clean marble bench with a wooden toilet seat lid and a little table with a basin and pitcher opposite that to wash up.

Good enough.

I get things sorted out quickly and feel refreshed when I exit the privy and return the lantern to its place. Turning to rejoin the group, I let out a yelp. "Sorry, you startled me."

Helene stands in front of me patting her throat. "Apologies. I meant only to share a private word, not to give fright."

I chuckle at my reaction and wave away her concern. "Maybe being stalked by Hecate set me on edge."

"I imagine so." She twists her hands together, and I realize as awkward as all this is for me, it is for her as well. "Nikon asked me to clothe you properly. Would you care to join me in my dressing room?"

"Of course...and thank you. Your grandson did a great job with the tablecloth, but I admit, I feel a little exposed."

She gestures to the right, and we walk along a stone colonnade toward the back of the house. On our left, birds swoop into the enclosed courtyard to settle in the greenery for the night. The house is essentially a large square with an open courtyard in the middle.

With no roof, rainwater is free to water the plants and fill the shallow bathing pool in the center.

"I regret Nikon's troubles have drawn you all into such a dangerous situation. He says you have a betrothed and family who will be desperately missing you."

I look down at the silver Claddagh band and smile. "I do. Somehow we have to convince Hecate to take us back to our time and let Nikon live his life."

Even in her declining years—the life expectancy of the time being seventy years—Helene moves with poise and grace.

She's petite with smooth, silver hair pulled up and held with decorative pins that match the green of her dress. Her bodice is embroidered with bronze, gold, and blue threads, weaving a pattern of leaves so intricate that it must have taken the seamstress weeks.

As we walk, her gown flutters behind her making her look

like a delicate faery. "I wish he would confide in us what acts to take to keep this from happening. The poor boy endures too much."

"No argument, but he's right. If you try to change things, there's no telling what else might change. He's a strong and intelligent man. I trust his instincts."

"You care for him a great deal."

I nod. "He's a good friend. He and Andromeda have become a part of our family."

The two of us pad silently across the smooth, stone floors and I'm dazzled by how quiet it is here. No buzzing of city sounds or white noise or electronics to interrupt the peace.

The world is still.

Another bird flutters by and I smile. It reminds me of Gran's birds flying through the skylight to get their fruit.

Helene's bedroom is another large, rectangular space with torch stands in the four corners and a few key pieces of furniture. The walls are painted beige, but on top of that, they've been frescoed in *trompe l'oeil*.

Lovely outdoor scenery covers most of the room with a peacock perched on the edge of a fountain and soft, mossy hills, but the lusty mural painted on the wall at the head of the bed has me doing a double-take.

Helloooo nurse.

A naked couple is in a moment of rapture: heads back, hands groping, a swath of fluttering green fabric strategically twisting between them to cover the X-rated bits.

Wow, maybe this as bedroom décor is perfectly normal for this time, but I can't imagine my grandparents having something like this over their bed.

Ew, nope. I don't *want* to imagine Gran and Granda having something like this over their bed.

Titillation has its place. It's nowhere near grandparents.

When did humanity become so prudish?

"Do you like art, Fiona?"

My cheeks flush hot as Nikon's grandmother catches me staring, mouth agape. "I was thinking how much Kevin would love this. He's an artist and works in a gallery. He would appreciate the beauty of this painting."

She smiles and gestures at her closet. "What type of dress were you thinking?"

I giggle. "I couldn't hazard a guess. Anything you think is appropriate to cover my parts will work."

"Do you prefer a bodice or a free waist?" She reads my expression and her silver brows arch. "Are the fashions of your day so different?"

"Yes, very much. As a rule, I only wear a dress if I'm going to a ceremony of some kind, a wedding, a funeral, or if one of my brothers or my father is receiving an award."

"Then what do you wear?"

"Yoga pants mostly, as well as jeans, or slacks, or khakis." She doesn't seem to understand so I demonstrate. "You know if the fabric went around my legs and fell to the floor separately."

"Breeks? Like the gladiators wear?"

I shrug. "That's not a loincloth, is it? I don't wear that."

"No. No. I believe I understand your meaning. I am, however, surprised women of the future wear them."

I nod. "If I wore skirts, I wouldn't be able to train."

"Train to do what?"

How do I explain being a druid? "You understand about goddesses and magic, right?"

"I do. Nikon—my husband, Nikon—was touched by magic. I have witnessed the workings of it in our lives. He doesn't age, and he doesn't fall ill."

"Right. Your husband encountered what we call fae prana—a pure source of nature magic. I possess the same magic but in a smaller amount and I am a guardian of nature—a warrior of sorts to ensure the innocents of my world remain unharmed by other people with magic. My brothers, my father, my boyfriend, and I are what we call druids."

"You mention your family often. You are close?"

I nod. "Very. My mother died when I was a young girl. My father raised my five older brothers and me."

"I had sisters." She shifts through the dresses. "I think that's why I loved being a mother of boys so much. They are such a different beast, are they not?"

I chuckle. "Absolutely. I'm sure if I had sisters, I would be a very different person. Instead of learning how to fight, I might've learned to embroider or act like a lady."

"Acting the part of a lady is mostly that—acting the part." Helene grins and selects a blue dress. "I think a free waist would be best. We are not so close in size that my fitted dresses would suit your frame."

I laugh to myself.

I think that was a really nice, Greek way of saying she's skinny and I have too many curves to fit. "This will be fine, I'm sure. Thanks so much—"

"Mistress!" One of the handmaidens rushes to the doorway and stops the moment she sees we're chatting. "Forgive me. When you have a moment, mistress. A matter of importance demands your attention."

Helene frowns. "I'll leave you to dress while I check on whatever this is about." When she strides off, I step behind her dressing screen and rid myself of Hecate's tablecloth in exchange for an actual dress.

It's a little tight in the shoulders, but it hangs to the floor and considering I'm going commando, that's all right by me.

"You clean up good, Red." Nikon is leaning against the iron banister in the corridor with his back to the courtyard. He straightens and checks out the dress up and down. "You look like a true Greek lady."

I snort. "I was just talking about that with your grandmother. 'Look like' is the operative part of that phrase."

"You fancy some fresh air? The boys and I thought we'd stare at the stars for a little before we turn in. You can let Bruin out for a stretch too if you're game."

"I'm definitely game."

He bends down and lifts a brown crock from the floor beside the column. "Are you lady enough to try Papu's liquid lightning?"

We are the escaped captives of Hecate.

Getting tipsy and letting our guard down is likely a terrible idea. "Hells yeah, Greek. Point the way."

CHAPTER EIGHT

"Fi, wake up." A gentle hand on my arm jostles me free from the warmth of my illusion of lying nestled in King Henry with Sloan. Only I don't want to wake up. I like where I am. "Open your eyes, sleepyhead, or you'll miss it."

I blink at the gray haze of morning giving way to the brilliance of morning sun. Sitting up, I scrub a hand over my face and follow Nikon's pointed finger beyond the edge of the cliff and out across the waters of the sea.

"A Mediterranean sunrise." Calum yawns.

"It's beautiful." Kevin rolls to sit up and take it in.

"I forget how beautiful sometimes."

The four of us sit in silence for a while, absorbing the natural wonder of a world barely touched by man. There's no overpopulation. No pollution. No nuclear accidents or destroyed ozone or animal extinction.

It's a natural world before humans get their hooks into it.

"What sea are we looking at, exactly?" I ask.

"All of them," Nikon says. "Well, three of the Greek ones. This property sits on the southern tip of Rhodes." He points out to the left. "That's the Mediterranean Sea." He points straight in front of us. "That's the Sea of Crete." Then he points off to the right. "And that's the Aegean Sea."

Calum nods. "Your family home overlooks them all. That rocks."

"Yep."

The sun has bobbed above the horizon now and is casting a fiery reflection across the Mediterranean waters.

"Check it." Calum points. "It looks like the all-seeing eye in *Lord of the Rings*."

"Damn, I wish I had my phone to take pictures," Kevin says. "I'd love to try to capture some of this on canvas."

I nod. "If nothing else, it's the silver lining of Hecate dragging us here at this moment. You were a lucky boy to grow up having this as your playground, Greek."

"That I was."

We sit in silence a while longer—well, it's almost silent. Bruin is snoring like a buzzsaw behind us. "Hey, Greek?" I ask a while later.

"Yeah."

"All bullshitting aside, do you see us getting home?"

He sits, staring out at the splendor of the sunrise for a long while. "I honestly don't know. It's a shitty answer. I get that. I simply don't know what it'll take to convince her to send us back."

The thought of never seeing Sloan, or my dad, or my other brothers again makes my sinuses sting with the onset of tears. It feels like someone is reaching inside my chest and squeezing my heart into mush.

If I let it, thinking like this will turn me into an emotional puddle of tears.

"It's too soon to start worrying, Fi." Calum reads the emotion in my expression. "You've been dragged through time before, and it always works out. This time, you're not even alone. We've got this, sista."

I swipe the moisture from my cheeks and inhale. "Yeah, we do. Of course, we do."

Kevin reaches over and squeezes my bare foot. "If we can't give Hecate what she wants, maybe we can lie or stroke her ego, then see where we are."

"Or we give her what she wants," Nikon suggests.

I crank my head to the side to glare at him. "Exsqueeze me? No. You're not giving up your life to become Hecate's beck and call boy. Screw that. Surrendering is not an option so get that out of your head right now."

"It could get you guys home."

"At what cost?" Calum snaps. "You? No deal."

I'm with Calum on that. "We don't sacrifice friends—we fight for them. What do you think it would do to us to know you're condemned to an eternity of being that bitch's plaything so we could go home to our happy life? How could we be happy? No way. I'd rather stay and get my Greek on."

Kevin nods. "We fucking rock the toga. Bring on the wine and sculpting."

"What about Olympic sports?" Calum asks.

"It's all Greek to me." Kev laughs and points at himself. "See what I did there?"

Nikon rolls his eyes. "We'll table it for now, but if it means me staying under her thumb or you three living your lives, I know what my vote is."

"Only it will be three votes against one, Greek. Sorry, not sorry. You lose." Calum flashes a smug smile and returns his attention to the sunrise. "Off the table."

I nod. "It's like that old spaghetti-and-meatball rhyme for kids. That option is off the table and rolled across the floor and under the door. Bye-bye, meatball."

"Bye-bye, meatball," Kevin laughs, joining in.

Nikon chuffs. "*You* are a meatball, Fi."

I grin. "Hecate can't be our only Olympian option for getting home. Surely there are other gods or goddesses with the power to send us there."

Calum nods. "Maybe someone who wants to put the screws to Hecate. The enemy of our enemy is our friend."

Nikon tilts his head and considers that. "You might be onto something there. When we were together, she was having problems with a couple of the other members of the pantheon."

"She's a selfish dick. I'm not surprised."

Nikon chuckles. "Fi, most deities are selfish dicks. They're omnipotent, so why do they care about us?"

Calum leans back and stretches his legs. "Okay, Greek, so who's lower on the dickdom scale but might have equal or greater juice and would send us home to piss off Hecate?"

Nikon frowns. "I don't think you guys understand how powerful she is. Hecate is one of the only free Titans. Her powers rank right up there with Zeus. She has power over all domains and witchcraft to top that off."

Kev straightens the two empty jugs we polished off through the night and sighs. "She has to have enemies. Maybe someone she's afraid of?"

Nikon stares out over the waters for a while, then shrugs. "Clytius, one of Gaia's sons, was a giant created to absorb and defeat Hecate's magic. They faced off in the great battle of Gigantomachy."

I nod. "Sounds promising. Where do we find him?"

"She torched him."

"She killed him?"

"Yeah, she literally torched him and burned him alive."

I groan. "You knew this about her and thought, yeah, I think I'll hit that. What could possibly go wrong?" I regret the pain I see in his eyes and exhale. "Sorry. That was shitty and uncalled for. I'm frustrated."

He leans sideways and bumps my shoulder. "It's fine. I understand. How do you think I've felt every day since?"

Poor Nikon. Teenaged boy. An uber-hot goddess wants him. I see how it could happen. "So, she's one of the most powerful forces, killed the giant specifically crafted to take her down, and is pretty much invincible."

"Now you're getting it. Welcome to my living nightmare." Nikon falls quiet as he drinks in the sights. His eyes are glassy, but that could be from staring into the sun.

"We'll figure it out, Greek." Calum squeezes his shoulder. "She's never come up against the Cumhaills. By the time we've finished, she'll regret taking us on."

"True story." I meet Calum for a high five.

Kevin reaches over to squeeze his arm. "You look tired, Greek. Did you get any sleep?"

"Who needs sleep? It's not like I can get sick or die from not taking care of myself. Honestly, there are times I wish I could. I've done all I can do in this life. At this point, being immortal is more of a prison than Hecate ever put me in."

I have no idea how to help him or what I can say to make any of this better for him.

"That's only because you're under her finger," Calum counters. "We'll get that sorted, and you'll be free to live life to its fullest and take full advantage of all immortality offers."

"From your lips to the gods' ears."

I roll to my feet and smooth the fabric of the dress Yaya lent me last night. "Let's head inside, make a plan, and start our day. Ancient Greeks drink coffee, don't they?"

Kevin groans. "Please say yes. The only answer to a question like that is yes."

Nikon snorts. "Sorry, guys. You're a few centuries too early for java. The caffeine craze won't start until the rise of the Ottoman Empire.

Kevin sighs. "Okay, now I'm pissed."

. . .

After waking Bruin and getting him nestled away inside me again, Nikon and I fold the blanket from the ground and leave the majesty of the sunrise to head back to the villa.

Seeing it in the light of day with the land dropping away at the cliffs and the three seas mixing and mingling around the island's point is even more spectacular than I expected. The sound of waves breaking is dramatic and with the view and the mist in the air, and the sunrise…

Perfection.

The grumblings of his grandfather have us changing course and veering toward a large citrus grove near the edge of the slope. Nikon senior is walking the aisles between the fruit trees and muttering.

"Good morning, Papu." Nikon greets him as we approach. "You only talk to yourself when things weigh on you. If it's our arrival, I apologize. Perhaps we shouldn't have come."

He shakes his head and pulls a branch down to sniff the limes. "Nonsense. Having you here is a blessing. You are as welcome today as you are centuries from now, I'm sure."

"Then what makes you wander and mutter like a man gone mad?"

He gestures to the tree. "A streak of ill health hit our land in past months. It began with an infestation of moths in late spring. We defeated the pests, yet I fear the grove may still succumb to the damage suffered."

"I'm sorry, Papu."

He scrubs at the back of his neck and exhales. "Then this morning, I noticed trouble with the vines in the vineyard. I fear you are not the only Tsambikos to fall out of favor with the gods."

I step in and look. He's not wrong about the damage. The leaves of the fruit trees are compromised. The ones not chewed away have waxy, silver patches of damage. "Would you allow Calum and I to try to heal this?"

"If you wish to try, I would be most grateful. Helene mentioned you spoke of a gift with nature."

I nod. "Like you, our lives have been touched by fae energy. Our powers are focused on being caregivers to the natural world. If Hecate didn't block our abilities when she took our tattoos, we should be able to help fix this."

Nikon senior dips his chin. "Gratitude."

Stooping low, I lift the hem of my dress and shuffle under the branches to kneel at the trunk of the tree. The grass is damp and cool with morning mist, but I don't mind. It's nothing like the cold we've had at home the last few months.

Calum joins me and smiles. "You're way ahead of me on nature healing, Fi. You lead. I'll follow."

I place my hands against the peeling bark, and my heart goes out to the poor thing. "You're really not feeling well, are you? Let's see what we can do about that."

I think back to the very first spell Gran had me work on and smile. It took me ages to get that little bean to sprout in my pot, but once I understood the connection druids have with living and growing things, I grew strong quickly.

I'm proud to have inherited even a fraction of Gran's natural affinity for plants. While I didn't arrive with my casting stones to amplify my power to influence the natural world, the purity of nature here is a power boost in itself.

Reaching out, I acknowledge my connection to the fae energy I've been gifted with and ground myself in this setting.

The rich, dark soil beneath me is full of the nutrients needed to promote growth. The tree trunk beneath my palms is strong, a healthy conduit to carry those nutrients as well as water to feed the leaves and branches above.

Closing my eyes, I connect with the living energy of the entire orchard and speak my spell aloud.

Your health is drained from moths and blight,

Yet still, your branches hold your might.
Recovery has been hard and slow.
We lend you gifts to heal and grow.
Nourish yourself from soil and sun.
And bear your fruit the battle won.

When I open my eyes, Calum is watching me and taking it all in. I'm used to people outside my circle looking at me with awe and wonder when I use my powers, but having Calum look at me like that is weird.

"That should get us started," I say. "So now, we'll wander around and check on things."

Papu bows his head and smiles. "I am honored by your efforts, Lady Fiona."

Nikon offers me a hand to help me up and winks. "Thanks, Fi. You rock."

"My pleasure. It felt good to get out of my head for a little and focus on fixing something I have more control over."

Calum and I wander off for a while, winding through the aisles, touching trees, and checking fruit. I repeat the spell at a few more intervals through the grove, and he does the same. Then, we come together, and I cast overall healing.

"May your branches bear strong, healthy fruit for years to come. May your roots find rich soil to nourish your growth. May you thrive evermore. Blessed be."

"Blessed be," everyone repeats.

When that's taken care of, I straighten. "Now the vineyard. Let's get the Tsambikos lands back in order."

The five of us make our way toward the crest of the "slope" Nikon keeps mentioning, and I get my first view of the extent of the Tsambikos lands. When they mentioned the vineyard, I imagined it as a few rows of vines to keep the family in ample stock of homemade wine.

I was mistaken.

The Tsambikos vineyard is extensive and takes up the entire southeast face of the slope down to where Nikon senior subdivided the property for his son's homes—which Nikon said was a five-minute walk.

That's a lot of grapes.

I realize now how Nikon's family makes their living. "How big is this vineyard?"

Nikon smiles. "Papu has sixty-two acres. Which is massive for these times."

"No doubt." With the blue waters nearby, the smell of sea air all around, and the lush green of the vines stretching off into the distance, this has to be the most beautiful spot on Earth. "Where are the sick vines?"

"Off a fair distance," Papu says. "Should we perhaps wait until after first victuals?"

After breakfast, I want to work on getting home. "If you tell Nikon where we need to be, he can flash us there, and we'll be quicker."

His grandfather shakes his head. "I have so many questions about your power. The boy I know as Nikon hasn't accessed his abilities."

Nikon looks at me and shrugs. "We seem to unlock our powers around twenty-one when our adult lives set in. I am only seventeen in this time."

"Seventeen? That's how young you were when Hecate tried to bind you into a lifetime and froze you in time?"

He nods. "Although seventeen in this time is considered to be adult, times changed."

I'd never believed he looked nineteen when he insisted he could get away with it. I simply played along because it's obviously a sore spot for him. Seventeen makes more sense.

"We'll fix it." I'm more determined than ever that Nikon is set free. "First, flash us to the sick plants."

Nikon and his grandfather take a moment to discuss where we're going, then Nikon nods and holds out his hands. I take one without hesitation, but his grandfather hesitates. Nikon chuckles. "Trust me, Papu. Other than the odd person having their hands fall off, flashing is perfectly safe."

The horrified look on his grandfather's face is hilarious, and Nikon cracks up.

"Oh, Papu. On my honor, no harm will come to you. It's an amazingly easy way to travel."

Nikon senior chuffs and takes his hand.

The moment we flash to the location, two things become blatantly clear at once. This area is very ill, and the trouble is not a natural occurrence.

My shield flares the moment we take form, and I spin to assess the danger. "Guys, we have hostiles! Bruin, I need you."

Bruin bursts free from my chest and finds our foe a few rows over. "I'm here, Red."

I call forward my armor and Birga. Neither reply.

Calum has the same problem and curses not being able to access his bow and quiver. "Fucking Hecate."

I grab a wooden landscape stake and follow Bruin's snarls. Running in a gown and sandals isn't my favorite—hell, it's not even in my top one hundred. "How many, Bruin?"

"Seven…no six…make that five…"

With every scream of panic, my battle bear counts down, and the opposition dwindles. He's amazing. He's a one-man offensive team.

He's cutting down bad guys, and we're still *en route*.

Rounding the end aisle, I join the battle already in progress. Bruin's chasing down a runner, and that leaves the four of us with only one each.

My guy might be a gladiator in his spare time because he has that musclebound brute thing going on and looks damned like a tank wearing only a leather skirt. He seems confused about fighting a woman at first but gets over the moral pause quickly enough.

I block the swipe of his sword with my stake and front kick him to the gonads as hard as I can. It's not a very technical melee maneuver, but it's effective.

Except when it's not.

My sandal connects with a solid shield in his skirt, and my brain spins out. "Have ancient Greeks got bronze balls?"

Nikon snorts on the next aisle over. "Metal codpieces."

"Rude."

Nikon grunts but he's still chuckling. "I'm sure he thinks it's rude you're targeting his junk."

Blocking the next swing of Spartacus's sword knocks me staggering back. *"Beastly Strength."*

As my muscles sing with magic and swell with strength, I send up a word of thanks. Hecate hasn't negated my powers completely, only stolen my tattoo mods.

When the guy comes in hard and fast, I take advantage of his mass and momentum and drop to the ground to scissor his legs. He grunts and falls like a cut tree, face-planting hard before rolling to the side.

I'm there before he gets up and I crack him on the side of the head with my stake. When he's down, I relieve him of his sword and press the tip of the blade to his chest. "Who sent you? What's this about? Who's trying to ruin Nikon?"

He spits at me.

"Nice manners, dude. You're gross."

Calum chuckles beside me. "Miss Manners is a bit after his time."

Nikon rushes around to the end of his aisle with a bloody sword in his hand. "Good. You've got one to question. Mine just—"

My brute thrusts forward, gripping the blade with both hands, and impales himself on his sword.

"—sacrificed himself," Nikon finishes. "Well, shit."

He drops to the ground, panting as the life ebbs out of him and his eyes go blank. "What did you do that for, dumbass? You were going to be the one who lives."

Calum glares down at my guy sputtering his last breath. "I guess we don't get to find out who they're working for."

"Unless Nikon's granda recognizes them," Bruin offers, trotting back with a grin on his face.

I repeat Bruin's comment for Nikon, and he nods in agreement. "Good point, Bear. I'll ask him."

Nikon rushes off, and I check my bear over. He's wet and by the smell of salt, freshly dipped in the ocean. At least he's not all covered in blood as he usually is when we finish a battle. "You good, buddy?"

"Couldn't get much better. I have a battle under my belt and a swim in the sea, and it isn't even breakfast yet."

Well, I'm glad he's enjoying his vacay.

Nikon returns with his grandfather, and he shows him the state of things. "Any idea who these guys are, Papu?"

Nikon senior frowns and steps over to look at the hacked-up heap that Bruin handled. "They wear the uniform of mercenary muscle, but who hired them to attack my livelihood, I couldn't say."

I leave the boys to their sleuthing and settle in with the affected vines. "It's okay, pretty plants. We're onto the plot against you now. Don't worry about tampering anymore."

Reaching out, I start the healing. Connected as I am with the plants, they tell me what the intruders did to them. When I finish cleaning them and restoring their health, I search for…

"Yeah, okay, here." I pick up what looks like a fireplace bellows and take it back to where the men are standing. "The vines say men come and spray them with molds using these."

"Molds?" Papu says. "And here I thought the Fates were displeased."

Nikon shakes his head and gestures at the acres of rows growing up the slope. "Grapevines do very well on sunny slopes and if there's a breeze, that much better. A steady breeze keeps leaves dry and prevents molds from taking hold. I knew people were envious of Papu's success, but sabotage? That's unbelievable."

"What do you want done with the bodies?" Calum asks.

Nikon looks at his grandfather. "Throw them over the cliff or leave them here as a statement?"

"I vote door number two," Bruin says.

I chuckle. "Of course you do. You'd probably have us stake them up like scarecrows too."

"A fine idea," Papu says. "I'll have my men tend to it after first victuals. Perhaps while we break bread, we can come up with a way to keep this from happening in the future."

I have a sudden stroke of genius. "Hey, Greek? I think it's time for another experiment with the old Leviticus theory. Fracture for fracture, eye for eye, tooth for tooth, remember?"

Nikon grins. "Eager for another FiNikon Mess Around?"

"Exactly."

He grins. "I like the way your mind works, Cumhaill."

He holds his palm open, and I slap mine to it.

"We solemnly swear we are up to no good."

CHAPTER NINE

Helene waves from the portico off the back of the house as the five of us return to the villa. She has a small basket of fresh veggies hooked over her elbow and a look of worry on her face. "Sweet mercies, Fiona. What foul deed have you endured?"

I look down and wince. Her pretty blue dress has been reduced to rags. "I'm so sorry. Somehow, I'll replace this."

She waves that away. "The dress is of no concern. Are you well and whole? What have the Fates thrust upon the lot of you now?"

I look at the men and chuckle. They look as poised and composed as ever in their tunics. It's me who's the hot mess. "There was trouble in the vineyard, but we took care of both the damage and any further tampering."

Nikon waggles his brow. "Whoever is behind the foul play will have a run of misfortunes himself if he tries anything again. Fiona and I made sure of that."

Yeah, we did. "Mischief managed."

Nikon chuckles, and it's obvious his grandparents don't know what to make of us.

"As long as you aren't hurt, all is well."

I nod. "I'm as whole as I've been since I arrived. Hecate stole a few things that I intend to get back, but other than that, yes, I'm fine."

Nikon puts an arm around his gran. "Fiona told you she's a warrior in our time, didn't she, Yaya?"

Nikon's gran nods. "Yes, that's right, she did."

"In truth, that doesn't do her skills justice. If she had to face even the most prized gladiators of this time, I would wager my coin on Fiona without question."

"Plus, she has a magical spirit bear," Calum adds.

Nikon senior nods. "He is a truly massive beast that bends to her will."

I wave that off. "No. Bruin definitely has his own will. He's my friend and my partner, not my beast of burden."

She nods. "I noticed the beast with you out by the cliff. Nikon, you must take better care of your friends. The pallets in the guest quarters may not be down-filled, but they offer more comfort than hard ground."

Nikon nods. "You're right, Yaya. We talked about coming back inside, but the night was warm, and the stars were out in multitudes. We enjoyed an evening out in nature. I don't know how long we'll be here, so I'm absorbing the things I loved most about my childhood here."

"Which includes sleeping on the ground?"

He chuckles. "No, it includes watching from the cliff as the sun rises like when I was young."

"An early riser, were you?" I say.

"Not at first." He looks toward his grandfather and chuckles. "I used to grouse and complain when Papu pulled me out of bed. He'd say, 'Come, *agoraki mou*. The only way to make your dreams come true is to wake and get started. You are Nikon Tsambikos, and we have a name to live up to.'"

"I stand by my words," his granda says.

"Then we'd come out and sit right there on that patch of grass and eat boiled eggs, cheese, and bread dipped in wine. In all the years Hecate forced me to be alone, those moments have meant the most to me."

Nikon senior stares off toward the sunrise, his eyes glassy. "I am touched to know they meant so much."

Now I'm blinking fast and turning toward the water.

Helene shakes her head. "Enough drama of the heart. Come inside and eat. Fiona has need of a new dress, and we must make plans to right the wrongs done to you."

The six of us arrive at the symposia's entrance, and I'm excited to see the platters of food spread across the low tables: eggs, cheese, olives, pears, grapes, and bread.

"Matera," Nikon breathes, his gaze locked on a slim, blonde woman looking out the window.

She turns at the sound of his voice. "My dear boy."

He manages a couple of steps, and his knees give.

She rushes to where he's kneeling on the floor. "Helene sent for me and explained your plight. Whatever help I can offer, you need only speak the words."

Nikon lets out a gasping breath, and Helene lays a hand on my wrist. "A good time to find you another dress and leave them to themselves, yes?"

I swipe my cheek and nod. "Great idea. Otherwise, I'm going to melt into a puddle of tears. Guys, come with us. I want Kevin to see the painting in Helene's room."

Helene leads the three of us to her private quarters, and Kevin and Calum take in the beauty of the X-rated fresco. They have the same reaction as I did to that being the inspiration for Nikon's grandmother and wander off to check out the paintings in other rooms.

After getting changed, Helene sweeps my hair up in the Greek style and pins it so that only a few strategic tendrils dangle down against the bare skin of my collarbone, and I'm ready to face the world again.

When we return to the symposia, Nikon has pulled himself together and stands as we enter the room. "Come in, guys. I want you to meet my mother."

"Matera, this is Fiona, Calum, and Kevin, three of my dearest friends. Fiona, this is my mother, Melina."

"A pleasure." Calum strides in to shake her hand.

Kevin is next to greet her, and when Nikon's mother raises her hand to me, I give it a gentle squeeze. The woman has warm, hazel eyes and a delicate handshake. She's blonde and beautiful, but in a natural beauty sort of way and not the blonde Hollywood starlet kind of way Andromeda is.

She doesn't have the same vibrancy as Nikon and Andromeda do. Maybe it's the fae prana that runs in their veins, but Melina's children radiate a magnetism their wholly human mother lacks.

We take our seats from last night, and I smile when Nikon sits with her. "Despite the danger and desperation of the situation itself, if nothing else, this trip back in time has had some spectacular family moments for Nikon."

Nikon grins. "Even when her future is at risk, Fiona takes time to find the silver lining for a friend."

"It's easy to find the silver lining with you smiling like that. S'all good, Greek."

"She speaks the truth, buddy," Kevin says. "We're happy you get to have these moments."

Calum nods. "Fi and I can imagine all too well what it means to you. Can't we baby girl?"

"Absolutely."

One of the house girls comes forward with a jug. "May I pour, madam?"

Helene nods and leans forward to pick fruit off the platter.

"Please do, Tera, and tell Cook to bring out the hot food when ready. Everyone is here and seated."

When the house slave leaves, Nikon senior turns to us and frowns. "Now then. How do you intend to rectify your situation and make your way home?"

"I've been thinking about that." Nikon plucks a small strand of grapes and pops a globe of fruit into his mouth. "Hecate may have brought me back to speak to my younger self and change the course of my life, but I won't do that. Knowing who she is, I know I made the right choice."

"Agreed, but she wants you to be hers again."

He frowns. "She thinks she can sway my forgiveness for the past and for the lives she took to keep me under her power."

His mother reaches over and touches his hand. "Helene mentioned that Hecate killed a woman you cared for."

He nods. "My wife, Kallista. If there is one thing in life I would change, it is that. Kallista should be spared. Papu, if I write a letter to myself when the time comes, will you give it to me and impress upon me that leaving Kallista to a happy future is worth everything I'd be giving up?"

Nikon senior lifts his chin. "I swear it."

"Thank you."

"That means you will never know the love of a wife," his mother says.

"Not for the first twelve centuries no, but maybe after that. Honestly, if I know Kallista lives, it will lift an immeasurable weight of guilt and anger from me in the years to follow."

"If I speak to you now..."

He sits up and takes her hand. "No, Matera. I beg of you. This is what I want. I will build a good life with Andromeda and Politimi. Once the New World is established, I make a home in a place called Canada. Then I meet Fi and her family, and I'm happy. I much prefer that to being Hecate's consort. Don't change the course of things, please."

"A man either accepts his fate or is destroyed by it." Papu sends Melina a poignant look.

Nikon nods. "I learned that long ago. Even with the chance to do it differently, I choose the same path."

"Time has yet to set you free."

Nikon shrugs. "Maybe Hecate thought waiting a thousand years would be long enough for me to forgive and forget, but she's delusional. I'll never forget, and I'll never forgive."

I don't blame him.

"So where does that leave us?" Calum asks.

He turns his attention to us and smiles. "You guys asked me earlier if Hecate has any enemies in the pantheon who might side with me or simply want to cause her grief. I think that's our move."

"Which god will you attempt to rally to your cause?" Papu asks.

"Dionysus. After breakfast, we'll go to his temple. I'll lay an offering for him and try to enlist him to our cause. Perhaps he has insight on what it will take to get us back to our own time."

"Will he have the power to take on Hecate?" Papu asks. "He's only a demigod and Hecate is quite a bit more."

"True, but he's the only Olympian demigod, and he's quite a bit more too."

"Are you sure he'll respond to you?" Helene asks.

Nikon finishes his wine and sets the goblet down on the table. "Not at all. Hopefully, he's open to stirring up some trouble because it's my only idea."

I learned during our drinking hours last night that the Isle of Rhodes is the largest of the Dodecanese Islands, and while Nikon's family all reside on the land on the southern tip, the walled city of Rhodes is at the northern end. That's where the bulk of the population lives, and that's where the prayer temples are.

Nikon flashes us there after breakfast, and we materialize behind one of the structures and out of sight. Hecate's temple is in an area with ten or twelve other columned buildings littered around a hill's crest.

The first thing that shocks me is that there are so many people here. The second is that the temples are so vibrantly colorful. "I thought Greek temples and statues were white. The Parthenon and all the buildings in the Acropolis are white. The statues I've seen when visiting the ROM are all white too."

"Not originally." Kevin studies the sights with a lusty gaze. "When archeologists discovered Pompeii and Herculaneum under the ash of Mt. Vesuvius's eruption, the cities were almost entirely preserved. They learned a lot more about what life was really like."

Calum chuckles. "They could've asked Nikon."

Nikon winks at me. "You're right, though, Fi. After a millennium of sun and rain, yes, everything was white. Here and now, they're painted as works of art."

"Painted maybe," I say. "I wouldn't say works of art."

Almost gaudy amounts of reds, yellows, and oranges cover the marble surfaces. Not all. Some are gold, black, and green.

"The color choices are something else."

Nikon shrugs. "It's a different time."

As we meander the temple site's grounds, Kevin and Calum wander off to explore, and Nikon and I absorb the bustle around us. Locals carrying bows of evergreen, food, and small coin purses are paying their respects and kneeling at the altars of whichever Greek god or goddess they hope will look upon them with good fortune.

"Do most people come to worship one god or do they have to make the rounds to all the temples? Do the gods get angry if they get passed over?"

He bends his elbow and lifts my hand to set it on his raised forearm. "Usually, people come with a specific plight in mind. For example, that couple there." Nikon points at a man and his wife cresting the ridge from the long climb up to the area's acropolis. "When they part ways, watch where they go."

I love to people-watch in my time, so doing it here is even more fascinating.

"The husband climbed the stairs and went into that one." I point.

"The temple of Hephaestus. As the god of fire, he's a prodigious and revered craftsman. I'd guess that man is likely a maker of armor and shields worshipping him in the hopes that the god's favor will help him produce fine armor. Or he's off to battle and wants Hephaestus to bless his armor and give it strength in the coming skirmishes."

"And the wife?"

"Which one did she go into?"

I point at the marble likeness of a man in front of a temple to our right. "That one with the nakey guy holding the snakey staff with the paramedic symbol."

"That's Hermes, and the snakey paramedic symbol is called a caduceus." I take his amusement as a win. He is proud of his culture and enjoys sharing it. If I can make him smile while his life is twisted up in the hands of a crazy lady, I'm happy to have him laugh at me. "Hermes is the herald of the gods, so the woman going in there is likely awaiting word of a loved one who hasn't returned from the wars, or she has family traveling here and is worried about their journey."

We walk through the scattered structures, and the disorder of the layout is driving me crazy. "Why not build these in a line or a courtyard? Their placement is so haphazard and willy-nilly, it's boggling."

He chuckles. "The temples are sponsored or built by different rich and powerful people of the area. They try to one-up their neighbors not to unify with them."

I catch the thickening of his accent as he speaks. His cadence and phrasing are changing a little too. It must be nice to be here and live as who he was all those centuries ago.

We pass the temples for Persephone and her mother Demeter for Heracles and— "Wow, he's popular." I point at Poseidon standing on the peak of his temple, his trident raised in the air. "He has ten times the visitors the others have."

"This is a Greek island, Fi. Many fishermen here depend on the sea for their livelihood and sailors who pray for calm waters for their journeys."

"You know...as much as I'm angry and afraid about being here and not getting home, I'm thankful for it too." I hug his arm as we walk and lay my cheek against his shoulder. "Your world is incredible. I'm so jazzed to witness it with you firsthand."

Nikon pats my hand and steps away from me. "Thanks for that, Fi, sincerely. Sadly, you shouldn't show me any kind of affection right now. If Hecate or one of her ghostly minions are watching, she'll be back to wanting to smite us both."

"Good point. Sorry."

He shakes his head, and his blond hair catches in the island breeze. It's weird seeing his skin golden and free of the tattoos and inkwork he normally wears.

"Hecate asked about your tattoos. Were they meaningful or were you simply trying to change the image in the mirror?"

"A bit of both. I got the first few through the military, and those meant a great deal to me. It's easier to be fearless in battle when you know you're immortal. I took great pride in keeping my brothers-in-arms safe on the battlefield, so when there were troop tattoos or celebration brandings, I wore them with pride."

"And when you realized Hecate wasn't going to reset you back to a clean slate the next morning, you got more."

"Got it on the first try." He winks.

He's back into clean slate territory now, so that must bug him. "So, back to the Hecate issue. Which one is hers?"

Nikon points at a temple straight ahead. "There. The one next to Apollo."

Hecate's temple faces a different direction, so I can't get a good look at it, but they've all been relatively similar. Tall marble buildings with measured columns along the front and sides, an ornately carved frieze over the entrance, and usually a sculpture of the god or goddess being honored either in front or perched on the peak of the roof.

At the next temple, I point at the sculptured form of an effeminately beautiful man tipping his head back to look at the bunch of golden grapes he's holding overhead. "Here we are. Dionysus, the god of festivity, pleasure, and wine."

Nikon laughs. "Of course, you know him. He's your soul mate. Your spirit animal of the gods."

I fist my hand over my heart and grin. "Preach."

I watch a local man come down the steps of Dionysus's temple and make my guess. "He owns a vineyard and wants to ensure a great crop of grapes this year."

Nikon nods. "Or he could be planning a massive celebration and be asking for a blessing for the event."

"We should get his name. I'm up for a massive Greek celebration."

Nikon laughs and taps my Claddagh band. "If you want to ensure you leave this time with your commitment to Irish intact, it's best not to attend any Greek parties. Our ways are a lot more hedonistic than those to which you're accustomed."

When he waggles his brows, heat warms my cheeks.

Stupid Celtic complexion. I can't hide anything.

Changing the subject, I point at the sculpture of Dionysus. "Answer me this. If you're a sculptor trying to honor a god, why carve him such a small penis? It seems to me, if you wanted to flatter the guy, you would take creative license and leave a little more marble up front to make things impressive."

Nikon barks a laugh. "How long have you been thinking about that?"

"Since we got here. None of them have what I would consider godly endowments. I doubt all of them are grow not show, so what's the dealio?"

Nikon's still chuckling as he wipes his eyes. "Oh, Red. You never cease to make me laugh."

"Glad to keep you amused."

"You do. You always do."

We stop walking, and now all I can do is look at Apollo's carved junk, *annnd* my point is made again. "So, oh wise, Greek sophist, the answer to my question is what?"

"Greek society believed men with the biggest cocks were the boorish, brash assholes. Cocky, you might say. It was a sign of respect to carve them smaller genitalia than they possessed to symbolize them being reasonable men."

Hilarious. "Well, thank goodness, because if Dionysus is the god of hedonism, I was feeling bad for him—and his orgy partners."

Nikon places a warm hand on the small of my back and chuckles. "Only you, Fi...only you."

The moment we crest the top step to Dionysus's temple, I glance sideways at Nikon and smile. "This is going to work, Greek. I feel it."

"Even if it doesn't, I'm thankful you guys are here to help me try. It means a lot, Fi. Thanks."

Stepping between the line of columns, we stride across the polished marble floor and head toward the altar.

"Are you sure we brought enough of an offering?" I whisper close to his ear.

He lifts the jug he's carrying and nods. "Papu's wine is the best in the Dodecanese Islands—likely all of Greece. Dionysus will appreciate it almost as much as he'll enjoy my little plot to stir up trouble. Hecate is very rigid and autocratic—the polar opposite to Dionysus and the way he lives life. I think he'll enjoy messing with her."

"While at the same time helping us."

"Right you are. Come on. It's our turn."

CHAPTER TEN

Nikon approaches the altar with an air of respect I think is wise. After meeting Hecate, dealing with everything to do with addressing gods and goddesses with an air of caution is a good idea.

"Dionysus, my lord, I come bearing gifts. An oinochoe of our finest family vintage and an offer of mischief. I have a problem with Hecate and pray you might wish to help with its resolution."

We wait, and I look around to see if anything is happening. Nope. Nothing.

Be patient, Fi, Nikon says directly into my mind. *Gods are propositioned for help a hundred times a day. It takes a moment to get their attention.*

Patience isn't my best event.

Stepping back, I wander the temple, letting Nikon take his shot. If not Dionysus, then maybe one of the other gods will take time out of their busy schedules to help.

What do gods and goddesses do all day, anyway?

"I am Nikon Tsambikos of Rhodes, immortal grandson of the master vintner of the same name." He tips the jug and fills the golden goblet on the altar. "Hecate has plagued my life for over a thousand years trying to force me to love her. I want to be free of her. In return for your help, my grandfather promises a large amphora of his finest wine from every harvest for as long as the vineyard produces."

Oh! Good offering, especially for a male like Dionysus.

I'm about to say so when an invasive chill runs the length of my spine and leaves me wanting to screech and shake it out of me. The ghost passes through me in an instant, and I freeze.

Crappers. Does that mean Hecate knows we're—

Power flares across my skin and goosebumps take me over. I'm transported to another temple, and I don't even have to guess whose. How has Nikon put up with this woman for so long? She's delusional and drunk on grandeur.

I draw a deep breath and give myself an internal gut check. This is stupid. No question. But if Nikon is ever going to be free of her, something needs to be done.

Stepping into the light beaming through the sun window above Hecate's temple, I tilt my face to the heavens and absorb the warmth of the sun's rays. "You wanted me here, so here I am. What's on your mind, Hecate?"

No reply. Honestly, I would've been shocked if she replied to me on the first try. I'm well-versed in shakedown tactics of interrogation. She's letting me sweat.

Only, I'm not sweating.

"I may be a measly human who holds no value to you, but if anything happens to me, Nikon will never forgive you. You made that mistake once and look where you are."

Nothing but crickets.

"Yes, he's angry and hurt, but you can start to earn his forgiveness. We're close friends. He confides in me. If you want him to hold you with any affection instead of unyielding disdain, I'm your best chance."

I look around, but still nothing. I'm starting to feel dumb, but maybe that's her play. Perhaps she wants to make me feel insignificant. Bending over, I pluck an orchid bloom from one of the dozens of bouquets and twirl it between my fingers.

"What will it take to end this? What do you want from him? You're smart enough to realize his love is off the table, so why do this?"

When my inquiries do nothing but echo off the marble, I replace the flower where I found it and stride off toward the colonnade and the stairs beyond.

Why bring me here if you don't want to chat?

I've almost reached the exit when magic washes over me and the interior of the temple transforms. Instead of stark and white, it's opulent and gold. Richly colored tapestries hang along the roofline depicting Hecate throughout history.

I follow the chronology of the images woven into the fabric and my gaze winds around the space. I find the goddess sitting upon a throne behind the altar. Raised to oversee her temple, Hecate sits in a burgundy and gold cushioned throne with her sandaled feet crossed on a stool in front of her.

As she looks down at me, she taps her fingers on the ends of the chair's arms. "You claim you know how to douse the fire of Nikon's fury? Give voice to thoughts."

To start things off right, I lower my gaze and curtsy. When I lift my chin, I pull a labored breath through tight lungs. "Free him to live and love again."

One of her ebony brows arches. "Why would I do that?"

"Because at some point, I believe the two of you shared genuine affection. The problem didn't stem from him choosing to stay with his family. The problem is that he's human and his place is here while you're a goddess and your place is among the gods and goddesses of the heavens."

"I offered to take him to Olympus with me. We could've been together all these centuries."

"Yet he still believes he made the right choice. I saw him with his mother and grandmother today. He didn't say no to you as much as he said yes to them. Intimate love is powerful, but familial love can be more than that."

"If that were truly the source of his protest he would join me now. All of his mortal family is dead. Nothing ties him to that life any longer."

"But since he chose them, you killed his wife and child. His love didn't survive that."

Hecate kicks her footstool. It shoots past me and crashes somewhere across the temple. When she stands, she points at me, and a pulse of her power hits me. "You claimed I could earn his love again."

I'm pulled to the ground by an invisible force, my knees hitting the marble hard. Stars blink in and out in my vision as the pain subsides. "His forgiveness…not love."

"I care not about his forgiveness. I did nothing wrong."

"You know that's not true. I saw your face when the two of you spoke of the loss of his child."

Hecate lifts her hands out to her sides and rises into the air. Drifting forward, she glides over the altar and lands on the temple floor before me. "Why do you involve yourself?"

"You know why. Nikon is a dear friend."

"How dear? What would you risk for him?"

"Don't answer that!" Nikon shouts behind me. By the thundering footsteps, he's running up the stairs of the temple, and he's not alone. "Dammit, Catey. I told you not to do anything to Fi, and yet here we are again."

"She knows your heart's truths and how to make you love me again, *agape mou*. I summoned her for information, not retaliation."

Nikon steps around me, and he looks murderous. "There's nothing to be done, Catey. I've told you that."

"Face it, Heckler. He's just not that into you."

I twist to see behind me and find a hottie with deep brown curls and a mischievous grin standing with Kevin and Calum.

He's wearing an ivory tunic with two gold bands at the neck and bottom hem and a swatch of navy-blue fabric over his right shoulder and pinned at his hip.

I know him immediately. Yes. Well, done, Greek. "Dionysus, thanks for joining the chaos. It's such a pleasure."

The god bends to offer his hand. The moment he touches me, Hecate's magic fizzles out and no longer pins me to the floor. When I'm once again on my feet, he winks. "Pleasure is what I'm all about, *carissima*."

The tingling in my fingers where he touches me grows and creeps up my arms and through my body in a rush. When it zings into something sexual, I reclaim my hands and take a step back. "You have quite a reputation."

"It's all true, I assure you." He grins, flashing me a panty-dampening smile.

Shaking off his seductive jumpstart, I ease my way over to stand beside my crew. "So, you'll help us?"

"Anything to stir a bit of trouble. Nikky said I might enjoy jumping into this mix. I wasn't sure until I saw how riled Hectic is. Now I think this might be good fun. And, in the spirit of efficiency, I know how to end this."

"You do?" Nikon asks. "Let's hear it."

"A challenge of trials," he says matter-of-factly. "Everyone knows how we Olympians love a good competition. The Twelve Labors of Hercules. The Trials of Psyche. Sisyphus and his rock. Challenging people to seemingly impossible tasks is a time-honored Greek tradition. Challenge Hecate for your freedom."

"No," Hecate snaps. "I won't allow it. You have no grounds for a challenge."

"What are the criteria?" Calum asks.

Dionysus shrugs. "I'm a broad-strokes thinker. I leave the minutia to those who care."

Nikon's smile wavers when he studies our faces. "What do you guys think?"

"I'm in," I say. "If it's our best option, let's go for it. We've faced demons, tricksters, dark witches, and a dozen other powerful opponents and pwnd their asses."

Calum grins. "Yeah, we've got this."

Nikon considers that for a moment and nods. "Yeah, let's do it." Tipping his head back, he shouts. "I, Nikon Tsambikos, demand a challenge of trials to end Hecate's claim on me once and for all."

"No!" Hecate shouts. "I don't agree. I *won't* agree."

"Not your call to make, Heckler. A challenge has been made against a member of the pantheon. The fire is lit."

Dionysus snaps his fingers, and another goddess appears. Man, being in ancient Greece is hard on a girl's ego. Everyone here comes in such a pretty package.

The new goddess looks annoyed at first but then spots Dionysus and her temperament shifts. "A gift of unexpected pleasure."

"Title of my sex tape." Dionysus grins.

I cover my mouth, coughing to hide my laughter.

"Oh, I like him," Calum says.

"I guess not all gods are stuck in ancient Greece," I say.

Dionysus chuckles. "How boring would that be? Who do you think inspired the hippie movement? Hedonist retreats? *Fifty Shades of Grey*? That's all me, baby."

Things just got so much more interesting.

Dionysus gestures at the goddess. "Kids, this is Themis, Goddess of Justice. Since you challenged the goddess bitch of everything for Nikky's freedom, it's best to make it official. This way, no one can go back on the terms, right Heckie?"

Hecate's green eyes are glowing with fury. "There are no terms because there will be no trials. This is a private matter between Nikon and me. It has nothing to do with anything actionable by the laws of challenge."

Dionysus smiles, undaunted. "Nikky, state your case. Themis will decide."

"No, Themis will *not* decide," Hecate stammers. "I killed her brother. How is she an impartial judge?"

Themis casts Hecate a derisive sneer. "Unlike you, I have a code of justice and am respected by the gods. I seek truths beyond personal desires and do what is right even when I don't like it."

"Snap, Heckler." Dionysus shakes his fingers. "She burned you good on that one."

Hecate glares at him like a petulant child. I half-expect her to ball her fists and stomp one foot. "You meddlesome halfwit. You shall ruin everything."

Dionysus claps his hands together. "Excellent. Ruining everything was on my to-do list." He turns his attention to Themis. "The challenge has been made and accepted. Are you ready to hear his complaint?"

Themis nods. "I am."

Nikon starts at the beginning and tells his tale to Themis, who looks bored for most of it. When he finishes, she frowns. "I hate to say it, but Hecate is correct. The romantic troubles between the two of you are private and do not qualify you to raise a challenge against her—even for your freedom from her stalking you."

Hubba-wha? "That's bullshit," I snap, stepping forward. "Check your rulebook again, or better yet, let me check it. I'll find something actionable to use against her."

Themis shifts her gaze to me and arches a brow. "I wasn't finished."

Oops. "Sorry. My bad. Go ahead."

Themis takes the floor once more. "Hecate's mistake was bringing you—three mortal humans—back to a time in which you do not belong and threatening to leave you here. Taking you from your family and loved ones affects your life trajectory, and that *is* grounds for a Challenge of Trials."

"Booyah! We're in it to win it, Greek." I raise my hand for Nikon to give me a high-five.

Only he doesn't.

"Why are you leaving me hanging, Greek?"

"Because there's more Themis hasn't explained yet, isn't there? Something about me being immortal and this being a world I *do* belong to. I don't lose my chance with my family. If anything, it gives me a second chance."

Themis dips her chin, and the rush of our win curdles in my gut. "The challengeable offense is against the three humans, and therefore they will stand as the challengers and face the trials to come."

"Us?" Unfortunately, Kevin's voice squeaks out much more mouse than lion. Poor guy.

Themis nods again. "Do you wish to continue with your challenge?"

I study Kevin and consider Themis's question. Kev is both talented and skilled in his way, but these trials will be incredibly dangerous. "Kev, you know I love you and think you're a kick ass and take names kinda guy, but—"

"You think I should sit out on this one."

I hate the hurt in his eyes, but he seems to agree. "I don't want you hurt, and if Calum and I are fighting, we'll both be distracted, worrying about you."

He nods. "I get it. I don't like it, but I get it."

I catch the relief in Calum's gaze as I face him. "What do you say, bro? You and me against the mythical might of ancient Greece?"

Calum shrugs. "We'll consider it a working vacation."

I chuckle. "Cool. I'm not much of a sunbather anyway."

With that decided, we turn to address Themis. "Count the two of us in as Nikon's champions."

"You're going down, witch bitch," Dionysus taunts.

Hecate laughs and rakes us over with a dismissive glare.

"Surely you jest. They are weak humans. Do you truly think they can rise to a Challenge of Trials?"

"They will need the resources empowered to them by their world and calling as druids," Dionysus says. "Hecate must return what she took from them."

Hecate is smiling now and flicks her fingers toward us.

Our tattoos are back. My dragon band, Birga, Calum's bow... All our mastered spells.

Thank goodness.

It's hard to believe I hated them as much as I did when I first got them. Now they're such an integral part of me.

To test things, I call for my armor and Birga. When they appear, I send a prayer of thanks and release them to return to their rightful place. Calum does the same with his bow and quiver. He seems equally relieved.

"Is this everything taken from you? Themis asks.

I shake my head. "I'd also like the clothes we were wearing when she brought us here. We carry natural stones in our pockets. If I'm battling, I'd like my boots."

Themis nods. "Return their clothes and their belongings."

Hecate shrugs. "It won't matter. They won't last ten minutes into the first trial. Then this will be over, and I won't have to deal with them poisoning Nikon against me."

Nikon rolls his eyes. "You're psychotic."

Before Hecate can respond, Themis holds up her hand. "What I need now is a clear statement of the terms of reparation for which the three of you fight. The weight and measure of your claims will determine the appropriate challenges."

Hecate practically growls. "If they fight to take Nikon from me, the weight and measure will be satisfied by nothing less than them performing the Herculean Labors."

Themis blinks. "Truly? You value this male so highly that you think the Twelve Labors is just?"

"Give it up, Catey," Nikon says. "That's ridiculous."

"It's not," she snaps. "I demand they achieve all twelve of them."

Themis points at an empty spot on the temple floor and Lady Justice's scales appear. She signals for Hecate to stand beside one of the weigh scales and Calum and me take our place beside the other. Reaching to the pile of loose stones at the base of the scales, she hands Hecate and me each one.

"Now then, Fiona, state your terms and what they mean to you."

I look at Nikon and draw a deep breath. "We fight for Nikon Tsambikos to be released from Hecate's obsession. He will have the freedom to live and love who he chooses, he will age normally, and Hecate can't stalk him or have her ghosts or minions watch him or act on him or anyone in his social circles. He will be free. For us, we fight for the four of us to return to our time without retaliation. We will continue living on our natural course with those we love."

I check with Nikon and the boys, and they nod.

Yeah, I think that sums it up.

Themis points at the flat plate hanging at eye level. "Set the stone on the scale."

I do, and the scales tip heavily to my side.

Themis nods and turns her attention to Hecate. "Speak to your defense and the value of what has driven your actions."

Hecate spins a tale of first love and promises made and how she's waited long enough for Nikon to live his life and how even now he disrespects what she sacrifices for him.

When she's finished, she sets her stone on the golden plate of the scale. The two plates tip and adjust until they find their point of determination.

They come to rest in Nikon's favor.

Booyah, bitch!

Hecate frowns and picks up another rock. "I didn't know his wife was pregnant and he has vilified me and judged me ever since. I have suffered because of it." She sets her rock on the scales and grins before picking up more stones.

"I'm an all-powerful goddess. It's very difficult to find a suitable lover who will live a lifetime and make an appropriate partner." She sets that one on too.

"In all this time, I've never loved another. Nikon has ever been my heart's true passion." She sets that one on too.

Now the scales tip in Hecate's favor.

Rude.

I pick up a couple more rocks. Hell, if she can ad-lib, so can I. "Hecate stalked the man I love and me, invading my privacy while we were in bed together and stole me away from a romantic weekend with him. If we're talking about pain and suffering, I can guarantee you, Sloan is out of his mind with it." I set that one on my plate.

"She gave Nikon an ultimatum to love her or else. That is *not* love. That is obsession. Love doesn't involve ownership of another person whether you're an all-powerful goddess or not." That brings the scales back a bit to our favor, but they still favor Hecate.

I want to yell, "Rigged!" but figure that's a bad idea.

Themis looks from Hecate to me, and when neither of us says anything more, she picks up a handful of rocks. "Each weight I place on the scales represents one trial. They won't be Herculean Labors because that trial was created with Hercules and his strengths in mind. We shall see how many tasks are to be completed and I shall build the challenges to suit. The trials shall begin at dawn tomorrow."

She places the first rock on the scales and waits a moment, then a second, a third, and a fourth…

She pauses as the scales adjust and settle. Placing one more rock tips them in the other direction, so she removes it. "Four."

"Not good enough," Hecate shouts. "I demand more."

Themis lifts her chin. "You'll accept four or I'll nullify this challenge and declare them the victor and Nikon free from your interference for breach of the agreement."

Hecate's gaze narrows. "Enjoy this while you can, Themis. When this is over—"

Themis laughs. "Threatening the judge of your fate is unwise. You should leave now, Hecate, before you do yourself more harm than good."

"One more thing," Nikon says. "I want it in the official challenge that neither Hecate nor any of her minions can follow, threaten, or interfere with us or our families and friends before or during the challenges as well as after. They stay out of it, and we get a fair fight."

Themis nods. "Your terms are accepted. Agreed."

CHAPTER ELEVEN

"You did what?" Papu looks at us with wide-eyed panic. "A pantheon Challenge of Trials? Has madness taken you? Them, I might understand. This is not their world, but you know the gravity of such actions."

Nikon closes his eyes and plops on the couch. "It's not madness, Papu—it's desperation. Four trials. Fi and Calum can do it. I know they can. Then the four of us can go home, and my life can be my own for the first time since I was a stupid boy."

Nikon's faith in us is touching, but honestly, now that the adrenaline of the standoff has faded, I'm a little panicky too.

"Was it an official challenge?" Yaya lowers herself to sit on the couch next to me. "Perhaps you are not bound to the agreement."

Nikon leans forward and pours each of us a glass of wine. "No, it's binding. Dionysus called Themis there to officiate, and we locked our terms in on the scales of justice. We're all in on this."

Papu scrubs a hand over his face, swearing into his palm. "This isn't right, boy. You should never have allowed it."

I swallow a gulp of liquid courage and enjoy the fruity body of it awakening my taste buds. "When we challenged her, it was supposed to be Nikon's fight, but Themis ruled Nikon's interest out as a personal matter and not an offense. She said the offense was against me, Calum, and Kevin."

"Then let the men face the challenge," Yaya suggests.

I sit straighter and smile. "Do you remember when I spoke to you about training and me being a fighter?"

"I do."

"I'm not only a good fighter—I'm a great fighter. I'm the strongest fighter among the three of us and more highly trained. Trust me. With me there and Calum at my back we can do this."

Nikon senior sits on the table opposite me and squeezes my shoulder. "Dearest girl. It warms my heart that you care enough for Nikon to risk this for him but think how he shall feel when you are killed in his stead."

"Papu! Don't say that." Nikon tips back his glass and empties it. "You are underestimating her. Stop envisioning her like Yaya or Matera and think of her more like Athena."

"Goddess of War?"

"That is a much more accurate comparison." Nikon sets down his empty glass and stands. "Come. We'll show you. Give us ten minutes to change. Then we'll go to the *ludus magnus,* and you will see."

I take Nikon's cue and stand. "What's a *ludus magnus?*"

"A gladiatorial training arena."

"Cool." Calum hands his wine to Kev. "Yeah, let's do that and work out before tomorrow."

I grab my pile of clothes and am ready to find somewhere to change when I catch Papu's horrified look. "Gladiators are training there," he says. "They will kill her."

Nikon waves that away. "No, Papu. That's what I'm trying to tell you. They won't. Come. You'll see."

"Watch your lead leg, Red," Nikon shouts from the stands. "You overextended there, girlfriend."

In my clothes with my armor and Birga back in my possession, I feel more myself than I have in two days. I wave to acknowledge Nikon's suggestion and ready myself for Moe coming at me hard from the front.

The three gladiators I'm training with right now are a big, dark-haired brute, a bald guy with slave bands, and a black guy who has more grace and finesse than the other two put together. I have named them Curly, Larry, and Moe.

I throw myself backward and do a back aerial, landing on a rock cropping built into the landscape of the training floor. Spotting my landing point, I plant my feet and absorb the momentum of my flip. I have barely enough time to get my feet beneath me before Curly swipes a wooden sword at me.

When we first began, they were reluctant to come at me and would only attack Calum. Over the last half-hour of different training drills, they've either learned to respect me as an opponent or despise me and want to hurt me.

I'm not sure which.

Either way, it means they're fighting with full force.

My shield burns a warning, and I turn to block at the exact moment Moe's staff arcs around to my face.

I drop to the rock below me and tumble down to the sand of the training floor. "Yikers."

"You almost got that one in the face, Fi. Be careful. We have no dental coverage here."

"You're hilarious, Kev."

"I try."

I evade the three for another couple of minutes, then I release Birga and do a tumbling run back to the stands. Calum hands me a water skin when I get there, and I gratefully accept it. "Okay, I'm done."

Nikon jumps down from the bench they're sitting on and

grins. "I don't blame you. That was some damned good fighting, wasn't it, Papu?"

Nikon's grandfather looks stunned. "I am relieved your skills are as impressive as Nikon boasts. I have yet to witness the female gladiators of Rome, though I expect you would best them in combat."

"They have female gladiators?"

Nikon grins. "It's a new craze in Rome."

I chuckle. "I'm not joining the circuit, Papu. This is a one-time gig. Four trials and home we go."

"Hells yeah." Calum holds up his knuckles.

I meet them with a bump, then bow to my sparring partners and wave goodbye. "Thanks, guys. That was fun."

Nikon lays a heavy arm over my shoulder and kisses the side of my head. "You guys are going to kill it tomorrow. I know it. I'm so fucking grateful to have the Cumhaills in my corner. I can't even tell you. I owe you guys."

I lay my head against his shoulder and smile. "How about you repay us with a celebratory dinner out at Blue Bloods when we get home?"

Calum chuckles. "This time, you could try not to throw it all up into the flowerbed."

Nikon squeezes my shoulder and smiles. "It was totally not your fault you puked in the black-eyed Susans. An evil grimoire possessed you."

"True story."

"You still have to think of a long-term solution for that damned book, Fi," Calum says.

"Yeah, remind me to put that near the top of the list when we get home."

"Will do. So, what's on the top of the list tonight?"

I grin and pat my tummy. "Dinner and a hot bath. You have hot baths, don't you, Greek?"

Nikon nods. "I'll even make sure you get to have it by yourself."

Kevin chuckles. "Aw, you spoil her."

I roll my eyes and laugh. "Yeah, and I appreciate that."

The next morning, Nikon wakes us up when it's time to get ready, and I make a quick trip to the indoor outhouse. After a cold breakfast, I splash some warm water on my face, and we're good to go.

At the door, Yaya hands Calum and me each a satchel and hugs us tight. "May Athena's light shine bright in you both today. Be well, sweet girl. Speed and strength, son."

"Thank you, Yaya," Calum says.

"Please don't worry." I ease back from the hug. "This is kind of what we do. Trouble seems to find us. Although we've had lots of scrapes with danger, we come through. We'll see you soon."

She looks like she might cry, but Papu turns her toward the courtyard and shoos her off. "I cannot decide if you are more brave or foolish."

Calum barks a laugh. "That's a point of distinction often argued at our house. It's usually too close to tell."

I stick my tongue out at my brother, and he flashes me a loving smile.

"Either way," Papu continues, "Even with your skills and your need to return home, taking on Hecate goes beyond the weight of what is yours to carry. The two of you do this for Nikon, and I shall never forget it. No matter the outcome, you are now members of the Tsambikos family."

"Thank you, Papu."

He pulls me into a tight hug. "To the stars, fiery one. Take it to the stars."

"I'll do my best."

He shakes Calum's hand and dips his chin. "May the Fates be kind to you, son."

"Thank you, sir."

Nikon tilts his head, and the four of us walk out to stand on the edge of the cliff to watch the sunrise.

"How do you feel about things, Fi?" Kevin asks.

"Good. Today we take a step toward getting home. As spectacular as it is here, I want to go back."

"We'll get there," Calum soothes.

Nikon nods. "Agreed. Eyes forward. Whatever happens, we face it together."

I chuckle. "Except for the part where Calum and I have to manscape a minotaur or dip a lion in gold or some other bizarre task."

Kevin laughs. "Yeah, except for that."

Nikon makes a face. "FYI, no Greek ever manscaped the minotaur. That's just weird."

We stand in silence and watch the sun pop over the horizon. Then, once the day has begun, Nikon holds out his hands to transport us. "Let the games begin."

Nikon snaps us back to the Rhodes acropolis, and we wander the grounds of the temples. The family villa's location on the island's southeastern tip means we watched the sunrise before it hit here on the northern end. That's fine. The few extra minutes give me time to settle in.

"You have your stones?" Kevin asks.

"Check." I pat my pocket and find the druid stones I always carry: my peridot from Patty, my swirly poop from the Ostara rabbit, an amethyst from Sloan, rounded out by the obsidian, rose quartz, ruby, and citrine Calum has in his pocket.

"Good morning, all." Dionysus swaggers out of Hecate's

temple and leans against one of the two primary columns at the top of the stairs. "Everyone ready for the first trial?"

I roll my eyes and chuckle. "More ready than you. It seems you forgot your clothes when you woke up this morning, dude. You're nakey."

Dionysus grins. "Wrong on all counts. I didn't forget. I am nakey as a show of irreverence in Hecate's sacred space, and also, I didn't wake up because we haven't been to bed yet, have we lovelies?"

Five more naked people stumble out to say hello. "Not to sleep, anyway," the other guy says.

"Right you are, Marcus. Not to sleep."

I chuckle and make it a point to keep my gaze lifted. "Well, thanks for coming. I appreciate the erotic send-off as well as your determination to piss off Hecate. You are all officially invited to be part of Team Trouble."

Dionysus grins. "Nikky was right. I like you, Red."

I eye Nikon. "Singing my praises to the god of drunken revelry, were you? Should I be flattered or worried about what that means?"

"Flattered," Nikon says. "Only ever flattered. You know I love you, Fi. Also, I may have mentioned to Dionysus that you were concerned about his sculpture's shortcomings at his temple. I think part of this display might be my fault."

Dionysus barks a laugh and sweeps a hand down toward his junk. "Naturally. I can't have people questioning my endowment. I'm the God of Pleasure, for heaven's sake."

My cheeks flare hot.

Nikon, Calum, and Kevin all bust up.

"Yeah, yuck it up, boys. I'll remember this."

Nikon doesn't look at all repentant. "Well, if your curiosity is satisfied, Dionysus can shield his mighty, godly sword."

"Yes, thank you. I'm sure that will make things easier with Themis as well."

Now it's Dionysus who's laughing. "Oh, sweet Celt. Themis was as naked as the rest of us until a moment ago. She only got respectable because she takes the rule of her dominion seriously."

I give up on trying to reason with them and start climbing the stairs. "Well, I'm glad she does. It makes me feel better about things to know she'll stay on top of what's fair."

"That I will." Themis is standing poised and at the ready beside the weigh scales. "You have my word."

When the four of us stop in front of her, Dionysus and his naked groupies gather around. Hecate is the last to arrive, but I have a feeling she was already here, watching from behind her veil of privacy.

"Now that everyone is assembled let us begin," Themis says. "I have weighed the error of bringing you here against all you wish in reparation and am confident the trials I designed will serve justice well."

Hecate frowns. "I wish to restate my objection to only four trials. It's simply not enough."

"Your objection is noted and overruled. Four is the number the scales demand, and four is what there shall be."

Dionysus grins. "Tantrum over, little mouse. You may stop your squeaking."

Hecate's glare falls on Dionysus. "I am not a child."

"Then why do you act like one?"

A surge of power charges the air and the hair on my arms stands on end. "This is none of your business, you drunken whore. Back to your temple."

He winks. "I think I'll stay and cheer for my team."

"You are not part of this," Hecate shouts. "Get out of my temple."

"We *are* a team." Dionysus flips his hand through the air, and suddenly everyone on the sidelines is wearing a "Team Trouble" t-shirt with a picture of him striking a pose on the front. "We have t-shirts."

That he knows what t-shirts are is funny.

That five naked Greeks are staring down at their t-shirts looking baffled is even funnier.

Themis arches a brow, but there is genuine affection shared between her and the god of feasts and fun. When she turns her attention to me, she sobers and extends her hand.

"This is your challenge scroll. Each trial will appear as you progress. Your support team may accompany you to provide counsel, but the tasks themselves must be completed by the two of you alone using only what skills and gifts you possess within."

I reach out and take the scroll. "Understood."

Themis sweeps her hand through the air, and an image of a labyrinth appears. "The most famous and dangerous labyrinth in all Greek history was designed by Daedalus to contain the half-man, half-bull known as the Minotaur. Your quest begins there. May the Fates be kind."

"Thank you." Calum and I exchange a smile, and I turn back to our support team. "Thanks for your help. I guess we'll see you when it's over."

Dionysus waves his hand, and his five playmates disappear. "They don't need to stay, but there is no way I'm missing this. You are about to navigate the Labyrinth of Crete. This will be epic. What was it you said, Red? Booyah, we're in it to win it."

I'm not sure I like his enthusiasm for us facing a deadly maze guarded by a bull beast but try not to take it personally.

"You'll need pants." I point at his naked half. "The t-shirt is great, but to be on the team, you gotta cover your man bits."

"Less entertaining, but I suppose slightly more practical."

When he complies with my request and gestures toward his suede pants, I hold out my hand to Nikon. "Okay, then. Let's go be epic."

In a snap, Nikon takes us to the entrance to the Labyrinth of Crete. I stare at the pillared entry into the side of a hill and frown, disoriented. "I imagined one of those tall hedge maze kinds of labyrinths."

"No," Nikon says. "In his *Natural History,* Pliny the Elder described it, *"containing passages that wind, advance, and retreat in a bewilderingly intricate manner. It is not just a narrow strip of ground comprising many miles of 'walks' or 'rides,' such as we see exemplified in our tessellated floors or in the ceremonial game played by our boys, but doors are let into the walls at frequent intervals to suggest deceptively the way ahead and to force the visitor to go back upon the very same tracks that he has already followed in his wanderings."*

I blink up at him. "Thanks, that is very comforting."

Calum squeezes my shoulder and meets my gaze. "We've got this, Fi. What's life if we're not testing our mortality and putting everything on the line?"

"Peaceful."

Nikon doesn't laugh.

"What's up, Greek? You okay?"

He shakes his head. "I hate this. Maybe we should call it and find another way to get home."

Calum makes a face. "And let Hecate win? Hells no."

"He's right," I say. "There's no way we're backing down now. This is how we get rid of Hecate."

Nikon shrugs. "Maybe that's a secondary concern. Maybe I need to accept things and keep you guys safe."

I wave that away. "Hells no. She's tormented you long enough. We've got this. Calum and I will crush this, and you'll be free of her."

"At what cost? She's darkened my door for my entire life. I hardly know anything else. I can deal with that. What I can't deal with is the idea of losing you guys."

I shake my head and draw a deep breath. "Not gonna happen."

I lock onto his worried gaze and straighten. "We can do this. Easy-peasy lemon squeezy, right bro?"

"You know it, sista."

"I love that you think that," Dionysus says. "The creature feeds on human flesh and can neither be tamed nor controlled. It knows every turn of the maze, and you will be lost and disoriented."

Nikon turns and scowls at him. "Either help or leave."

Dionysus lifts his fingers and a glass of something candy apple red appears in my hand. "Fine, I'll help, but only because you asked so nicely. Drink this, Alice."

I take the glass and inspect the liquid. It's not natural. I know that for sure. Magic pulses within it, and when I sniff it, the hair on my entire body stands on end. "What is it?"

"It's a drink of my making. I call it the Inner Vixen."

I look at Nikon and frown. "Am I being roofied by the god of ecstasy right before I go on stage?"

Nikon eyes up Dionysus, who seems to be having entirely too much fun for the situation's gravity. *Your instincts are good. What does your shield say?*

Nothing. All's quiet. With that revelation foremost in my mind, I press the glass to my lips and swallow every drop of Dionysus' Inner Vixen.

The fruity tang tweaks my taste buds as the drink flows over my tongue and down my throat. Magic tingles in my cheeks as the liquid rushes through my system. It's invasive and unstoppable.

Dionysus takes the glass from my hand, watching me intently. "Let it flow, *gliko mou*. Fighting it makes it unpleasant. My gifts are meant to be enjoyed."

Makes sense. Dionysus is all about pleasure and indulgence. Since it's already done, I decide to trust him.

The moment I relax and accept what's happening, things start happening in triple time. I gasp as the world around me spins. No, wait, it's me that's turning.

Calum shouts, but I can't make out what he says.

I'm off the ground and spinning like a top in the air. The blurring view of the boys, trees, pillars, door, pillars, the boys, trees, pillars.... Oh, I'm dizzy. I take a lesson from dance class and focus on one spot as I spin.

I find Calum and lock my gaze on him each time I turn.

My cells are bursting to life like kernels of corn popping in the microwave. *Pop, pop, pop...*

It's not painful. It's more like an awakening. As if the percentage of my cerebral activity was at the normal ten percent for humans and now I've doubled that—tripled maybe.

It's as if my mind and body have come fully under my control for the first time in my life. With that control, I will myself back to the ground and take a knee. Breathing to the depth and breadth of my lungs, I try to reel it all in.

"What's happening to her?" Calum shouts, kneeling beside me.

Kevin brushes my hair out of my face looking furious. "What did you do to her?"

"She's fine," Dionysus says. "In human terms, I doped her on ambrosia. She be trippin', yo."

Nikon's eyes blow wide, and he spins to glare at the god. "Ambrosia! Ambrosia kills humans."

"Simmer down, sexy. The girl has goddess running in her veins—I feel it."

That's true. Fionn was the great-grandson of the Tuatha De Danann and the goddess Boann said she could sense the strength of that lineage too. I want to reassure Nikon, but I'm barely holding myself together.

"You're freaking me out, Red. Talk to me."

"I'm good," I gasp, totally unsure if that's true. Does a person about to spontaneously combust know they're about to detonate? "Calum, don't drink the Kool-Aid."

Dionysus chuckles. "He doesn't get the Kool-Aid, Red. I don't think he'd survive it. For him, I brought this."

I look up and see him handing Calum a wicked knife and a thigh sheath. When the spinning stops, I relax and force myself off the ground. I push to stand and then—holy schmoly—I'm looking down at the three of them from above.

I'm a helium balloon threatening to fly away. Someone grab my string. "How do I get down?"

Dionysus chuckles. "Focus. Ambrosia only releases your inner potential. This is all you."

All me? Then I want to slow the ride and catch my breath. Focused on the horrified look on my brother's face, I take control and rejoin those bound by gravity.

It takes a moment, but I get there. When I do, Kevin grabs my wrists and holds me in place. "Are you okay, Fi?"

"I think so. Bruin? Are you okay?"

I could use some air.

I release him, and when he materializes, he staggers in circles until he stumbles and flops on his rump. With his head hanging down, he lets out a long grumble.

I kneel next to him, set my forehead on his broad, muscled shoulder, and breathe in his outdoorsy scent. "Sorry, buddy. The next time I get powered up by a mischievous god peddling ambrosia, I'll let you out first."

"I'd appreciate that."

Dionysus claps his hands together looking pleased. "Outstanding. Another player on the field. Welcome to the trials, Bear. Where did you come from?"

Nikon explains Bruinior the Brave to Dionysus, and the god chuckles. "Excellent."

"Unacceptable." Hecate flashes in and joins us. "There was no mention of her having a battle beast helping her or of Dionysus gifting her with greater strength."

Themis appears, looking annoyed. "The agreement was the girl could use all abilities and tools within her. The bear was within her as were her powers, which Dionysus released but did not alter or enhance. I find no conflict."

Hecate screams and lightning cracks above.

A bolt snaps from the heavens and I raise my palms. "*Command Lighting*." I clench my teeth, fighting to absorb the massive amount of raw energy bombarding my body.

Hecate may have conjured it to take me down, but my druid connection allows me dominion over nature. I groan as power vibrates in my cells and rattles in my bones.

It seems to last forever, but when it's over, I straighten.

Her eyes widen as our gazes lock. Yeah, my freaky fae eyes are glowing. I feel it. "Nice try, bitch. How about you go back to your temple and sulk while I kick your scrawny ass in these challenges? I think Themis mentioned something about us being granted the win if you interfere."

Hecate's gaze narrows. "I don't need to interfere. You're going to die a violent, horrible death without my help."

"Likely, but it won't be today."

Themis steps between Hecate and me and waves her off. Before she flashes out, Themis looks over her shoulder and smiles. "We're all rooting for you two. Hecate has thought herself above reproach for too long. Prove her wrong, and we will celebrate you throughout Olympus."

Calum chuckles. "Well, good because having the entire Greek pantheon watching makes things so much easier."

I laugh. "Right?"

Nikon chuckles. "Forget them. Pull out your scroll and let's read what the first trial is."

CHAPTER TWELVE

I shrug the cloth satchel Yaya prepared for me off my back and untie the ribbon holding things closed. The trial scroll is at the top, so I retrieve it, unroll it, and read aloud.

"Trial of the Labyrinth: While the Minotaur of legend is long dead at the hands of Theseus, in the past centuries, many dangerous creatures have made the labyrinth their home. The first stage of your trial is to navigate the maze within, evading capture and death, to find the garden of the dead at its core.

"There, you will find the rare Titan Arum. While the plant smells like the rot of death, the oil it excretes is the first prize for your quest. Collect the oil of the Corpse Flower without disturbing the plant, and escape the maze."

I roll up the scroll and hand it to Nikon. "Get to the center, collect the oil of the stinky flower, and get back. Got it."

Nikon takes the scroll and frowns. "Don't forget the 'evading capture and death' part. That was important too."

"True story." I pat my chest and Bruin joins me.

After tying up the satchel's ribbon, I sling it on my back and get ready to leave. "You ready, Freddie?" I ask Calum.

"I was born ready and just got better."

"Here, take this." Dionysus slips a silver flask into my bag and winks. "Where would you be without me?"

I chuckle. "I doubt I'll be taking the time to get my buzz on, but thanks."

Dionysus winks again. "I was thinking more about what you're going to collect the oil in to bring it back."

"Oh, good catch, dude."

He gestures at himself. "More than a pretty face and godly endowment, right?"

I roll my eyes. "Am I ever going to live that down?"

He grins. "Likely not."

"On that note." I lean in and hug Nikon and Kevin.

"Go, team," Kevin says. "Love you both."

"Love you too."

"Take care of them, Bear," Nikon says. "I'm counting on you, big guy."

I pat my chest where my bear is fluttering around. "We'll all take care of each other. Don't panic, Greek. S'all good."

Nikon nods. "Hells yeah, it is. Knock 'em dead, kids."

With that as our send-off, we step into the labyrinth's entry and wait a moment for my fae night vision to kick in. "*Tough as Bark.*"

With my body armor activated, I step deeper into the first hall. "Many dangerous creatures, eh?"

Calum chuckles. "Let's get in and out as quickly as we can and meet up with as few of those as possible."

"Sounds good to me."

"How do you think we should navigate in here?"

"When I thought it was a shrub maze, I figured we'd send Bruin to scout ahead. Now I'm not so sure."

No. I don't like the idea of leavin' ye.

"Agreed. Until we get a sense of what's down here, I say we stay together."

Before I step out of the pool of light cast inside the entrance, I reach out with my gifts to see if I can get a sense of the creatures within. If they're animals, I should be able to connect with them or at least detect them if they're close enough to engage.

Closing my eyes, I reach out. "*Beast Sense.*"

I'm not sure whether it's the ambrosia boost or the lightning bolt, but my druid powers are buzzing like damp Pop Rocks in my veins. I merely think the spell, and it bursts forward. My range is heightened too. Where I usually sense things within a couple of hundred yards around me, that radius has tripled. "I agree with Themis' warning. There are some strange energies down here."

"How close?"

"Not so close that I'm worried." A moment later I add, "The closest stirrings are from a mischief of rats."

"Rats in a maze." Calum smiles.

"I like the way you think." Shucking off the satchel slung against my back, I take out one of the small loaves of bread Yaya packed.

"*Animal Friendship.*" I send out my call for aid and encourage the swarm of subterranean squeakers to come to make friends with the nice Canadians bearing gifts.

A moment later, the high-pitched excitement of a dozen, long-tailed, scraggly-looking rats breaks the entrance corridor's silence.

"Hello there," Calum says.

I rip pieces off the crust of the bread and toss it down. There's a barrage of chatter, and I toss down a couple more pieces, gaining their trust. "I bet you guys know your way around in here, don't you?"

"Yeah, they do," Calum confirms. I pass him a chunk, and he makes sure the little ones in the back get some too. "My sister and I need to get to the center of this labyrinth to where the stinky plant is. Do you guys know how to get us there?"

I chuckle as they chitter and chatter in excitement. "Yes, I have more food for when we finish. First, we need the stinky plant, though, 'kay?"

When they turn and scurry straight down the corridor, I shove the last of the bread in my mouth, call Birga to my palm, and jog after them. "Quick and quiet, everyone."

"Good plan," Calum whispers at my back. "Let's not spook the natives."

As we navigate the warren of corridors, doors, and entranceways, I remember a conversation with Sloan from months ago. We were in the underground tunnels of Fionn's fortress beneath the Hill of Allen, and I said the place was a labyrinth.

Sloan being his annoying, super-intelligent self had to correct me. "Actually, it's a maze. Though the terms maze and labyrinth are often used interchangeably, the directions in mazes are betwixts-and-betweens instead of a labyrinth's opposites. Also, a labyrinth most often has one path that winds through it, while a maze has many."

At which point, I told him he was annoying and ridiculous, and he needed to pull the stick out of his ass.

"No, *yer* ridiculous. While traveling through a maze you don't go in any particular direction, and this randomness allows you to reach destinations that you can't locate by using the points of a compass."

I told him if that made sense to him, it only proved how whacked he was.

"According to Celtic lore, some species of fae cause men to lose their bearings, and only when the voyagers are truly turned around and lost—would they find themselves in the wondrous isles."

Leave it to him to pull something like that out of his ass while we were on a quest.

An ache flares in my chest. It's the ailment I've attributed to me being "Sloan sick." It's a debilitating infliction if I let it take hold, so I fight back the fear and loneliness it brings with it and keep my head in the trials.

Sorry, broody. I can't fall apart at the moment. Missing you will have to wait.

Fleet of foot and making great time, Calum and I follow the bouncing butts of my rat pack as we wind deeper into the belly of the Minotaur's Labyrinth, a.k.a. maze.

"It's freaky passing these closed doors, isn't it?"

I nod. We've watched enough horror movies to expect them to swing open and some demented beast to jump out and try to eat us. Thankfully, that doesn't happen.

After a while, the paranoia eases.

It still freaks me out when the rats pass through a slightly open door, and I have to open it wider and peek inside the next corridor.

Most of the doors are open or taken down. Likely because the creatures down here get tired of closing them on the most frequently used paths. What I worry about is if it comes to a chase, I don't want opening doors to slow me down.

I push that thought away.

When things are going well on a quest, the last thing you should do is imagine the worst-case scenario. That's when the world goes to shit. Instead, I focus on how well things are going. "We're Pied Pipering the hell outta this trial."

Calum shoulders a door, and it squeaks as it swings open. He pans his bow and arrow through the dark space as I move into the chamber behind him. "I think the rats get all the credit for things so far."

True. Our fuzzy friends are leading the way through the maze of tunnels, banking left and dropping down steps and climbing stone ramps and turning right and climbing through passages and opening doors and making shit look easy.

Then it happens.

The roar of a deranged beast echoes from every direction at once, and I freeze. Our little guides scatter. "Cat crap."

Without them, we don't know which way to go, and we have no idea how to maneuver the passageways. I reach out with *Beast Sense* for the second time. The moment my heightened senses come back to me, my pulse triple-times it and starts pumping like a mofo. "I have six incoming."

"Can you bond with them?" Calum asks.

Or maybe confuse them? Bruin adds.

"I can try. Calum, connect with the rats and get them back. We're lost without them." I bend to touch the dirt floor of the maze and start with confusion. Now connected to my surroundings, I send out a pulse of mixed inputs radiating from me in centrifugal rings: spatial disorientation, conjured scents, random noises, and gusts of wind.

I spare the rats because they're the one bunch of creatures here that I don't want to be confused.

My shield is tingling, but I don't need my Fianna mark to tell me danger is coming—I hear it. The bellows of the beasts are something out of a prehistoric movie. It's as if they're calling friends to the party.

Which they likely are.

I can do things to keep them from getting to us, but if I collapse passageways or throw up stone walls, I'm going to alter the pathways.

Will that screw us in the long run? I think it will.

While searching the corridor, I assess our position for the imminent battle. Thankfully, the Minotaur was a big guy, so the pathways are wide and tall. The problem is there are so many archways and doors to other corridors it's practically impossible to defend.

"If we backtrack a little and block off the passageways the rats didn't take, we can improve our defensive position."

"Good enough," Calum says. He releases his bow and jogs back twenty-five feet. "*Wall of Stone.*"

I tackle the ones closer and work my way toward him. Placing my hands on both sides of the openings, I envision the passageway being closed by solid stone. "*Wall of Stone.*"

When I finish that, I pivot and do the same thing with two passageways on the other side. With the doors, I press my palms on the frames and bind them shut.

"Are you ready to join the party, buddy?"

You know it.

When I release Bruin, he takes form and surveys the lay of the land. "We're takin' our stand in the center of a chute, are we?"

"Yeah. I figured that way nothing can surprise us from behind. It also blocks two of the six with dead ends. That might give us an extra few minutes while the beasts double back and find a new way to come at us."

A roar in the darkness brings the hair up on the nape of my neck. "Okay, that's close." Calum calls his bow and quiver forward.

I join Calum and call Birga. Bruin takes our back. I twist around and run my fingers through the deep guard hairs on Bruin's muscled shoulder. "Have fun, Killer Clawbearer."

"Ye know I will."

"Love the enthusiasm, Bear," Calum says.

I locate the three closest threats, lift my palm, and push the magic thrumming up my arm. "*Beast Bond.*"

Whatever is closing in on us is strong-willed and cunning. It recognizes my effort to gain access to its will and fights back. I try to connect with both of the ones coming in from the front and the one coming at Bruin behind me.

"I got nowhere with bonding. Sorry guys. It's on."

Before the beasts turn the corner, I throw my hands toward the seam of the ceiling line. "*Faery Fire.*"

The fireballs I toss out aren't any bigger than lacrosse balls, but they cling to the seam between the wall and ceiling and are bright enough so we're not fighting in darkness.

The beasts coming at us round the corner and let out a string of hideous screams. One rears back and recoils into the shadows, while the other raises a clawed appendage to swipe at the faery fire.

"It's too bright. It doesn't like it."

Faery Fire burns with magic and singes each time the beast makes contact. It bellows but doesn't stop trying to snuff the light.

Calum takes advantage of the distraction and starts loosing arrows. "Go for the brilliance of Times Square, Fi."

I throw up more *Faery Fire* at our end of the chute and Bruin's as well. While our welcoming committee is freaking out about that, I reach out with *Beast Bond* again to see if maybe they're more receptive to my suggestion.

They're not. Not even a little.

Calum's curse brings my attention to his arrows deflecting off the beast's skin and falling useless on the dirt ground.

The arrows might not be penetrating its skin, but they're pissing it off. It lashes out with its tail and takes a wild swing at us. I see the barbed point and my tattoo flares with a full warning. "My shield says, don't get barbed by the tail."

Calum snorts. "I wasn't planning on it even before your shield weighed in."

"Smartass."

Bruin's opponent has joined the thick of the melee and is moving in fast.

I grunt while swinging Birga to hold the thing at a distance. "You are one ugly son of a gun, aren't you?"

These things have no pigment in their skin and are weirdly translucent from living underground. They have two legs, four arms —two long and two short—and that barbed prehensile tail. They're bare of hair and have a long, whiskery snout that looks like a mole.

They're giant naked mole-rat men.

The one that backed out of the light is back, and it's pissed. It charges forward, and I spin to defend Calum.

"The eyes," Calum shouts. "Go for the eyes, Bruin."

I see how he discovered that since one of our beasts is wailing and flailing with its claws ripping at the arrow sticking out of its face. In a wild swipe, it swings its tail at me.

I evade the barb, but I catch the tail across my thighs.

The force of the contact knocks me back against the wall and pins me against the stone. "Frickety-frack, these things are strong." I release Birga for the moment and shift my focus to *Bestial Strength*.

As my muscles receive the influx of power, I realize I'm not tiring out. I'm not even winded. As much as I train to win battles, there is a great deal of care taken to ensure I don't overextend energy when and where I don't have to.

Right now, I don't think that's an issue.

I call on *Faery Fire* again, but I don't cast it. Building up power within, I wait until the energy grows strong—until it's hot and burning inside me like a miniature sun.

I duck another swipe of that tail and call Birga to intercept. Her Connemara marble spear tip slices through the appendage, and it falls to the ground with a *thunk*. The full-throated screech of the beast is damned satisfying.

Enraged, it comes at me without care or consideration.

I release the built-up *Faery Fire* and throw it forward with all my might. The passageway bursts bright as a sun going supernova.

While the thing reels back, I grip Birga with both hands and bury her marble spearhead deep into the gut of the other beast ahead of me.

Calum comes in close behind me, taking it down and putting it out of its misery. With a grunt, I lift my foot and kick it off my weapon.

It stumbles back into the long arms of the next opponent. The creature winces at the light and screams, pulling its gutted friend back into the shadows.

Swiping a bead of sweat off my brow with my forearm, I reach out to sense any more incoming trouble. Nope. The others are moving back.

I breathe deep and turn to check on Calum and Bruin. They're finishing off two and making sure they are good and dead. "I think you're good, buddy."

Bruin grunts. "Aye, I think yer right. Never hurts to make sure they're thoroughly dead though."

I chuckle. "I suppose not."

After a minute or two of assessing the scene, my rat pack scurry back and start climbing over the fallen.

"Yeah, you guys are free to nibble on them all you want once we finish what we started. We're still heading to the center of this maze. Everybody remember that?"

Calum chuckles. "They remember."

"Yeah, who can forget searching for a stinky plant?"

After taking a swatch of fabric from the satchel, I wipe the blood off my face, then Bruin's, and off Birga's tip. Calum is doing the same and tucks his scarlet-stained rag into his pocket for the next bloody cleanup.

"Sometimes I can't get over how glamorous our lives became after we realized our druid heritage."

Bruin snorts. "At least it's not boring."

Calum grins. "Right you are, Bear. That is true."

With my rat brigade back in full swing, the tour of Crete's underbelly continues. I'm not sure exactly how big this place is because there are so many twists and times we double back but even without the dimensions, I know it's enormous.

How long do ye think we've been in here? Bruin asks from within.

"I'd guess close to two hours, maybe three." It's hard to tell, tromping along in the dark.

Are ye confident the rats know where they're goin'?

I repeat the question to Calum.

He nods. "I think so. They seem confident."

I've no sooner spoken the words when our furry friends come to a scrambling halt.

"What's wrong, guys?" I sense their fear as acutely as if it were my own. "Is something coming?"

They confirm that. I reach out and try to sense the danger. I don't feel any beasts nearby. There are, however, a few lesser creatures and a lot of scurrying, scrambling, slithering types. I don't want to think about all the creepy-crawly things living down here.

"My shield is flaring, but I'm drawing a total blank." I draw a long breath into my lungs but pick up nothing beyond musty stone and stale air.

What is it, Red? Yer pulse is racin'.

I don't know. The rats are scared, and my shield is burning, but I have no blips on the radar.

A booby-trap maybe? Or a spell lyin' in wait?

Maybe. I cast *Detect Magic* and *Find Traps,* but nothing comes back to me.

Or ghosts?

The mention of ghosts makes me think about Hecate. "You don't think Hecate would be stupid enough to send her ghostly minions in here to interfere with us when Themis made it clear she'll give us the win, do you?"

Calum shakes his head. "Not on the first trial. There's still plenty of time for her to win without cheating."

"Then what is freaking out the rats? I've probed for traps, and magic, and creatures, and spells. If it's not ghosts, what's left?"

"Poison?" Calum suggests.

I reach out to detect for poison and venom and—"Okay, I have a hit." My shield's getting angry and the burn is intensifying. "Whatever the danger is, it's escalating."

With my senses heightened and my feelers out, I catch the scurrying of many legs coming my way. The twist in my gut isn't comforting at all. "I have the converging of many legs plus a warning of venom."

Calum makes a face. "I don't like the picture you're painting there, Fi."

The rats are squeaking and scrambling to turn back.

"What's wrong, little dudes?" The response that comes back to me is more impression than words.

"What are they saying?"

"I'm getting a dominant sense that, *She is coming.*"

"Whoever *she* is, I don't want to be here when she arrives, so let's heed their warning and get the hell gone."

"I'm good with that."

The two of us turn tail and run.

It takes a ten-minute sprint before my guides settle down. They stop next to an old, broken skeleton and I sink against the wall and ass-plant on the dirt floor. I'm not nearly as winded as I should be, considering the run we finished.

Still, Calum's winded, and my little guys are tired, so we take a break. Casting a small ball of *Faery Fire* up to the ceiling, I light things up and pull some goodies from my satchel. "It must be around ten, I'd guess. Time for second breakfast, don't you think?"

"Sounds good to me." Calum catches his breath.

The rats agree, so I pull out another loaf of bread and a cloth wrapped around smoked meat and some cheese. We share a little underground picnic. Then I pull out Dionysus's flask. I pass the mouth of the vessel under my nose and give it a whiff.

"Checking to see if it's spiked?"

"After the last refreshments, do you blame me?"

Calum chuckles. "You went full-on Linda Blair there for a bit, Fi."

"Yeah, and I'd rather not make a repeat performance."

The fruity aroma of the wine has a hint of honeysuckle but doesn't smell at all like the ambrosia he surprised me with earlier. Deciding to trust that he's not trying to dope me a second time today, I take a cautious sip.

When that goes down easy, I drink a little more and pass it to Calum. "Okay, boys and girls, let's get to the core of this beast. I want to be home by dinner if I can."

The rats chatter for a little, and we're off again.

CHAPTER THIRTEEN

It's another hour before the endless tunnels and pathways open up to a large, square chamber. We can't see much inside except a black void, four Greek gargoyle statues, and a couple of pillars. The rats stop at the opening of the doorway but don't venture in.

"Dudes, what's up?" Calum asks them. "We've come so far. Why stop now?"

"I think the answer to that lies somewhere in what has my shield tingling to life."

"Damn. The thing was quiet for almost an hour. I liked the reprieve."

"I guess that's over now." Focusing on the chamber beyond, I sense nothing. No beasts. No poisons. No heartbeats other than mine and the little tickers of my faithful friends. "So, what's making our resident rodents jumpy about racing to the finish line?"

Deciding to err on the side of caution, I release Bruin. "Buddy, can you do a mystical recon sweep of the chamber while I shed some light on the sitch?"

Happy to. He circles me once with a loving breeze before shooting off into the center core of the Minotaur's Labyrinth.

When he comes back, I brush my hair off my cheeks and peer into the room. "Anything?"

Nothing I can see. Is yer shield burnin'?

"Not burning, but definitely tingling hot."

So, maybe caution and not danger?

"Maybe. Hey, did you happen to see a smelly plant while you were in there?"

His laughter is filled with an easy amusement that helps unwind a bit of my tension. *Och, I don't think ye'll have any trouble locatin' the plant.*

"Did he see it?" Calum asks.

I shrug. "He laughed when I asked and said we won't have any trouble finding it."

"Does it smell that bad?"

It's no bouquet of roses, but that's not what I meant. Why don't ye cast a little light on the room? Ye'll see what I mean.

"He says to cast a little light and see for yourselves."

Honestly, it would be nice to see with my own eyes for a bit. Having my freaky fae night sight activated for the past three or four hours is giving me a headache.

"*Faery Fire.*" I take the ball of crackling blue flame in my palm and hold it high. I notice a stone gutter above my head. If we're in luck... I lob the fire into the trough and *whoosh,* flames burst up and spread in a long line along the wall to my right, up the side, then across the wall opposite me, back across the other sidewall, and back to my left.

"Amazeballs. Coffered lighting."

Bruin manifests to his grizzly form beside me and tilts his boxy head toward the middle of the room.

"Holy shitters," Calum says.

My jaw drops. "Are you freaking kidding me?"

"I'm surprised ye didn't see it with yer fae sight, Red."

"I did. I thought it was a support column in the center of the room."

"Nope."

Nope is right. I've never seen a plant this big— like, ever.

"It's gotta be close to twenty-five feet tall," Calum observes.

I step forward, check our surroundings, and get entirely drawn in by the Titan Arum. "How is it possible? Is it a magical plant?"

"Rare but not magical," Bruin says. "It's a natural Earth-created plant."

"That's hard to wrap my brain around." Calum stares straight up at it.

The Titan Arum is growing out of the labyrinth's floor with a large, bulbous base that gives way to a massive, dark purple petal collaring the towering spike that reaches toward the ceiling.

The purple flower petal reaches well over my head, and when I'm looking straight up, the spike is seriously four times my height. Staring straight up, I see a round opening in the ceiling above.

"By the positioning of the opening, I figure light only comes through when the sun is at its zenith because there isn't any coming in at the moment," Calum says.

"It must still get enough sun and rain to allow it to grow. It's huge." My bewilderment with the size of the flower has drawn me in close.

The stench of death snaps me back to reality.

"Oh, barf, that *is* disgusting." I take a couple of steps back and cup my hand over my mouth and nose. It does nothing to stop the gag reflex.

Calum grimaces. "How can a plant be worse than decomp at a crime scene?"

"*Gust of Wind*." I swipe my hand through the air and direct the current of airflow to circle us. We're at the eye of the mini-tornado, and that's fine. It doesn't stink in our conjured wind funnel. "Okay, so how do we get to the oil in the center of that without disturbing or damaging the plant?"

"No idea."

"Yeah, me either."

"How's the shield warning, Red? Any worse?"

"Nope. The same. It's a heads up but don't panic."

"Yet," Calum adds.

"Yet." Chuckling, I pull out Dionysus's flask. I take a couple of sips and Calum has a drink, then he holds it up and tips the rest into Bruin's mouth.

When the flask is empty, he shakes the last drops onto the ground and holds the flask toward the flower as if to conjure an idea. "Do you have a 'come here stinky oil' spell?"

I run through my mind, thinking about the spells I've learned from Granda, Sloan, and Dora. I can't think of anything that will help us out.

"There are quite a few dung beetles around, no doubt drawn by the reek of death."

"How does that help?"

"I can ask them to gather oil in their little mouths and come spit it in my flask."

Calum snorts. "That will take decades."

"Well, what will bring the oil to us without disturbing the plant?"

Dust motes shift in the air, caught in the first rays of light starting to show in the opening. An idea strikes me then. "Thank you, Gran. Always an inspiration."

"*Commune with Nature*." I close my eyes, release the wind circling us, and call any nearby hummingbirds that are up for doing us a favor.

It's hard to focus on sending them a calm and reassuring invitation with my back tingling with fiery nettles, but I do my best. I take the moment of waiting to clear my mind and connect with the soil beneath my feet. I press a hand to Bruin's shoulder blade and recharge.

"Given all the casting I've done down here, I'm surprised I'm not more drained than I am."

"It must be Dionysus's power boost of ambrosia."

"We need to honor him more often in drinking games and toasts going forward."

Calum chuckles. "I'm sure that won't be a problem."

The *buzz* of wings vibrating brings our attention to our volunteers. There must be close to two dozen. "Hello, there. Thank you for your help. Inside this big plant is a pool of oil. I need to take some with me, but we must be very careful not to disturb the plant. Can you do that?"

Their response equates to a hyper-active "hells yeah," and away they go.

It takes fifteen minutes before I feel the flask's weight alter enough to give it a shake. A few inches are sloshing around in the belly of the container, and I nod. "Thank you all so much. Blessed be."

"Blessed be," Calum and Bruin add.

I release them from my cause and smile as they fly off and out the opening high above. Golden sunlight is now streaming through without restriction, so I figure it has to be midday. "Time to take our leave. Let's get gone. Half a day to get in. Another half to get out."

I tuck the flask into the satchel and pat Bruin's shoulder as we turn toward the exit. We haven't taken ten steps when my shield bursts into a full warning, and I stop in my tracks. "Heads up, boys. My shield just kicked up ten notches."

Looking around, we search for the source of danger.

"Is it beasts again?" Calum asks.

"I'm still not picking up any incoming dangers…."

The sharp crack of stone has us pivoting and turning back toward the plant.

"What was that?" Calum asks.

Bruin twists his gaze around, his ebony nose twitching in the air as if he's trying to sniff out the source. "Not sure."

I adjust the strap of the satchel and gauge the distance to the exit. "How about we get out of here and not find out?"

"Great plan."

The three of us strike off with more speed, heading back to our rat pack and hopefully our escape from this place. We're halfway back to the entrance when the crack of stone echoes from all around us.

I catch movement, and my heart drops. "The fricken statues are coming to life."

"Shit." Calum frowns, his head cranking around to take in the danger. "They must be guarding the plant."

"We didn't disturb the plant."

"Maybe stealing oil is considered a punishable offense."

I huff. "Well, we're boxed in by four homicidal stone statues."

"Isn't this a scene in *Tomb Raider*?"

"I haven't seen that one yet," Bruin mentions.

Calum frowns. "Fi, I'm disappointed in you."

"What? It's on the list. We haven't gotten to it yet."

"Hello, Cumhaill kids, what do ye want to do? Is this fight or flight?"

As the gargoyles crack and stretch and start swinging six-foot-long stone axes, I lose interest in fighting. "Definitely flight. Run for it."

We barrel toward the doorway we arrived through until the shrill screeching of rats has me turning. "Change course, guys. Detour. Our guides have adjusted our route."

I duck the stone blade of one of the guardian's axes. The *whoosh* of air past my face makes my stomach churn. Armor or not, that would've hurt.

I'm almost past him when I'm knocked from behind with enough force to launch me into the air and twenty feet across the room. "*Feline Finesse*." I land on my hands, tuck into an awkward roll over my satchel, and slide on my ass.

Calum grips my wrist as he passes and yanks me to my feet. "You got great air on that one but duffed the landing."

"Everybody's a critic."

The roar of my bear has me turning.

"No, Red. Go. I'm right behind ye."

My every instinct screams within me not to leave Bruin, but he's right. He can vapor out and catch up.

Taking his advice, I nod to Calum that we're still retreating. We race to the exit where the rats are waiting and beat feet as far and as fast as we can move.

My heart is racing, but it has nothing to do with a lack of endurance and everything to do with panic over Bruin.

I'm here, Red.

The whip of my hair into my face has never been so welcome. "Thank the goddess."

Sadly, I'm not alone.

The thundering of stone footprints pounding into the ground behind us has me hitting my internal NOS and gunning it as if it's life and death.

Which it is.

My shield flares. I sense the booby-trap as the release mechanism triggers. There's no time to stop.

Diving forward, I wrap myself around Calum and take him to the ground. He grunts and I cage him as much as I can, rolling through the rigged area.

Two ejected blades catch me in the back, ripping my shirt, but my armor saves my skin. I turn my face and block a third. It catches me in the side of the head.

If I had been mortal, that would've crushed my skull.

Rolling to my feet, I check Calum. He has a blade sticking

from his thigh.

"Shit. I'm sorry."

Calum curses, tugs the knife free, and keeps going. "Not your fault. You can't expect to take all the hits."

The rats are chattering about it not being much farther, but it took four hours to get in. I can't see how we'll be able to outrun the stone sentinels while taking hits and evading the other creatures in here.

Especially with Calum limping.

Still, Da didn't raise quitters.

Arms pumping at our sides and muscles in our legs burning, we follow our teammates, praying they know a shortcut.

Down!

I shout Bruin's warning and Calum and I both drop to the ground without question. My shirt rucks up and my back skids on stone. The stone ax flies over me as I slide.

That would've decapitated us.

Run!

"Bruin says run."

"You don't have to tell me twice."

With a grunt, the two of us scramble back to our feet and race forward, hurdling over the stone weapon and banking a hard right to keep up with our rats.

When I see the vine-covered stone wall straight ahead, I curse. "It's a dead end. Shit!"

The rats are chattering, and at first, I'm too panicked and disappointed to listen. Then I see them climbing up the vines, and I look up. "Oh, you beautiful rodents."

Calum sees it too and smiles.

On the run, I jump as high as I can and grab hold of the foliage. Hand-over-hand and pushing up with any toehold I can take advantage of, I lift myself closer to the small opening above. Calum is right at my hip.

With my heart pounding in my ears and the salt of sweat

burning in my eyes, I clamber up the wall. I want to check on Bruin, but all my focus is on upward propulsion and getting both of us through the opening before the stone guardian catches up.

Another roar of fury tells me my boy is buying me more time. Man, I love that bear.

My fingers grip the last vines available, and I pull at the debris and growth grown over our escape route. "Damn it."

"Move, Fi." I swing out of Calum's way as he draws the knife Dionysus gave him and hacks at the vines. While he cuts, I clear, and soon I'm cursing at the brilliance of daylight tunneling into my retinas.

I'll take it. I clench my eyes shut, pull myself onto the grass of the exterior world, and scramble to pull Calum out with me. When we're both clear, I tug on him until we get as far away as we can before we collapse, heaving for breath.

"Bruin? Are you with us?"

My lungs are burning as I roll to the side and heave. I haven't got much in my belly, but whatever is left from my rat picnic comes up in a rush. Swiping my mouth with my hand, I clean myself up and wipe my hand over the grass.

After flopping onto my back, I stare up at the blue sky and get reacquainted with life outside the maze of death.

"Bruin, talk to me, buddy. Tell me you're all right."

The kiss of the breeze to my cheek dispels my worst fears. *I'm here, Red, and in one piece.*

"Couldn't have done it without you, buddy." I close my eyes and exhale heavily. "One trial down. Three to go."

"Fuck," Calum grumbles.

"Too soon?"

Bruin's bass chuckle makes me smile. "How about we celebrate today before we worry about tomorrow."

"Yeah. I can do that." I lay there for a few more minutes before I figure we're verging on being lazy. "As much as I'd love to lay on the grass beneath the warmth of the sun on an ancient Greek isle, there are trials to go before I rest." I snort at my joke. "See what I did there? Trials to go before I rest."

Calum palm-smacks his forehead and groans.

My grizzly swings his head toward me and grins. "Aye, I caught the gist. Yer a funny, funny girl."

I push up to my feet, pull out the rest of the bread and pastries and drop them down to my rat pack. "Mischief managed." I snort again.

"Fi, that's bad. Stop."

"You got that one too, did you? A family of rats is a mischief... mischief managed."

"You forget, I've lived with you for almost twenty-four years. Yes, I got that one too."

Feeling pretty pleased with myself, I turn and look around. "Do you think Nikon and Dionysus will know we're done and pick us up? They're our ride home."

"Och, I'm sure they watched the whole thing on the big screen in Hecate's temple. Odds are, they're on the way to collect us as we speak."

The hairs on the back of my neck rise as a surge of magic brings Themis, Hecate, Nikon, Kevin, and Dionysus to the party. "Good call, Bear."

Nikon breaks from the group and is about to hug me when I catch the fire in Hecate's gaze and sidestep him.

Instead, I reach into my satchel to retrieve the flask. "Oil of the Titan Arum. Plant undisturbed. Labyrinth complete."

Themis takes the container and nods. "Thank you, Fiona. Rest now. Tomorrow brings your next trial. You two did well today. Congratulations."

She disappears, then Hecate, and after a wink and a pat on the shoulder, Dionysus leaves us too.

When the coast is clear, and it's just us, I fall against Nikon's chest and accept that hug. "Damn, Fi, you look like you've been chewed up and spit out."

I look at the little mouth of the labyrinth escape hole and chuckle. "You're not that far off. It's Calum who's bleeding though."

I point at my brother. Kevin is already pressing the fabric rag from earlier against the wound. "We need to get him home and get this looked at."

"Is it bad?" I ask.

"Nah. Only a poke. Once it's washed and dressed, I'll be as good as new."

I nod. "Okay, Greek. Home. Bath. Food."

He squeezes my hand and reaches for Kevin to complete the connection to Calum. "As you wish, Lady Cumhaill. Bruin, are you ready?"

Bruin dematerializes and swirls around us once before settling in my chest. When the flit and flutter in my sternum subsides, I nod. "All is as it should be. Take us home."

CHAPTER FOURTEEN

The following day comes too soon. For not being a morning person, seeing three sunrises in as many days is exhausting. I could also be a little tired and cranky-pants from the first trial. Maybe.

Thankfully, Nikon wakes me with as much enthusiasm as I have to share with him. "Hey, Red. Ready for round two?"

"Yeah. Looking forward to it. How is Calum?"

"Right and tight." My brother scrubs a hand over his face on the pallet he and Kevin share on the floor. The two of them roll to their feet and shuffle off to get ready.

I yawn so wide my jaw cracks.

Nikon's gaze is sad, and I'm not sure why.

"What's up with the sad face? Did you lose your puppy?"

He touches my hand and squeezes my fingers. "You were talking in your sleep when I came in…crying in your sleep actually."

I swipe at my cheeks, and yep, they're as damp as my pillow. "I do that sometimes. Don't read too much into it. I really am fine."

He sits on the edge of my bed and pulls me into a hug. "No,

you're not, but you've done well fooling everyone. I won't break the illusion."

I close my eyes pinching them against the sting of tears too close to the surface. "I miss them, Greek. Da, and Sloan, and my brothers. I know they're getting used to shit like this happening, but they still worry—and I worry about them worrying."

"I know. I'm so sorry."

I sit back, swipe my cheeks, and shake my head. "You can apologize a thousand times, and it'll never be your fault. This is all on Hecate. I don't blame you for any of it. Not one bit. The part about the four of us being stranded here together and experiencing your world is the only good part."

He leans forward and kisses the top of my head. "You're one in a million, Red."

I absorb the love and let it soothe my aching heart. After a deep breath, I point at the tied fabric bundle at the end of my bed. "What's this?"

He smiles and gets up to bring it to me. "Your clothes didn't fare well yesterday, so I thought you could use a fresh new warrior outfit for the trial today."

"Oh, I lurrrve new clothes." I grin and accept the package, pulling the tail on the string holding the material together. Flipping back the flaps of fabric, I smile at the rich brown leather. After bringing them to my nose, I breathe them in. "Mmm, that new leather smell."

When I unfold them, the bodice takes a little figuring out, but I get it. "Damn. These are spank."

"All the rage in female gladiator garb in Rome right now. Only the best for my champion."

I blink at him. "You flashed to Rome to get me new fighting leathers?"

"You and Calum. His gear is there." He points to another wrapped bundle beside the pallet.

"You didn't have to do that."

He blinks and shakes his head. "Fi. You guys are doing all this to give me my life back. I would do anything for you. Flashing to Rome for new leathers doesn't even scratch the surface of what you deserve."

I squeeze his hand. "If I got jammed up by an ex, you'd do the same for me. Now, give me two minutes behind the dressing screen to get ready. And Greek?"

"Yeah?"

"Thanks for these. I love them. It was very thoughtful."

He dips his chin, opens the flame of the oil lantern a little wider, and when the light in the room grows, he steps toward the door. "Doesn't scratch the surface, Fi. I heart you guys."

Left to ready myself for battle, I grin at his parting words. Not everyone grasps our vernacular, but Nikon truly has become one of the family.

The four of us arrive at the Rhodes acropolis a little early, so to walk off our nerves, we wander the temples and comment on the statues and buildings.

"The sheer dedication to craft amazes me." Kevin runs a loving caress over the horns of a goat gazing up at Pan. "Every line of every fluted column, every leaf on every carved laurel... It's all crafted with both skill and pride."

"I can barely whittle a stick for a marshmallow."

Calum laughs at my comment and nods. "True story. Dillan or Emmet usually do it for her."

With my arm linked around Nikon's elbow, I rest my cheek against his shoulder and think about his life. "It must be hard for you in Toronto, seeing skills dwindling and the value of art being part of everyday life diminishing. After living like this, it's sad to see how far our art and trades have fallen."

"True, but I've also witnessed amazing innovations. I'm in awe of humanity in the twenty-first century. People may not know how to carve marble like Michelangelo, but there are other things they do well."

I tilt my head to where Kevin is pointing something out to Calum and smile. "You should teach Kevin things you know about in this time. He's so talented and I bet he could pick up techniques of sculpting and painting and bring about a Greek revival."

Nikon watches the two of them and smiles. "I never thought about it, but yeah, that's a great idea. I used to love to paint frescos. It would be fun to get back to that."

"Kev rents a little studio space near his old apartment where he works. He says it's cramped, stanky, and is stupid expensive, but the natural lighting is amazing and makes it worth it. I'm sure he'd make space for you."

He chuckles. "Fi, if I'm breaking back into art, I won't be sharing a cramped space that smells. I'll find us a place more suitable as a studio for inspiring the muses."

I squeeze his arms. "I'm sure he'd be thrilled."

"I suppose we should head inside." He pats my hand and calls to the others. "Everybody ready for round two?"

I gesture a sweeping hand down my front. "Looking like this? Hells to the yeah, I'm ready. I feel badass."

He grins. "You look badass too."

"Sloan would lose his mind if he were here," Kev says.

I smile, wishing that were possible. "Yeah. He would."

"Sorry, maybe I shouldn't have said that."

I wave that away. "Nonsense, he's on my mind whether we talk about him or not. I'd rather imagine him ripping these leathers off and having his way with me."

Nikon waggles his brow. "Great visual. Now I'm imagining that too."

Calum frowns. "Ugh. Me too and me no likey."

Nikon waves that away. "Me likey a lot."

I bark a laugh and point up the marble steps of Hecate's temple. "Get inside, Greek. You're an incorrigible sexpot."

"Did someone call me?" Dionysus grins wide as he steps between the entrance columns. "Incorrigible sexpot happens to be one of my official titles."

I roll my eyes and leave them chuckling while I continue inside and meet up with Themis. "Good morning. What's on the agenda today?"

"Do you have your trial scroll?"

I pull it out of my satchel and hold it up. "Yep. It was blank this morning, so we figured it would power up once we got here."

Themis's smile is warm and genuine. "First, let me congratulate the two of you on your accomplishments yesterday. I am thoroughly impressed. It's easy to see why Nikon holds you both in such high esteem."

I dip my chin and place a hand over my leather bodice. "That's kind of you to say. Thank you."

With that, she steps back and sets a rock on the scales, and the weight shifts, bringing us closer to balanced. "There now. The second trial should be powered up, as you put it."

I take out the little scroll, unroll it, and read aloud.

"Trial of the Fates: The Moirae are the three Goddesses of Fate, Clotho, Lachesis, and Atropos. These sisters weave the fate of humanity and gods alike, with no being powerful enough to influence their judgments. Clotho is the origin of life, and her thread is spun upon the birth of all. Lachesis is the second sister, and she allocates the fate of lives in progress. Atropos is the cutter of thread, and with her shears, she determines how and when a life will end. The second trial is to track down a tapestry stolen from the loom of the Fates and return it before sunset. Make haste. The cloth stolen belongs to a beast of a male attempting to prolong his life for ill purpose. Atropos has seen his intentions. He must die this day.

"And for him to die, she must have his tapestry to cut the thread of his life," I repeat, to make sure I got it right.

Themis nods. "In this case, yes. Dionysus may escort you into the lair of the Fates and provide transportation and information only. Once you arrive at the trial location, you must accomplish everything without aid."

Calum nods. "Understood. Thank you."

I tuck the scroll back into my satchel and step over to Nikon and Kevin. "Looks like you get the morning off."

Nikon doesn't seem keen on that. "Dionysus, we'll hang around your temple. Once they're ready to start the trial, do you mind coming to get us?"

"For you, Nikky, I'll make the trip back."

Dionysus, Calum, and I step out of the temple to greet the first rays of morning. "Any pep talks or power drinks this morning?"

Dionysus grins and holds out his closed palm. "Since you asked, I do have something for each of you."

Calum and I extend our hands, and he sets a gift into each of our palms. I examine the silver pendant and attached chain. The pendant has his likeness etched in black with leaves, vines, and bunches of grapes weaving around the outer edge. On the back, there is a penis with Greek lettering around the outer rim.

I chuckle. "I'm honored to wear your talisman. What does the inscription say?"

Nikon leans in and smiles. "It says, Divine Ecstasy, Revelry, and Fertility."

"All the good things in life," Dionysus says.

I put it on and lift my hair so it falls against my neck. I'm about to tuck it under the bodice of my leathers to keep it safe when he stops me.

Reaching for it, the curly-haired god bends to kiss the pendant. I don't miss how close that gets him to my boobs, but I don't make a big deal of it. Players gotta play. When he finishes, he sets it between my breasts. "I hope having my blessing brings you each endless joy. I appreciate people who embrace life and live outside the norm."

Calum tucks his under the new leather battle vest Nikon got him in Rome. "Thanks, man. We appreciate your endorsement and all your help."

He grins. "When this is over, I expect a drunken feast to celebrate our win."

"Done," Calum agrees, much too quickly.

Okay, now I'm terrified. I'm all for a party but have no idea what a drunken feast with the god of wine and fertility might entail. Still, it would be rude not to accept after everything he's done. "Yeah. I look forward to it."

The three of us arrive under Dionysus's power at the entrance of an underground cave. Its mouth reminds me of the opening for the original dragon lair set into the Cliffs of Moher. Except, instead of looking out over the Atlantic Ocean, this one looks out over the Mediterranean Sea.

"How much do the two of you know about the Moirae?" Dionysus asks.

I shrug. "Not much. They were known as the three one-eyed crones who determined the course of a person's life, amirite?"

Calum nods. "In a movie I saw once, they were blind hags that had to share the eye by passing it around."

He chuckles. "Then prepare yourself. Come. I'll introduce you."

As we enter the cave, Dionysus whistles a tune and the song sounds as crisp and full in note as if he is playing the flute. He really is an upbeat guy, which is a nice addition to our ragtag team.

At the cave's mouth, the walls, ceiling, and floor are rough with protrusions of stone juts and jags. Navigating the floor for footholds goes slowly. It smells of mildew and brine, which in my humble opinion, is a million times better than the death heaps of the dragon lair entrance that first time.

As we pick our footing and make our way through the minefield of the cave floor, I wonder how Dart and my other dragon young are doing. The last time I spoke to him, Patty said all was well on that front, but being grounded from seeing them has been hard.

I miss my blue boy and worry he doesn't understand why I haven't checked in on him since our big adventure behind the veil.

After a long period of creeping forward with slow progress, Calum catches my wrist and points forward. He's spotted a path past the teeth of the cave's mouth, and it leads us quickly into its throat. "This is better. At least here we can walk. How annoying was that?"

Dionysus smiles. In truth, the dodgy footing didn't seem to bother him. Either it's a god thing, or he's done it a few times and has picked his path. "It slows the approach of intruders enough that the ladies can prepare for guests."

"Do they get a lot of visitors?"

Dionysus shrugs. "I can't say. I've never been interrupted when I've been here."

He flashes me a sassy smirk and carries on.

From that point, we move forward at a much more progressive pace. Now and then, I throw a flame up to light a torch resting in a steel cage on the wall. They're spaced out at quite a distance, but never are we in total darkness.

"How far is it?" Calum asks. Normally that's Dillan's line, but sadly he's not here.

"If you imagine this is the gullet, there are still the winding passages of innards to navigate," Dionysus says.

Perfect. Themis said to make haste, and yet we'll waste hours making our way to the scene of the crime. Thinking about the task gets my hamster back in its mental wheel. "So if we had to plod through the stone jags at the mouth of the cave, how did the thief manage to surprise them enough to not only find and claim his tapestry but steal it?"

Dionysus shrugs. "I suppose that's part of the mystery to figure out."

We come to a fork in the path, and I'm about to pause until Dionysus strides down the left path without hesitation. I shrug and smile at Calum. "He seems confident."

He chuckles. "I have a feeling he's been here before. Maybe a few times."

"Agreed. He seems jazzed about being here now."

"Either that's because the life of a god is tedious and we've given him a distraction, or he's looking forward to visiting the Fates."

"Either way, I'm glad he's here and is having fun."

"Speaking of having fun with Dionysus, why did you sound so guarded about having a drunk-fest with the man when this is all over?"

"Nikon warned us about Greek festivities. With Dionysus there, the wine and food will be as endless as the naked revelry."

Calum grins. "And the problem is what?"

I chuckle. "We'll deal with that when the time comes. Right now, we have to catch a thief before sundown, complete the trials, get Nikon free of Hecate, and get home."

Calum lets out a long-suffering sigh. "That's quite a honey-do list."

"I know, right? No time to plan drunken Greek orgies."

We turn the bend, and I yelp and abruptly stop so I don't run into Dionysus, who is naked again. "Did someone say drunken Greek orgies?"

I giggle and avert my gaze. "Yes, but the context was that we currently don't have the time for one. Things to do. Thieves to apprehend. Time and place, my friend."

He waggles his eyebrows at me suggestively, and I can't even believe I'm talking orgies with Dionysus.

My life is cray-cray.

"And just to be clear, I'm a monogamy girl, and my guy is Sloan Mackenzie back home."

Dionysus flicks his hand between us and rolls his eyes. "Monogamy is a social construct humans placed upon themselves to convince themselves they are happy living within the boundaries of the status quo. Realizing desire is the path to true happiness."

I chuckle. "We'll argue that point later. First, let's finish this trial."

So, like many lore stories, the part about the Moirae being blind, one-eye-sharing hags is way off base. The Fates are lovely, nubile women who live in a cave of wonders in the belly of stone. An abundance of torchlight brightens the walls, the floor is polished and smooth, and their loom set up is like walking into a massive textile factory.

"Okay, so not what I expected," I say.

Dionysus chuckles. "They are Themis' daughters. How could they be anything but breathtaking?"

I didn't know that, but now that I do, it's not hard to see.

They have the likeness of their mother, although it still blows my mind that in the pantheons of gods and goddesses—and immortals as well—the visual cues of age and lineage are lost because two people who look the same age could be generations apart.

"We have guests, sisters," one of the women says.

The woman seated at the loom sends the shuttle through the

threads and stomps on the foot pedal, tightening the weave. "Too many hours have passed since your last visit, *gluko mou*."

Dionysus grins. "I bring you my champions against Hecate, Fiona and Calum Cumhaill. Did Themis tell you of their Challenge of Trials?"

The third sister rises from where she works a spinning wheel and nods. "She did. She said two human warriors would be tasked to return the tapestry of Theostratus of Sparta before he is set to die at sundown."

I nod. "That's the gist of it."

Calum steps forward and presses his hand to his chest. "While I have experience tracking people down and bringing them to justice in my time, with no Internet or security cameras or tracking technology, we're at a bit of a loss. We'll need all the time and details you can give us."

The sister at the loom giggles and the sound is a melodic chirp of songbirds. "Life tapestries are our domain, child. We know where it is. The task we need you for is to recover it and return it to us."

"Oh, that's fantastic." I grin and high-five Calum. "Where is it?"

They go on to describe in great detail a mountain with a long, Greek name, a cavern that drops to the center of the world, and a chimera conjured to guard the entrance of where he's hidden the tapestry.

I'm completely at a loss, but Dionysus is absorbing it all and nods. "I know where it is, kids. I've got you covered."

Thank you, baby Yoda. "Okay, so what happens if he doesn't die today? How badly does it change the intended timeline if he dies tomorrow?"

The three frown. "Tomorrow will be too late. Theostratus is a wicked and powerful man who desecrated and destroyed the temples of many gods to steal the ingredients to a potion that makes him invincible. The prophecy Atropos foretold has him starting a battle of gods that will last decades."

Awesomesauce. "So he's invincible?"

Clotho shakes her head. "No. He ingested the potion only hours ago, and it has begun its workings. It will take hold in full strength by the setting of the sun tonight."

"So he has to die before that so you can stop his plans."

The three nod. "If it's that important, why is it our trial? I'd think the gods would be swooping in to *deus ex machina* the hell outta that."

"Hell is the problem," Clotho says.

Apothos nods. "The tapestry is hidden within one of the back entrances of the underworld. That is the domain of Hades, and no god will enter because there is no leaving. Using my shears to end this is the only way to end him."

"Hecate could," Calum says. "Nikon said her power as a Titan plus as an Olympian goddess, plus the queen of witchcraft equate to the might of Zeus himself. With her rule over the domain of death and ghosts, she could withstand the curse of entering the doorway to the underworld."

Dionysus nods, smiling expectantly. "Buuuut..."

When he looks at me, I get it. "She wants us dead anyway, so if she declines, Themis has little choice but to volunteer us as tributes."

He nods. "The gods need this win, *carissima*."

"Since Hecate won't step up to take one for the team, we have to do it as one of the trials to free Nikon and get home."

Dionysus nods. "After watching you two in action yesterday, Themis truly believes this stands a fair test of your abilities."

I appreciate the vote of confidence, but I'd feel better about it if my entire posse was here and we could do it together. "What about the guard? You mentioned a chimera guards the tapestry?"

Clotho nods. "Theostratus is undergoing a metamorphosis

and is lying in a state of rest. He conjured a chimera to guard him and the tapestry while he undergoes his change."

I look at Dionysus. "Can I get the crib sheets four-one-one on a chimera, pretty please?"

"Imagine a ferocious, fire-breathing monstrosity that possesses the body and head of a lion with the head of a goat protruding from its back and a serpent for a tail."

"Amazeballs, a guardian beast turducken. All righty then, you know where we're going?"

Dionysus nods.

I hold out my hand to connect with Dionysus and Calum. "It was nice meeting you. And, if it's cool, can I ask a favor? Do us a solid and don't cut our threads."

Atropos holds her hands up and smiles. "I won't, but I'm not the only force in play. If you die in battle, you still die."

I nod. "Understood. I'll be back."

CHAPTER FIFTEEN

It's crazy, but in Greece, even the back entrance to Hell offers a gorgeous scenic view. When Dionysus snaps us to the place the Moirae described, I look around for the horned demons and ground bubbling up with brimstone. Nope. All I see is a rocky mountainscape with blue sky above and turquoise water stretching off to the left.

"This is it, eh?" I ask Calum as the two of us get the lay of the land.

"He seemed sure this is where they said to bring us."

"So a quick trip in and out the back door and everyone is happy." I roll my eyes as I hear myself say that and blush. "I'm so glad Dionysus isn't here." The chortling behind me has my cheeks burning hot. "Never mind."

Dionysus raises his palms when I turn. "What? Why give me a dirty look? You were the one who said it. You dirty, dirty, girl."

Nikon and Kevin look relieved to be reunited but hey, we haven't even done anything yet. They didn't miss anything.

"Back to the problem at hand," I say. "We need to focus on finding the rear entrance… the back door… uh, damn it, where am I going?"

Dionysus and the boys are laughing at my expense, so I tromp off in a huff. "Fine. I'll find it myself. You guys stay here and act like childish asses."

"I heart you, Red," Nikon calls after me. "You're my girl, and I accept you for who you are."

"Yeah, yeah." I wave my middle finger over my head and study the grassy landscape. If I were placing a back door into the realm of the underworld, where would I put it?

Not in the ground. Anyone could fall in. I turn, searching the gentle rise of volcanic rock before cluing in. "Right. A volcano could lead down to the fires of hell. Maybe the way into the underworld is by jumping into the volcano."

I climb the rocky terrain for a little and cover my face with my hand. The cloying stench of sulfur is enough to choke me.

There's no way anyone could climb this volcano, reach the top rim of the crater, and make their way in.

They'd pass out and suffocate first.

Abandoning that plan, I step back down the slope and release Bruin. "We're looking for the entrance to Hell, buddy. A chimera will guard it, so don't get too close."

On it.

I hike up a hill and look down at the other side. Only rocks and more hills.

"Any luck?" Calum asks. He seems to have sobered, so maybe he's ready to get down to business.

"None. What good is it to tell us to make haste if they send us to a spot where we can't even find the entrance?"

Bruin comes back and takes his physical form on the grass beside us. "I don't see anything interesting, Fi. Maybe it's glamored?"

"Oh, good idea, buddy. Yeah. That might explain it."

I close my eyes and focus. "*Detect Magic*."

My receptors overload and I back it off a little. "Okay, lots of magic. Too much magic, honestly." The bombardment of my search spell is too broad.

"Too bad we don't have Sloan's bone ring so we could see what's going on behind the scenes," Calum says.

The mention of Sloan's ring has me glancing at the platinum Claddagh band on my finger. My heart aches to be back home. Even him being here would be okay. He's so stupidly smart he's always an asset on quests.

However, he's not here, so we have to figure it ourselves.

I think for another moment before I come up with my next attempt. "*Beast Sense.*"

I wait while my senses expand and—"There it is."

"Did you find it?"

"Sort of. I figured if I couldn't find the doorway, maybe I could find the beast guarding the doorway."

"Good enough."

We strike off, using the information I'm receiving similar to echolocation, zoning in on what I hope is the chimera. "If Theostratus of Sparta is as powerful as they fear and ballsy enough to steal from the temples of the gods, he might have more than one line of defense."

Calum calls forward his bow and quiver, and with the leathers Nikon bought him, he's the whole package. Except it's a little damaged.

"How's your leg?"

"One hundy."

I chuff. "I call bullshit for six hundred, Alex."

Calum arches an ebony brow and shrugs. "The wound isn't so bad. It really was only a poke."

"But?"

"But it stings and burns a little. I think maybe with the tunnels and the crawling up vines and rolling in the dirt it got a little infected. No biggie."

I nod. "Good to know. You gotta be straight with me, dude. If something's up, I can't help if I don't know."

"Right back atcha, sister mine."

We follow the magic thrumming in my veins and end up standing in front of an innocuous tree growing from an isolated grassy patch. "According to my senses, the beast should be ten yards that way." I point, searching the air for any sign of a magical mirage or glimmer of glamor.

Calum follows my gesture and shakes his head. "Sorry. I've got nothing."

"Bruin? Are you getting anything?"

"No, but that doesn't mean it's not there. Let me take a look around." Bruin plods forward, his ebony nose twitching in the air as he sniffs. "I smell something odd. It's magic, for sure, but I'm not sure what it is, exactly."

"Could it be the beast turducken?" Calum asks.

He chuckles. "Could be. I'm movin' in fer a closer look."

I watch as he lumbers farther away from me. When my shield flares to life, I step forward to stop him, but he's gone. Somehow, between one step and the next, he disappeared.

"Did my bear just get sucked into the glamor?"

"All signs point to yes." Calum scowls at the flawless scenery in front of us.

"Well, if he's on the other side of things alone, I'm certainly not staying here."

"Agreed. The chimera and the tapestry are on that side of things anyway. All for one and one for all."

"Good luck, D'Artagnan." At a jog, I call forward my armor and Birga, bracing myself for the veil of glamour either Hades or Theostratus erected to keep people out.

Passing through the veil isn't something I enjoy or care to do again. It stings and makes my legs feel like over-extended rubber bands. Shaking them out, I take in the scene on this side of the glamor.

Bruin has engaged in fighting the beast, and I point at the

dark, gaping maw of the cave ahead of us. "There, that's what I'm talking about. That looks like an entrance to Hell."

Calum snorts while reaching over his head to grab the shaft of an arrow. "Glad you feel better."

Letting the sense of triumph go, I jump into the mix and dig in to help Bruin. "Where do you want us, buddy?"

"I have left," he says.

"I have right." I scurry to shift into position, assessing the creature as I engage. When Dionysus described the thing, it sounded weird, but looking at it up close, it's much stranger. It's a lion with a goat's head growing out of its spine and a snake for a tail. "Who thought this Frankenstein combo platter was a good idea?"

"Not me." Calum has shifted position so he can continue to shoot arrows without catching us with friendly fire.

Bruin grunts as the three of us fall into a rhythm.

It doesn't take long until Bruin and Calum have the furious lion rearing up on its hind legs, and I'm able to sink Birga deep into its belly. The wail of pain is regrettable. I don't get a beastly vibe off the thing. It's doing its job.

We are too.

When the beast falls to the ground, Bruin dislodges the head of the serpent with a mighty swipe of his claws and tosses it away. Calum puts the goat out of its misery.

I have no idea if the three animals are one life or if they live in a symbiotic link, but in the end, all three fall still.

"Nicely done, guys. The chimera is down and the day is still young. We've got this."

The three of us straighten and reorient ourselves toward the entrance of Hell. "If Theostratus is still out, maybe we can do a quick snatch and grab and—"

The roar of a lion startles us all.

I shout, twisting around with Birga to defend from a rear attack. The dead chimera is still lying there dead, but its body has split open, and now two more full-sized chimeras are crawling out of its carcass.

"Is that supposed to happen? Did anyone mention that might happen?"

"Not to me," Bruin says.

"That's just wrong." Calum winces. "It reminds me of Sloan and the festerbugs. Were those lions inside the first one waiting to come out?"

"I think it's more of a Hydra heads sitch."

"Every time we kill one, we'll get two more?"

"That's my guess." I gauge the distance from where we are to the mouth of the entrance. "Dammit, there's no way we can get inside before it attacks. We need to get closer."

Calum nods, nocking an arrow and readying for round two. "So, we put these two down, and during the lull of regeneration, maybe we can get inside and find the tapestry."

"If we're takin' on these two and rushin' inside, we're comin' out to face four more."

"It's not a perfect plan, Bear."

"Agreed. It's not even a good one."

The three of us jog toward the cave mouth anyway, the two chimeras now upright and in pursuit. "Serves me right for thinking that was too easy."

"That'll teach you," Calum says.

Bruin roars as the first of the abominations engages.

I'm hunkering down to ready for the other one but see an opportunity. With a one-handed grip and a wide arc, I swing Birga to sever the serpent head off Bruin's opponent.

The beast's tail falls to the ground like a dead rope, and I have barely enough time to reset my stance for my battle.

The serpent seems to be the easiest part of the beast to sever, the goat's head the least lethal, and the lion is the greatest strength and threat. Or at least that's my theory until the goat head lets out a satanic *maaa* and shoots a stream of fireballs at me.

"Dude. The goats belch fire."

Bruin clutches his goat by the throat. Blood fountains into the air and I get my focus back on my opponent.

"Or not."

Calum shifts and sends a massive volley of arrows in and pincushions both beasts. "Okay, new plan. We kill the goat and the lion but leave the snake. It's tied to the body, and maybe the beast won't regenerate if there's a part of it still hissing."

Bruin snorts. "Yer sister already killed my snake."

I command the ground below my attacker to cave in and pierce the lion as it stumbles into the crater. "Oops, sorry. You keep the goat alive and see—"

"My goat's dyin'. All I've got is the lion."

I grunt as a fireball hits my shoulder and knocks me back a step. "Rude. Can't you see we're talking?"

My lion is growling and gasping its last breaths. I close the ground around him and head for the entrance to make use of the time. "You do you, Bruin. I'm going for it. Calum?"

"I'm with you."

We leave Bruin battling his beast and bolt forward. It's not a blind run. I'm checking for dangers and have magical feelers out for any backup security Theostratus may have put in place.

Closing the distance is uneventful until I reach the shade of the cave opening. The heat of the day is lost, and a shiver runs the length of my spine.

When the hair on my arms stands on end, I take a moment. "Do you feel that? What's making me so jumpy?"

Calum back-flats against the stone and draws a few deep breaths. "Could be a natural response to crossing the threshold into the underworld."

"Could be." Yeah, that, in itself, is a majorly big hairy deal—but it feels like more than that.

Make haste, Themis said.

Right. No time to overreact.

I release my fae sight and step into the darkness. The air is heavy with the scent of char, and I try to wrap my head around the fact that I'm stepping into the asscrack of Hell.

Yes, it's a terrible visceral image, but that's where I am.

It takes a moment for my vision to adjust. Then I ease forward in a measured approach. "Where's Dillan and his cloak when you need him?"

"Likely bummed that he's there and we're here."

I smile. "Yeah, he liked getting sucked into the wake of my mystical mayhem last time."

"Except for being run through by a sword."

"You can't let a little rain ruin the whole vacay." I close my eyes and cast *Detect Magic* again. This time, I get a clear and definite direction.

I signal to Calum and get my feet moving.

Ready or not, here we come.

As much as I hope the icy chill of death and ghosts will dissipate once I ease away from the entrance, it doesn't. I suppose it was wishful thinking, considering no one should feel comfortable as they enter the underworld.

I'm working hard at ignoring the ghostly chill haunting me when the fog of confusion presses against my mind. I'm not sure if this is Theostratus at work or part of Hades' security measures, but I find it harder and harder to keep my wits about me.

I meet Calum's gaze and wince, circling my head. He nods. He feels it too. On the off chance we succumb to the influence, I figure we better have a Plan B.

I don't have any breadcrumbs, so I raise my arm and run my finger along the stone to draw an arrow to signal our way out. The stone responds to my will without resistance, and between Calum and me, we repeat the action every ten feet.

Bruin joins us in his spirit form, and I'm relieved to have him check in. *Are ye all right, Red? Ye look pale.*

A little weirded out. Do you feel like bugs are crawling under your skin?

No, but I don't have skin at the moment.

Good point. I make another arrow and flex my fingers in and out. *What about the chimeras? Are they coming after us?*

No. The one ye left half-buried in the pit is still stuck. The one I killed multiplied but the two replacements are waitin' at the mouth of the cave.

No need to come in here if they know we have to go back out there, eh?

Something like that.

Okay, at least that means there's no immediate danger bearing down on us. *I don't like it in here, Bear. How far in do you think he went?*

I don't know, but I could try to find out.

Okay, do that...and Bruin? Hurry, Bear.

I hear the panic in yer tone, Red. What's wrong?

It's a spell or something. It's confusing and terrifying, and I'm trying to get a handle on it, but whatever it is, it's powerful. I don't want to be here. Take a quick look around and see if you can find the tapestry.

Are ye sure ye want me to leave if yer on the verge of meltin' down?

That's why I need you to find that tapestry, buddy. Whatever is happening is getting worse, so we need to focus on our task and end this.

On it. Scream if ye need me.

Like a banshee. When Bruin leaves, I try to continue, but I don't make it any farther than a few steps before I turn to face the stone. My body is trembling, and I have to lock my knees to keep from ass-planting.

Calum steps in behind me and wraps his arms around me. He's shaking too, so I don't feel so bad. He's as brave as they come. It's only a spell.

Calum raises his finger to the stone and writes, WWBD?

I smile, thinking about my brother, Brendan. He was the wildest and bravest one of all of us, and since his death, WWBD has become a litmus test in our lives. What Would Brendan Do?

If Brendan were here, he'd squeeze my shoulder, kiss the side of my head and say, Tough times don't last, baby girl. Tough people do. Get on your horse and giddy-up.

I swallow and remember the gift Dionysus gave me yesterday. He unlocked my potential and told me I could access it and focus it with my will.

Straightening, I turn, hug my brother, and nod. We've got this. I press a hand on both mine and Calum's forehead and draw a steadying breath. *"Resist Influence."*

I close my eyes and envision whatever is tainting my perception as a layer of panic that I can pull off me and toss to the side. As much as I want it to be that easy, it isn't.

I am, however, able to step away from the stone wall. When I check with Calum, he nods that he's better too.

I found it. Thirty feet in, there's a fork to the left. Follow it to the end, and there's a small cavern. Yer man is there, and he has the tapestry lyin' over him like a blanket.

I signal to Calum that I know the way and follow Bruin's instructions. As we move, I still create stone arrows and fight the need to run away screaming.

Honestly, part of the reason I haven't lost my shit is that I know Dionysus and likely all the gods and goddesses of Greece are watching this on Olympus-vision.

Ohmygawd, I'm living in the *Hunger Games*.

I reach the mouth of the cavern Bruin mentioned and stop dead. Well, crud. Theostratus is there, true, but Themis and her daughters forgot to mention one thing—the guy is a giant.

A literal giant.

CHAPTER SIXTEEN

I stare at the mountain of man before me and shake my head. Long, straggly black hair and beard, a nose the length of my forearm, and muscle-banded arms as big around as tree trunks. I meet Calum's wide-eyed gaze and lean in to whisper. "Don't you think this should've come up? Hey Fi, you know the evil man who's morphing into an Olympian superpower, yeah, well, he's a giant so maybe take your slingshot."

Calum chuckles, but there's nothing funny about this.

Bruin laughs too, but it's definitely *at* me and not *with* me. *Yer overreactin', Red. He's a half-giant at most—likely a quarter.*

Are you seriously fractioning the giant I'm supposed to take down to make it seem more doable?

Ye don't need to take him down. Only steal his blankie.

I roll my eyes and test my surroundings. The guy seems to be out cold. The cavern is dark. My shield is silent.

Fine. Let's do this. I give Calum a nod and turn to face the cavern. *"Feline Finesse."*

After stepping through the entryway, Calum and I check the corners to secure the room and begin a stealthy approach. What's the big deal, right? We're only jogging over to a sleeping giant to steal the tapestry that means his life or death. I'm sure it's fine.

It's not like he'll kill to protect it or anything.

No matter what fraction of giant Bruin gave me, this guy is ginormous. Thankfully, a massive man has massive lungs, and even with his breathing soft and slow, it's easy to hear.

By what Themis said, he's not so much sleeping as transforming into a godly supervillain but hey, not my monkey, not my circus. They didn't ask me to kill him. They tasked me with getting his tapestry back so *they* can kill him.

Eyeing the tapestry in question, I sigh. He has it tucked under his arms and is holding onto it, even in his state of metamorphosis.

Do you think he's going to wake up if I pull it?

He might.

That's encouraging. Have we got a better idea of how to get it without waking him up? If I can avoid it, I'd rather not have an irate giant chasing me into the three chimeras guardian squad outside.

Let's try to avoid that if we can.

Still, I don't see any other way to get it but to pull it physically. I talk with my hands to see if Calum has any bright ideas. He shrugs and shakes his head.

Okay, I guess we pull it. If he wakes up, I'll grab the blanket and run while you manifest and hold him back to give me a head start.

Sound strategy.

Sound strategy my ass. It's the only thing I can think of. Assuming he's out cold is presumptuous, but I'm still suffering from underworld paranoia, and I need to get this blanket and get the hell gone. Direct approach it is.

The bottom corners of the tapestry are loose and hanging down his sides, so we start there. Gathering the fabric in both my hands, I start pulling it slow and steady. Calum mirrors my actions across the stone platform the giant is laying on.

The first couple of feet are easy enough to collect, but only because that was the part he's not holding. His arms are as heavy as marble columns, so I really have to put some power into it.

Breathe, Red. His breathing is steady. Yer good.

I don't feel good. I'm freaking out but don't want to let anyone down, so I fight to keep myself in check. *His arms are too heavy.* Even with *Bestial Strength,* and Calum's help, I'm not getting this tapestry pulled free. *Bruin, maybe a gentle breeze. Do you think if his hair gets in his face, he'll brush it away without waking up?*

No, but other than standing here until his transition is complete and he's invincible, I don't see another option.

Agreed. Give it a shot.

Bruin breezes past my cheek and blows my hair up.

I trap it and tuck it behind my ear without thought. See. That's all I need this guy to do. Just move your arm and give me a chance.

An unruly strand of hair shifts under Bruin's influence and I hold my breath, waiting to see if he'll move.

Nothing.

Try again. Maybe tickle his nose a little with the hair or something.

Ye realize I'm a fierce and honored battle beast and yer askin' me to tickle a man's nose with his hair.

I roll my eyes. *It's a giant. That's very manly.*

He snorts. *If ye say so.*

I do.

Bruin tries again. The giant's hair flutters against his cheek and up onto his cheek. I wince as Theostratus lets out a grunt and smacks his face. The slap of hand to face is loud in the quiet corner of Hell's entrance, and I highly doubt he'll stay asleep after that.

Right. Going for the snatch and run option.

Bunching up a wad of woven fabric, I give Calum a nod, and the two of us yank the tapestry. We don't get more than a few more inches. *Damn, this guy is made of lead.*

New plan, Bruin says. *I attack him, and while he's disoriented, you and Calum take the blanket and run like the wind.*

It's risky but worth a shot. *Okay, Bear. Let's see what you can do.*

Bruin takes form in the cavern and positions himself on the same side of the rock platform as me. I never thought Bruin's paws were small, but next to this guy's hands—which are the size of bucket seats—they sure look it.

Bruin doesn't go straight for the attack. He grips Theostratus' arms and tries to pry them off the tapestry. Calum and I pull back on the fabric with everything we have, but we don't get far.

The guy's arms must be made of lead. My muscles hiss against the strain. I brace my foot against the stone platform and try to use my weight to leverage it free.

Come on you huge piece of shit, move your arm and let go of the blanket.

His breathing stutters and I glue my gaze on his face waiting for the moment his eyes open. There's no longer a question of *if* they'll open, simply when.

It's no use, Bruin. We need him to move and let go.

Agreed. Get ready to run.

One sec. I'll try to give us an advantage. *"Confusion."* I cast the spell and wait to feel it take hold.

All right. On yer mark, Red.

Adrenaline is pumping in my veins as I envision the whole Fe, Fi, Fo, Fum, chase through the winding channels back to the outside world.

I meet Calum's gaze and raise three fingers so he gets the gist of what's to come. *Okay, buddy, it's a heave-ho on one. Three... Two... One...*

The bellow Bruin lets out makes me pee a little, and I was expecting it. Theostratus' eyes flip open at the same moment

Bruin's claws tear across his throat. Blood sprays and the giant reaches up instinctively to cover the four tears in his flesh.

Calum and I are ready and take advantage.

We yank the tapestry free, and he shoves it at me before calling his bow and falling back to defend my escape.

Turning on the run, I grapple for the bottom as I race out of the cavern and make my escape. Calum is right behind me, and I'm so thankful he is. I don't know that I could've faced the terror of this cavern without him here.

There's an inhuman scream of fury right behind me, but I can't worry about that. Bruin will slow him down as much as possible. The rest is up to us.

My gaze skitters and flips along the stone walls, watching for the arrows. The panic and anxiety forced upon me are almost debilitating, but somewhere in my mind, I've convinced myself that we're leaving now.

All we have to do is follow the arrows and get gone.

By the time I turn the last bend and see the light of day, I'm losing the tapestry. It's long and unruly, and if I'd had time to fold it up, I wouldn't be dropping it, but I didn't.

Reaching down, I pull on the length of fabric threatening to trip me. It's no good. There's no way I can run with it and call Birga so I can fight the chimera.

I have to stop.

"Cover me for a sec." At the mouth of the cave, I drop the tapestry and scramble to grab corners, fold it, and roll it into a manageable bundle I can carry under one arm.

"You good?" Calum shifts his stance to search the area outside the entrance.

Once I control the tapestry, I call for Birga and ready for the battle ahead. "Good to go, bro."

I know we'll be set upon the moment we rush outside, but I still yelp as a lion tackles me. It pounces from above, and the rocky ground comes up fast and hard to meet my palms. I'm still bouncing off the ground when the second chimera joins the fun.

Calum rolls to his feet beside me and grabs his bow. I drop the tapestry to grip Birga and defend. It's time to fight. There's no sense in dying trying to get home.

The whole point is making it back.

My face mashes into the graveled ground as one of the lions wraps its maw around the back of my neck and tries to break my neck.

Tough as Bark for the win.

Still, I'm in no defensive position and have now lost track of the tapestry. The fangs of the serpent crack against the shell of my skin and I fight to get my hands and knees under me to push off the ground.

It's no use. The freaky Frankenstein lion beast is on me.

"Bestial Strength." I push against the weight pinning me down but get nowhere. Growling, I wish with everything in me that I was a bigger, fiercer cat than him.

I would love a fair fight.

My body tingles with magical energy and my heart races. The sensation is similar to when Keldane negated my body armor and sliced me through the middle with his scimitar.

Rage burns hot in my blood. I won't die here.

The tingling morphs into a burn that erupts into an explosion of my cells. I push against the hold of the chimera and roar as it's thrown back. It crashes into Calum's opponent, and they both study me before turning to run.

Racing after them, I look down at the massive russet paws carrying me to close the distance.

Holy fuck, I've got claws.

My cranium floods with impulses I don't recognize. Random thoughts and instincts flash through my brain like some kind of crazy, evolutionary iPod shuffle.

What am I?

I don't have time for that now. This must have been like when Emmet turned into Kangaroo Jack—only I'm a cat. A really freaking large cat, considering I'm looking down at the chimeras and they're submitting.

I'm scaring the crap out of them.

Yeah, I am.

Red? Where are you?

The panic in Bruin's voice brings me back to the task at hand. I turn and race back to my bear. He tenses and takes up an offensive posture, and I back peddle to stop.

It's me, buddy. I'm a freaking cat.

He shakes his massive head, but there's no time to chat.

Theostratus is upon us, and he's pissed. Calum has the tapestry and looks torn between getting it to safety or joining the fight. Bruin engages the giant, and I hate seeing my boy dwarfed by such a violent opponent. The beauty of my bear's fighting strategy is that if he sees a damaging hit coming, he vapors out and repositions to his advantage.

He tears a chunk from the man's calf, and when the retaliation bears down on him, he vapors and claws him on another part of his body.

I dive in and join the fight, clawing and growling like a hellcat. He flings me off his arm, and I get air. Flipping in the freefall, I twist until I spot the ground and land on my four paws. With a growl, I go back at him.

Calum's arrows are sticking out from his chest, shoulders, and back. He's starting to look like a porcupine. I launch, catching his arm and rabbit-kicking his stomach with my back claws.

The fury of his bellow echoes all around us.

Before he can shake me off again, I release and drop to the ground. Bruin and I tag-team him hard. One of us from the front, one from the back, and all the while, Calum plugs him full of arrows. We're getting good damage though.

Theostratus spins, and I curse. *He's already healing. His invincibility transformation must be almost complete.*

The sun is growing low on the horizon, and a sinking realization hits me. Time must move differently in the caverns of the underworld. *Shit. It's later than we thought.*

Bruin growls and materializes to swipe his ankle. *This won't end if we stand our ground.*

My gaze shifts to Calum holding the tapestry at the same moment as Theostratus. Putting my new four-legged speed to the test, I bolt. *Slow him down. I'm going to get Calum to Nikon and Dionysus and end this. Be careful, Bear.*

Be careful, saber-tooth panther.

Hubba-wha? Is that what I am? There are so many things firing in my brain right now I can barely focus. I do, however, know I need to get the tapestry back to Themis to end this.

When Calum realizes I'm bearing down on him, he turns and runs. Cue another round of fury from the giant.

Suck it, Theostratus.

Running on all fours, I guard Calum's escape with the tapestry as a wildness that sings in my cells fills me.

The joy of wind blowing through my fur overcomes me. My massive pads grip and push off the stone-littered ground. The Mediterranean sun is heating my coat, and I look around, celebrating the stunning perfection of nature.

When we crest the hill and see Nikon and Dionysus, I race forward driven by the triumphant joy of our success and my current form.

Nikon flashes himself and Kevin back a couple of hundred feet, but Dionysus stands his ground and grins. "Well done, Red. You tapped into your powers most spectacularly."

"What the fuck?" Nikon snaps. "That's Fiona?"

Dionysus takes the tapestry from Calum and folds it over his arm. "It is. How about we discuss this back in the lair of the sisters? This is a time-sensitive delivery."

I shake my head. *We can't leave without Bruin.*

Nikon nods. "You take Calum and end this. I'll get Bruin and Fi reunited."

The ground trembles under my paws as the giant barrels for us. He's bloody and disoriented, but he's still a danger to all of us.

I'm here. I'm here. Bruin rushes to join us in a gust of wind.

The moment I feel him merge with me, I nod. *We're good, Greek. Tell Dionysus we're good to go.*

Dionysus snaps us to the loom room of the Moirae and hands Atropos the tapestry. When she runs off to do her thing, I sink back on my haunches and draw a few deep breaths.

Trial two. Done.

I've barely thought that when magic surges in the air around us and we find ourselves back in Hecate's temple facing the witch bitch and Themis.

Themis looks down at me and smiles. "You surprise me more with each encounter, Fiona Cumhaill."

Yeah, well, this was a surprise to me too.

I focus on changing back, but nothing happens. If this is still remnant power from Dionysus's Inner Vixen cocktail, what happens if the ability to release my untapped potential runs out? Will I be trapped like this?

Emmet was afraid of that too, and it worked out for him. He simply needed to calm down and focus.

It took three days, but he got there.

I don't have three days.

"Our gratitude extends to you both. We won't forget your service to the pantheon." Themis takes a stone off the pile on the temple's marble floor and sets it on the scales. It sets the plates into a teeter-totter until the weight adjustment is absorbed. "A victory well-earned. We'll see you at sunrise."

Perfect. I stand and rub my shoulder against Nikon's ribs. A red, saber-toothed panther, eh? That's pretty fricken cool. And I'm big—like, really big. When we were battling, I was almost as big as Bruin's massive grizzly when we stood shoulder-to-shoulder.

Nikon strokes the sleek fur of my shoulder, and there's no missing the protectiveness in his touch. That's funny because I'm a prehistoric battle beast now. "You did good, Fi. The Olympians definitely owe you one."

I don't care about that right now. Honestly, all I want to do is get back to the villa and change back to myself.

Nikon seems to understand that because he pats my side and in the rush of his magic, snaps us back to Papu's house.

CHAPTER SEVENTEEN

I let out a breath when the four of us arrive at the cliff of the Tsambikos villa. As much as I love his grandparents, and I know they're worried and waiting for word on the outcome of the day, I'm happy he brought us here and not straight to the house. My body is thrumming with inputs I don't know how to handle, and I need a moment.

"I thought you might need a moment." Nikon read my mind. Stepping back, he gives me space. "I'll go fill them in on the day's events. You take your time."

I meet his worried gaze and nod. *Thanks, Greek. Can you tell Calum I'm okay and that he rocked it today?*

"Will do."

Nikon relays my message, then Calum and Kevin take a seat in the grass a few yards away. I appreciate them worrying, and I get the message loud and clear. They're here if and when I need them but won't impose.

Staring out over the meeting place of three seas, I try to rein in the bombardment of power, chaos, and instinct. It's a lot. I feel bad for making fun of Emmet when this happened to him. It's scary and overwhelming.

Bruin, can I release you for a little while I sort through the jumble in my body?

Of course, Red. Whatever ye need.

Thanks, buddy.

Bruin takes physical form and flops down beside me. I shift so I'm leaning against him, and we settle in for some downtime. *You did great today, Bear. I'm thankful every minute of every day to have you with me.*

Same. We're a dream team, that's for sure.

True story. We sit together, watching over to the right as the sun dips low and sets. I can't get a handle on the turmoil reeling inside me. Are the emotions of a druid in animal transfiguration so different?

Emmet never mentioned that.

Neither did the Perry twins.

What do you think Theostratus dies from? Heart attack? What's it like when Atropos cuts your thread?

Never gave it much thought.

I have—although not through the lens of the Greek Fates. After Brendan died, I thought a lot about what it means to exist one minute and not the next. Did he know it was happening or was he unconscious? Did he pass with the unshakable understanding that his family loved him?

I like to think he did.

I draw a deep breath and feel the weight of anguish and sorrow building in my chest. Crime scene images of my brother shot and bleeding on a sidewalk fill my mind. Then other bloody memories filter in. Liam's chest hemorrhaging after he took the bullet meant for me in the subway. Dillan's body doubling over as a sword pierced him.

I feel the anguish of the violence they suffered.

Curling onto my side, I tuck my face into Bruin's long fur, the ache of loss and separation more acute than I've ever felt. I miss my family. I miss Brendan. I miss—

"Fi? What's wrong?"

I can't look at Nikon, who snapped back right then. The pained look of guilt and worry he's been carrying since Hecate brought us here is too much. Everything is too much.

"Okay, Red." He eases down beside me. "Talk to me. What's happening?"

"What's wrong?" Calum says as he and Kevin come into the mix. They look down at me and the worry and anguish in their eyes cleaves my heart in two.

"Something's not right," Nikon says.

"What is it?" Calum asks. "How do we help her here?"

"I have an idea. Stay with me, Fi." The snap of his energy takes us into a temple, and I glance around to figure out which one. It doesn't take long. The moment Nikon calls for help, Dionysus is kneeling on the marble next to me.

"All right, *carissima*," he says. "I have you now." There's another surge of magic that transports me again. My eyes are closed but I open them, sure that Dionysus brought me to a sauna. The air is warm and heavy with humidity.

"Nikky, stand back and let me get her into the spring."

"I'll help you—"

"You can't. The water kills humans."

"Hello? Fiona is human."

"Not wholly. The lineage of a deity runs in her veins. This water cleanses gods of foul influences."

"Does Fi have enough goddess for it not to kill her?"

"I think so."

Think so? That's not comforting. Dionysus's magical signature surrounds me a moment before I'm wet and held at the surface in his arms. "Relax, Red. You'll be better now. I'm sorry you suffered. I should've thought of this."

Thought of what? What is happening?

I hate not knowing what's going on in my life. With everything in me, I want to speak to him. I want to ask him questions. Not being able to makes me angry.

My body tingles and the vibrations across my skin go deeper. The tingling morphs into a burn that erupts into an explosion of my cells.

I recognize the sequence and sink into his arms. Yes, I want to speak and be heard. I want to be me.

The transformation back to myself is far less scary than the other way. When I'm sure I'm me, I stand on two feet and rake my wet hair over my head, smiling at Dionysus. "Hey, thanks for the save. I feel better."

His smile doesn't hold any of his usual smartass smirk. This time, it's a genuine relief and affection. "Welcome back, *carissima*. It's been a day for you."

"It has." I chuckle at the two of us standing in the center of a ground-fed fountain and gesture at the grotto beyond. "Are we done in here?"

He nods. "If you're feeling better, I'm relieved to say it worked. You gave us a bit of a scare."

I step over the rim of the basin, and Nikon sweeps me into a crushing hug. "Are you okay? What happened? I didn't know what was wrong or how to help you."

I take a moment to enjoy the strength of his hug then ease back. "I'm good now, but I have no idea what happened. One minute I was fine and the next I was drowning in sorrow and despair."

"It's called death dread," Dionysus says. "Part of the reason gods don't go into the underworld is that afterward we're bombarded with the dread and sorrows of our lives. Having endless lives, that's a heavy load to bear."

I rub the ache in my chest. "It was awful. I felt the horror of the people I love getting hurt around me—Liam, Dillan, and poor Brendan. I felt the pain of his death all over again. It felt like my heart was physically breaking apart."

"But it's over now?" Nikon asks.

I do an internal gut check and nod. "Yeah, I think so."

"It is," Dionysus says. "The dread of the underworld can't withstand the cleansing properties of the Fountain of Peirene."

I shiver, and Nikon puts his arm around me, extending his hand to Dionysus. "Thank you. I owe you a big one for fixing Fi. She's more than my friend. She's my hope."

He waves that away. "I saved her for her, not you. You owe me nothing—unless your undying devotion means wine, women, and wanton. Then you can owe me if you must."

I laugh and reach up on my tiptoes to kiss Dionysus' smooth cheek. "Undying devotion it is. Thank you."

Nikon flashes us back to the spot by the cliff, and even though we've been gone less than a half-hour, it seems like a lifetime and that things have gone badly since we left. Calum and Kevin look distraught, and Bruin is pacing and roaring at the night sky. I run to meet him.

"I'm here. I'm better."

Bruin lets out another roar and barrels toward me. Mid-run, he vanishes and swirls around me before settling in my chest. *Don't do that. I was scared.*

"I'm sorry, buddy. I didn't mean to leave you."

Nikon makes a face and looks at Kevin and Calum. "Fuck, I'm sorry. I took Fi without thinking. I didn't mean to leave you out of it."

Red, if ye could give the Greek the finger from me, I would appreciate it. He and I are not on speakin' terms at the moment.

I flash Nikon a middle-fingered salute and shrug. "That's from him. Not me. You are not forgiven."

Nikon purses his lips to keep from smiling and nods. "Understood. I'll make it up to him." Then he looks at my brother and Kev. "Am I in the hot seat with you too?"

Calum grabs him by the back of the neck and pulls him against his chest for a hug. "You acted without thought to save my sister. I'll never fault you for that."

I shiver, and Kevin turns me toward the villa. "Since we want you alive and well, let's get these wet leathers off you and get you warmed up."

I nod. "Like Dionysus said, it was quite a day."

I wake a little shaky, the memory of death dread still pressing on my heart. I understand that it was the underworld's dark magic, but the facts and the images weren't fantasy. They were real, and they remain with me. Brendan. Dillan. Liam. The truth is, bad things can happen to good people.

Look at Nikon and what he's had to endure.

Sometimes life isn't fair.

I close my eyes against the darkness, but my mind is spinning now. I sigh. There's no sense trying to sleep. I'll only lay here and drive myself crazy. Flipping back the coverlet, I sit up and let the coolness of the terracotta floor soothe the bottoms of my feet.

I miss my fuzzy blue bedside rug from home. I miss King Henry and sleeping with Sloan and even Manx when he gets lonely and needs cuddles.

Before I work myself up, I make my way out into the hall and visit the facilities. After I set the lantern back onto the little cabinet, I notice the whisper of male voices and follow the sound to the symposia.

Nikon and his grandfather are sitting alone drinking wine and chatting.

Deciding to return their privacy to them, I turn—until I hear my name.

"... I understand that, still, it's not their fight to fight. What kind of man does it make me to allow my dearest friends, one of them a woman, to fight battles in my stead? It's shameful."

"They don't seem to feel that way. From where I stand, they're determined to help you regain control of your life. As for Fiona being a woman, she does it for you because she is able and wants to. That speaks of a deep connection."

Nikon chuckles. "I know where you're going with this, Papu, but no. Fiona's heart solidly belongs to another. Sloan is a good man and adores her. They're building a good life."

"You could fight for her. She obviously cares for you."

"That's just Fi being Fi. She's the kind of person who lays her life on the line for another."

"That's a rare and special trait."

"She's a rare and special girl."

Papu grunts. "I've honestly never seen a woman fight with the strength and skill she possesses. I don't know what to make of her."

"That's a common mistake when dealing with Fi. It's best not to try to understand where she fits into things and embrace the fact that she *doesn't* fit into them."

I smile, liking that advice a great deal. *Point to you, Greek.*

Backing away, I leave them to chat and wander through the interior garden on my way back to the guest room. Nikon's grandparents are wealthy, and though their home isn't lavish by modern standards, it's definitely something special at this time.

The rustling of birds draws me to the enclosed courtyard. How awesome is it to have gardens in the center of the house?

Why not?

Meandering through the sleepy plants, I touch the leaves and focus on the vibrancy and health in their leaves. My fingers tingle with the vitality they bring me, and it hits.

Part of the reason I feel out of sorts is that I've been using my powers so much and have no access to my grove.

Nothing replenishes my strength and feeds my soul like spending time with my fae family either in my swing, sitting at the base of one of the trees recording spells in Beauty, or relaxing in the hot springs pool.

With that thought foremost in my mind, I pad barefooted to the door and unlatch the night bar.

"Milady?" Rastus, one of the main house guards, says. "It is very late to be outside. Is there a problem?"

I shake my head. "No. I thought I'd spend a half-hour in the grove. Lock up behind me. I'll knock when I return."

He shakes his head. "Master Tsambikos will be angry if you exit unguarded. I shall escort you."

The man is worked up at the prospect of me leaving, and I don't want to cause him more anxiety, so I relent. "All right, thank you, but I would like to be alone within the grove."

He grabs a spear from a bunch stacked behind the door. "If I can see you, I won't disturb you."

When we open the door, Rastus speaks briefly with the outer guard, and the other man shuffles inside to replace the wooden bar that braces things shut at night.

The evening breeze is warm and welcome. It pulls my hair and tickles my bare neck. "It's lovely here at night." I smile up at the brilliance of the stars above.

"It is." Rastus isn't a chatty guy.

We walk in silence to the end of the villa and into the orderly rows of citrus trees. True to his word, Rastus falls back and allows me to stroll through the trees on my own.

I close my eyes and draw a deep breath, filling my lungs and my sinuses with the fresh fragrance of lemon, lime, and orange. The aroma of fresh citrus is so much stronger and richer than when you find it at a supermarket.

I press my palm against the rough bark of one of the trees and connect with the energy within. It's been two days since Calum and I performed the healing and the trees are already much stronger and healthier. It's amazing what nature can do when given the tools to take care of itself.

Spotting a lemon tree laden down with a hundred beautiful, yellow fruits, I sit at the base of its trunk and close my eyes. Two trials complete. Two more and we'll be going home. Two more and Nikon will be free of Hecate.

We can do this. We can absolutely do this.

With my hands planted firmly against the ground, I take strength from the rich earth below.

I didn't realize how much I needed this. Back home, I was so caught up in the search for the leviathans and the answers to why they came to Toronto to murder Arthur Montclair that I hadn't taken the downtime needed to recharge.

This is a different kind of place—a different kind of life.

Leaning back against the trunk of the tree, I close my eyes and worry my thumb over the pendant Dionysus gave me. Oh, what a crazy life I live.

"Hello, *carissima*. Have you something on your mind?"

I meet the seductive gaze of Dionysus and smile. He's not the rugged, manly type of guy I'm usually attracted to, but I see the appeal. There's a beauty all its own in the softness of his features.

"Reflecting on the twists of life."

"So, keeping it light in the wee hours."

I chuckle. "I suppose."

"You decided to wax philosophical in a lemon grove all alone at night?"

"I'm not alone. Rastus is watching." I wave to the guard, who looks alarmed by Dionysus' arrival. I flash him a thumbs-up and wonder if that gesture translates. Considering he appears to stand down, I assume it does. "I miss my druid grove at home. It's a source of power for me."

He nods. "Today's trip into the underworld must've been draining. I'm sorry I missed the effects of the dread until it overtook you."

I wave that away. "Not your fault. You've been great. We couldn't have gotten this far without your help."

He takes a knee in front of me and holds out his hand. "Allow me to escort you back. You're tired, and as your biggest fan, I want you not to die tomorrow. I have a lot riding on you."

I chuckle and allow him to pull me to my feet. "What do you have riding on me, side bets of wealth and wine?"

He shakes his head. "Hope that the good guys can win against a power like the she-bitch."

I like that he doesn't speak her name.

She's not welcome here.

Dionysus tucks my hand into the crook of his elbow, and I smile at the warmth of his skin. He's not bombarding me with sexual energy, and it makes me happy to think we've gotten past the drama of what he shares with the world.

We exit the grove together, and Rastus looks like he might have a heart attack when we approach. I wink at him, and he strikes off toward the villa, leading the way and allowing the two of us to continue uninterrupted.

When we get back to the front door, I turn to face him. "Dionysus?"

"Yes, Red."

"I'm thankful you heard Nikon's call for help and engaged in our fight. I'm thankful we're friends."

He considers my words for a moment and lifts my hand from his elbow to his lips. He presses a chaste kiss on my knuckles and smiles. "I am as well, *carissima*. It's been a long time since I made a genuine friend."

"Well, you have. Thanks for looking out for me and know that if you need anything, I'll look out for you too. You rock."

He chuckles. "You rock harder. Now, go get some sleep."

CHAPTER EIGHTEEN

When Nikon comes into my room to wake me up, I'm already dressed and staring at the ceiling. "Eager for the day's trial, Red? Or did you not get any sleep last night? I heard a rumor that you were out star-gazing with a certain god of seduction in the wee hours."

I chuckle and shift over to give him space to sit on the edge of my little mattress. "Dionysus and I had a lovely walk through the citrus grove. No seduction involved."

He studies me as if he's trying to gauge the truth of my words. "He has a way with people. I wouldn't judge—"

I bat him with my pillow and giggle. "It was a simple walk and a talk, Greek. Nothing more than that. My virtue is safe, and he was a complete gentleman."

He grins. "Well, good. Honestly, if you're open to adding a Greek plus one to your bed, I would hope it would be me."

I point down at Kevin and Calum still spooning and sleeping on their pallet and chuckle. "Don't you have your Cumhaill quota filled for plus one already?"

He lifts his shoulder. "If you weren't in love with Sloan and I didn't respect the guy so damned much, I'd fight hard for what we could be, Fi."

"I get that, but honestly, once this whole Hecate disaster is behind you, I think you'll see things differently. I'm the first emotional connection you made in centuries, but you deserve another immortal to spend your life with. Someone who won't leave you suffering the loss of a mortal life."

"So you think you're my gateway crush?"

"Absolutely. When the time comes, and we find your perfect match, I'll be the first in line to celebrate your happiness. You deserve everything immortality offers, Nikon. Don't settle for anything less."

He leans in and kisses my cheek. "No matter who she is, you'll always be my girl."

"Damn straight." I wink. "Now, wake up the snuggle bunnies down there, and I'll visit the little tapestry room. We have asses to kick and trials to conquer."

After our usual routine of breakfast with Nikon's grandparents and them wishing us well, we watch the sunrise, and Nikon snaps us to the Rhodes acropolis.

"Does anyone else feel like this sunrise trip to Hecate's temple is getting old?" I smile at Dionysus, who's sitting on the top step wearing black leather pants, his Team Trouble t-shirt, and a wicked pair of black boots with skull buckles on the side.

"Looking good, dude." I make sure to eye him up and give him a boost. "Raising your game, are you?"

He tilts his head from one side to the other as if considering it. "I'm thinking about making some changes. I thought trying out a new look might spice up my life a little."

I laugh at the impossibility of that. "Says the guy who spends his days either drinking, sexing, or partying. I think your life is plenty spicy."

He stands, and I notice the tattoo on the inside of his wrist. I point at the Celtic tree with the triquetra at its heart and look up at him. "Why are you wearing the Fianna mark?"

He lifts his shoulder. "A tattoo is supposed to hold meaning for you, right? Remind you of something or someone important to you?"

I nod. "And?"

"This reminds me there are still people who are willing to stand up for other people no matter what the cost. People who embrace love and friendship without judgment. People who know when to fight and also when to celebrate and have fun."

Nikon squeezes my shoulders from behind and leans close to whisper in my ear. "Just a simple walk and talk, eh?"

"Whatever the reasons, I like the edge of dark and dangerous, my man," Calum says. "It looks good on you."

Nikon nods. "Calum's right, *adelphos*. As far as finding inspiration, Fiona and her family are a damned good choice. I'm thinking of starting a Cumhaill fan club."

Dionysus winks at me and gestures at the temple behind him. "Shall we? We still have a she-bitch to crush. No time to dawdle."

I catch Calum's wrist as Dionysus, Kevin, and Nikon head inside. "Another day in our crazy life."

Calum wraps his arm across my shoulder and presses his head to mine. "I love our crazy life. Sadly, I know the mayhem tends to hit you a little harder than the rest of us. How are you doing, Fi? Yesterday turned on you a bit."

I consider his question and give it an honest answer. "I'd say fair to fine. Nothing a grove healing and a week of lounging in King Henry with Sloan won't cure. Speaking of healing, how's your leg? Still tingling?"

He purses his lips and sighs. "Yeah. I don't want to hit any panic buttons, but I think something's not right. Do you think the blades in the labyrinth could've been tipped with something? Maybe poison or venom or magic of some kind?"

"I don't know. Nikon or Dionysus might know better."

He nods. "For now, don't say anything in front of Kev. I'll talk to the Greeks quietly after today's trial."

"Are you still good to do the trial with me? Do you want to sit this one out?"

He scrunches his face up and laughs. "Nice try, baby girl. You're not getting rid of me because I have a boo-boo."

I take his hand and tug him forward. "Oh, I'm not trying to get rid of you. I need you. What's the saying? You don't need to run faster than the beast. You only have to run faster than the guy next to you. Your bum leg improves my odds for survival."

"Noice." He laughs. "Florence Nightingale you are not."

The usual gang is assembled when Calum and I arrive at the Scales of Justice. Themis gives us a smile of welcome and raises a hand to hush the crowd. I study the dozen or so toga-clad people milling around behind the scales and wonder what's going on.

My first thought is they're a bunch of early morning worshippers here to honor Hecate. Then I notice almost all of them possess the "godly glow" of those of the pantheon.

"What's that about?" I ask.

"Pantheon paparazzi," Dionysus says. "After yesterday's close call with Theostratus, you've gone viral."

I roll my eyes and look at Calum. Seriously? "Well, it's nice to know the torment of our lives is at least entertaining."

Frowning, I pull out our trial scroll and get right to it.

"Trial of the Spider's Web: Arachne was a great weaver who boasted to all that her skill surpassed that even of the goddess Athena. When reminded that inspiration stems from the muse of the gods, Arachne refused the goddess any credit. Athena took offense and set up a contest between them.

"Athena's weaving represented four other contests between mortals and gods in which the gods punished mortals for setting themselves as equals. Arachne's weaving depicted how the gods misled, tricked, and abused mortals. Insulted by Arachne's lack of respect and enraged that the piece was far more beautiful than Athena's own, the goddess ripped Arachne's work to shreds and beat her with her shuttle.

"Terrified and ashamed, Arachne hanged herself. Thinking death too quick an escape, Athena sprinkled her with the juice of Hecate's herb. The dark poison brought her back to life and transformed her into a spider.

"Over centuries, the strength of Arachne's web has become legendary. The strands are so strong that to weave them together creates impenetrable armor. Recently, a group of demigod youths challenged those dangers and have yet to return to Olympus. The third trial is to find the missing youths and return them to safety."

Calum seems strengthened by the task description. "Infiltrate, locate, and rescue. I can get behind that."

I roll up the scroll and tuck it back into my satchel. The attentive gazes from the pantheon paparazzi make more sense. "How many of you have ties to the missing teens?"

All hands raise.

"All right, tell us what you know. Pointing us in the right direction improves your chances of getting them back."

As it turns out, the parents and friends of the missing teens know very little. Arachne is known to take travelers as prey and has created an impassable area of forest called the Forbidden Forest. The tales of horror are the plotline of any predictable horror movie. She captures people in her web, injects them with venom, paralyzes them, and wraps them in cocoons for later consumption.

Nothing new there—except that it's for reals.

"The Forbidden Forest, eh?" Calum says as the five of us stand at the edge of a tree line. "Not very original."

Kevin arches a brow. "I think it's a case of the keywords being in the title. Forbidden Forest paints a clear picture."

"Not for rebellious half-god youths," I say.

Dionysus frowns. "It's a tough age. Trying to keep up with the full gods but being looked down upon and not fitting in with the human kids because they look at you more like a circus freak or someone to fear."

The bite in his tone is more than compassion—it's bitterness. Nikon told me Dionysus was a demigod taken away from his family, turned into a goat, and raised by rain nymphs. He never fit in and was never really accepted.

"We'll find them."

With that, Calum kisses Kevin, and I hug everyone and call my armor forward.

"Okay, let's treat this like any kidnapping case." Calum calls his bow forward. "We go in quiet and calm. We watch for danger. We get the kids out."

Sounds good in theory. "All the while watching for an eight-legged vengeful weaver with a super-strong web."

"Exactly. Easy-peasy."

Both of us call on *Feline Finesse* and walk in single file, keeping an eye out for any line of web left as a tripwire. Spiders are crazy sensitive to any vibration of their web, and the last thing we want is to notify Arachne we've invaded her territory.

"I prefer beasts with fur," I say absently, searching the treetops for any sign of movement. "Give me a tarantula over a daddy long legs any day."

Calum shakes his head. "I'll take spiders off the table altogether, thanks."

"If that were possible, so would I but everything has a purpose, right?"

"That's what they say." He steps over a fallen log and turns to help me. "Are you sensing anything yet?"

I reach out with *Beast Sense* and shake my head. "Nothing yet. According to the parents, it's a fair hike to get into the dangerous parts of the forest."

"The parents who are gods or demigods who could come get their own damn teenagers back?"

"Yeah, them."

"Why put yourself out when you can get two displaced humans to do it for you, amirite?"

"Maybe they said, 'If you dumb kids do anything stupid, we're not going to come and save you.' Then it's a show of tough love parenting to let them rot in a cocoon."

"Oh, so they're being good parents by not saving them. See, I missed that. Thanks."

I chuckle, turning to scan the trees behind us before proceeding. "So, now I'm the dumb teen, and I hear there's a vengeful meat-eating spider who lives in a forest and traps anyone who comes into her area and my first thought is hells yeah, let's go there."

"Right?"

My shield wakes up, and I take a quick look around. "Okay, my mark is waking up."

Calum slows so we can take a serious look around. "Just waking up?"

"So far, yep."

We shut down the chatter and focus more on the sights and sounds of our surroundings. Or the lack of sounds. "Do you think it's always this quiet?" I whisper, looking toward the canopy of leaves above, searching for birds or squirrels or anything that signals there are still living creatures in this forest.

"I don't feel any mammals or birds, do you?"

I reach out and shake my head. "Nada."

That's sad and unnerving. A forest this size should be teaming with life. The animals are either gone by choice or by design. I hope it's the former.

I point toward branches above our heads, and an icy chill runs the length of my spine. An intricate web connects the leaves and branches of the canopy. As eerie as it is to walk through a silent forest and not see anything flitting or fluttering around, it's worse knowing the forest is choking and held prisoner too.

To make sure the forest still has some life, I reach out for bugs, worms, and beetles. Okay, so there are lots of decomposers. There would have to be, or this forest would die.

I'm still thinking about that when Calum stops in front of me and points.

At first, I look too far ahead and miss it, but when he turns to make sure I see it, I catch sight of the golden strand of thread strung knee-high across our path.

I nod, and when he steps over it, I do as well.

From that point, we move a lot slower, keeping our movements small and our attention focused.

"Check for magic," Calum whispers after another ten minutes of plodding through the forest. "If they're demigods, maybe you can pick up their signature and track them."

"Detect Magic." I let my gaze soften as my senses heighten. I don't get anything back from that, so I try another route. *"Detect Venom."*

If Arachne injects her captors with venom to subdue them, maybe that's the way to find them.

My fae eyes overtake my usual baby blues, and as my search starts bringing results back to me, the closest source throws me.

It's like thermal imaging and the pulsing orange splotch on Calum's leg does *not* make me happy.

"Are you getting anything, Fi?"

I lift my focus and expand my search. Dionysus' ambrosia boost seems to still be in play because I'm sensing a *ping* on my radar system that would normally be well beyond my range. "Two hundred yards that way."

Calum follows my gesture and frowns. "Let's stay on the path as long as we can and cut across. At least here, I can see what we're walking into."

"Sounds good. Now that we have a target, I'll send Bruin out for a recon trip." *You set, buddy?*

Ready and steady.

Looking for a bunch of teenager-sized cocoons two hundred yards that way plus any sign of Arachne if you come across her.

Got it. I'll be back.

When my hair flies up, and I nod, my brother continues along the path. It's slow going, but I'd much rather take our time and not meet up with a spider big enough to eat people.

At least until I absolutely have to.

When we come to the point on the path where we have to bank right, I tap Calum's shoulder and give him the signal. *"Find Traps,"* he whispers.

I feel the signature of his power surge in the air around us, and as much as I love him and believe in him, the reality is, he doesn't have the juice I do.

Find Traps. I cast it without words and hope there's nothing to find or if there is, he finds them first.

I don't want to be "that druid" and think I can do everything better myself because I know that's not the case. I simply have stronger magic.

Bruin swishes back and swirls around us.

We have a bunch of cocoons straight ahead.

Awesome, buddy. Great work. And the spider queen?

No sign of her. Do ye want me to take a look around to find her?

No. I don't think so. Spiders sense even a slight breeze along their network of web. If she's not between the kids and us, let's not go looking for trouble.

As ye wish. I'll keep an eye out for ye along yer path.

Thanks, buddy.

I tap Calum's shoulder and relay the info Bruin gave me. Thumbs up on finding cocoons. Straight ahead. No spider queen.

He turns back to the forest, and we work on cutting through the scrub to close the distance to those kids.

It feels like it takes forever before we get to the little clearing where we believe the cocoons are stored. We would know for sure what we're dealing with if we could get in there. At the moment, that's a problem.

The scene reminds me of those creepy images you see on the "why I'll never live in Australia" memes on the Internet where the entire scene is tented in a blanket of web.

"Seriously creepy," I say.

"Yeah, you're witnessing the horror feature of my nightmares for the rest of my life."

Directly in front of us are a crisscross of guard webs acting like laser beam security around an exhibit in a museum.

"How do we get in there? If we hack through, she'll be here before we can even cut them out."

Calum scowls. "Can Bruin cut them out?"

"Does he have that kind of precision?"

"Do we have that kind of time?"

I scratch the side of my head. Seeing the result of a massive spider woman's feeding grounds is giving me the heebie-jeebies. "How does *she* get through?"

Calum arches a brow and smiles. "Good question, Fi. Sure as shit she doesn't undo this every time."

From above, Bruin says. *A branch runs straight over the clearing with space below for her to drop and move around inside.*

I relay that to Calum, and he searches for our way to access things from above. "Climbing the tree and dropping isn't an issue for us, but how do we help them climb up and out if she poisoned them?"

"If her web is as strong as rumored, we could tie the cocoons together and sling it over the branch."

He chuckles. "Or coax the branches of the tree to braid together and give them something to climb up."

I nod. "Yeah, that's better. Okay. Let's do this."

CHAPTER NINETEEN

It doesn't take long for Calum and me to scale the tree's trunk and drop into the center of the clearing Arachne uses as her food storage. I rise from my landing, release *Diminish Descent,* and take in the mess of whacked and weird we volunteered for.

"When Bruin said a bunch of cocoons, I did not picture this."

It's like one of those sci-fi movies where the hero finally gets a glimpse at how bad things are for humanity, then the camera pans out farther and farther, and it keeps getting worse and worse.

Yeah, that's this.

"We're looking for six kids." Calum turns in a circle, his gaze unfocused. "How the fuck do we find them in this? There must be two hundred."

"Apparently, she bites off more than she can chew."

"Or she's a prepper planning for the apocalypse."

I chuckle, but it's not funny. "Thinking caps on. Do we try to find the six we need or start slicing them open and let everyone loose?"

"Sure as shit, cutting them all free will trigger a security breach to her somehow."

"So, we try to narrow it down first and cut as many free as we can during the evac."

Calum frowns. "It bites my balls that we leave any of them here."

"There's no way we can save them all. Besides, we don't even know if they're still alive and well in there. If she started doing this centuries ago, some of these meat meals might be more like jerky than prime rib."

Calum snorts. "You have a real way with words. You know that?"

"What? Am I wrong?"

"No. Your slant on things just makes me laugh. Okay, so going with your jerky versus prime rib theory, maybe we can go by heat or heartbeat or—"

"Detect Venom." I do a complete three-sixty turn and scan for something we can use to our advantage. "They would all have some level of venom in them, but if fresh venom is orange and it dissipates to purple as it ages, this section holds the new arrivals."

Calum turns to where I'm indicating and draws the knife he has sheathed against his thigh. "I'll roll with that, but what makes you think fresh venom is orange? What if it's purple? Then we're starting in the wrong place."

I shake my head. "No. I'm sure fresh venom is orange because that's what I'm picking up from your leg wound."

Calum frowns and drops his gaze. "Well, shit."

"Yeah. Sorry."

He nods. "Doesn't change anything. Orange it is. Give me your best guess on the new arrivals."

I point out five together. "These here."

"That's five. We're looking for six."

"I don't know what to tell you, bro. There are five that are bright orange and the others are noticeably less orange."

Calum positions himself at one end of the group, and I call Birga and start at the other.

"Slice them quick, top to bottom, and move to the next one. Once we have the cocoons open, we'll worry about getting them out and up to the branch."

"Oh, shit, the branch." I raise my hand toward the branch we used to drop here. *"Commune with Nature. Plant Growth."* My connection to the trees is sluggish at first, but it doesn't take long before I twine a thick rope of young branches to hang down to us.

When that's in place, Calum winks. "On one, Fi. Three... Two... One.

Slicing through the weave of the cocoon is like hacking through plywood with a butter knife. That's saying a lot because Birga is supremely sharp and I'm sure Dionysus's knife is too. "I can't decide which is worse, touching it or smelling it."

Calum finishes with his second cocoon and steps beside me to start his third. "Definitely the smell."

It seems that Arachne's venom does something gross to the insides of her victims because not only have they all lost control of bowels and bladders, but they've been sealed up with it for days.

"The glamorous life of a hero." I fight my gag reflex and blink against the sting burning my eyes. "How's your first one doing?"

Calum and I finish slicing simultaneously and start tending to the kids stuck inside the putrid pods. I release Birga and widen the gap, airing them out.

"Dude, can you hear me?" I pat his cheek a little rougher than I normally would, but if they don't start snapping out of it, there won't be five to save next time. There will be seven.

I seriously don't want to crap my new leathers.

"Damn, I wish Sloan or Emmet was here. I miss their healing mojo."

"Amen." Calum gives up trying to rouse his kids and pulls them from their husks to set them on the forest floor. "I'm concerned about the climbing out of here part of the plan. I have a feeling these five aren't going to be challenging Tarzan for the title of King of the Jungle anytime soon."

I almost palm my mouth but remember at the last minute where my hands have been and gag. "Okay, I need a bath." I try not to think about that and focus on the current worst problem. "Maybe Bruin alley-oops them up and over."

Calum blinks at me. "You think your bear should shotput five demigods over the feeding ground wall?"

"They're demigods. How bad could it be?"

He waves a finger at me. "You're winding down on this whole trial thing and getting a little scary."

I finish pulling my second guy free and let him flop on the pile of dumbass demigods. "Sorry. I'm tired and miss home, and the whole death dread drained a lot out of me."

Fi, I've got good news and bad news.

"Oh shit." I drop my head back and groan. "Bad news first, then the good news, buddy. Finish strong."

Calum straightens and frowns.

Bruin materializes, and the kids barely react. "The spider lady is coming."

"There's good news?" Calum asks.

"Now ye don't have to worry about tripping her alarms. Ye can run like hell."

I look down at the pile of kids and sigh. "I don't think running like hell is an option at the moment. Good enthusiasm though. Nice try."

Knowing Arachne is coming rouses the boys more than I expect. As Calum and I reassess the idea of how to get them out, they scramble to life.

"We were told there were six of you," Calum says. "Where's the other one?"

A kid with goat horns stumbles to his feet and grabs up the cocoon husks. "He bailed and went to his girlfriend's villa instead."

"Smart kid," Calum says. "Okay, according to the bear, we have about two minutes before the spider bitch is back and we're all in trouble."

"We won't be here when she comes," a hulk of a kid says. He shuffles to help his buddy gather the empty cocoons.

"Getting gone is a great plan, but we need to travel light. In an escape, you can't bring your web booty with you." I straighten beside Calum and test the branch rope. "So, are we going with climbing or alley-oop?"

"I think climbing. They're doing better." We turn as the guy with the horns kneels, and his buddies all slap a hand on him. Reality hits a split-second too late, and Calum and I are left staring at an empty forest floor.

"Those little shit weasels flashed out and left us here."

"Fucking hell." Calum sheathes his knife and jumps for the rope. "Those stupid, ungrateful..."

I stop listening as I double-check we have everything and start climbing up after my brother. "Bruin. Guide us out of here, buddy."

It takes us no time at all to climb the rope, scale the branch, jump down and book it back toward the exit. My shield is lighting up, and it really is time to take our leave.

"...piece of shit, goat-horned, asswipe..."

I don't disagree with him, but maybe saving his breath for running would be a good idea.

"...cocksucking, pant-shitting, selfish..."

She's coming, Red. Veer left of those fir trees up ahead.

"Stay left of the firs, Calum."

"...double-crossing, spineless, dipshits." I'm not sure if he's run out of steam on the insults or he's taking a time out not to get dead.

Either way, I like the part about us not getting dead.

She's gaining on you.

Calum's gait is shifting to favor his bad leg. We still have too far to go for him to slow down or go lame now. *Shit. "Plant Growth. Wall of Thorns."*

I cast the spells behind me, hoping to slow her down even a little. Arms pumping, legs burning, we've dropped the hammer. "Will she leave the forest to follow us out?"

"No idea."

"Bruin, tell Nikon we're coming out hot and need emergency transport. Have Dionysus take Kevin to safety."

Got it.

The thundering *crash* of brush and branches right behind me is not comforting. Calum's limping now, and she's only fifty feet behind us at most. "Not far now, bro. Haul ass. You want to give those little pricks a talking to, don't you?"

"Hells yeah."

"Good. Then be mad. Anger is powerful."

"I see the edge of the trees."

"Aim for the Greek. Even if we bowl him over, aim for the Greek."

My Fianna mark burns fiery hot.

Something sharp hits me in the back and yanks me off my feet. The change in trajectory is violent, and I land hard. My body armor protects me from the worst of it, but my skull sloshes in my head, and it knocks my hamster flying out of my cognitive wheel.

Shaking my head clears nothing. In a daze, I get Birga up in time to take a swipe at the belly of the beast. Arachne is a hideous monstrosity with the pointy legs of a spider and the head and chest of the woman she once was.

The woman is like a mermaid masthead on the body of a giant black widow. It's freaky as hell.

Two black fangs drop as she opens her mouth and leans forward to bite me. They clack together, dripping with venom, and I barely have time to get my elbow up.

Thrusting my arm into her face is messy and stings, but she wasn't able to puncture my armor, so I'm good.

Bruin roars as he throws himself at her and knocks her for one helluva tumble.

I scramble to my feet and grab Birga on the run. Calum was right. I see the edge of the tree line, and it's not far. "Bruin. Leave her. Don't miss your ride this time."

I run straight out of the trees, but it's not Nikon waiting for me. It's Dionysus. "Where's Calum? Is he safe?"

"Nikon took him. I came back for you. Can we go?"

I'm here. I'm here. Bruin hits my chest in a rush, and I stagger back a step. "Yeah. Go!"

"Take me back. For fuck's sake, I'm fine. Take me!" Calum's panicked tirade has me running across the marble floor to get to him.

"I'm here. I'm good."

There are times when brothers hug you hard to squish the air out of you to make you tap out and call mercy. Then there are times like this. Calum's entire body shakes as he holds me and I know it's not all anger.

After losing Brendan, we all made a pact that it couldn't happen again. No one dies.

I'm thankful for my armor. It's only because of my hard, outer shell that he's not crushing me. "It's okay. I made it out, and we're both still standing."

"Fuck, Fi," he whispers against my neck. "You can't do that shit to me."

I chuckle and rub his back. "Technically, I got sucked into a fight by Arachne's web-slinger. Not my choice."

He eases back and holds me by the shoulders, taking inventory. "You're whole?"

"Yeah. Her fangs couldn't pierce my armor."

"I thank Fionn every night for those protective greaves." Kevin joins the love-in. He hugs me and tilts his head toward a very upset and cautious-looking Greek. "He saw Calum's state when he came out of the trees and pulled him from the fight. As you see, that didn't go over well when Calum got here and realized you weren't with them."

I meet my brother's gaze and cup his jaw. "He made a tough call, and it was the right one. Things could've gone south fast if you came back for me in the shape you're in."

"Not his call." Calum's voice is hard.

I sigh, noticing the audience taking in the show. "We'll table our dysfunction until we get home. Let's end this leg of the trial and get cleaned up. We reek."

Calum chuckles and wrinkles his nose. "Yeah. We do. We should probably go spend some time with the parents so they can enjoy the fruits of our labors."

I nod. "A great idea. You go tell them their kids are a bunch of spoiled, spineless cowards, and I'll check on Nikon."

Calum looks over my shoulder and rolls his eyes. "Fine. Tell him I'll get over it, but I'm still pissed."

I squeeze his hips and step back from our hug. "Will do."

Wrapping up the end of the third trial goes off without much more drama. Themis declares us the victors, another stone gets placed on the scales, we thank Dionysus—again—for being there for us, and it's back to the Tsambikos villa to clean up and rest up for the last trial.

"Do you need anything else, Mistress?" A slender young servant girl with black hair and bare feet sets two folded towels down beside the private bathing pool.

"No, I'm fine. Thank you, Drixa."

She bows and moves to leave me. "At your convenience, Master Nikon the Younger awaits your company in the outer chamber."

Unlike the open pool in the atrium courtyard, the bath is very private. I've been sealed inside with the humidity and the fragrance of bathing oils for almost an hour, unwilling to let the serenity go. "Tell him he can come in."

"Mistress?"

I chuckle at her surprise. "I'm completely concealed beneath the milky water. There's no need to panic."

Nikon comes in a moment later chuckling. "You're going to scandalize my younger self. You and I may be accustomed to modern practices, but Drixa is beside herself out there worrying about me compromising your state of honor."

"I lost my state of honor years ago, and I'm sure your younger self will weather the storm. I'm too tired to face the world. I think I might laze in here until it's time to leave tomorrow morning."

Nikon sits on the wooden bench against the wall and leans forward to prop his elbows on his knees. "It's been a hard week for you. I'm sorry about that."

I wave that away. "I've accepted your apology enough times already. We're good. What has you hanging around outside the lady's bath?"

"I'm worried about Calum and wanted to talk to you privately about it."

"Is his leg bothering him?"

"Fi, you should've seen the look on his face as he ran out of that forest. My instinct to get him out of there was as much panic as it was a conscious decision to get him to the temple."

"Did he tell you the blade in the labyrinth was tipped with venom and that it poisoned his leg?"

"No! When did you find that out?"

"He mentioned it wasn't healing properly, and today, while I was detecting Arachne's venom, I figured out why. He said he was going to talk to you about it but didn't want Kevin to know yet."

He runs his hands through his long, blond hair and sighs. "I suppose he'd have to be talking to me to tell me about it."

"He was scared for me and pinned his anger on you. He knows it's not fair. He'll get over it. He told me to tell you as much."

He rubs his palms together, looking relieved. "Sooner rather than later would be good. It's eating me up that you two are doing all this for me—suffering because of me—and I'm contributing nothing but being a mystical Uber transport."

"Work on the venom problem, and I'll talk him down. We Cumhaills have a hot temper when brought to a boil, but we cool down quick."

Nikon nods and stands. "Thanks, Fi. I'll figure out what we're up against with his leg. You enjoy your lazing about. You deserve it."

I lift my toes so they peek out of the water. "Yeah, I do."

CHAPTER TWENTY

R*ed, wake up.*

I blink against the dim gray of pre-dawn light. *What is it, buddy? What's wrong?*

It's Calum. Ye asked me to keep an eye on him, and I think ye better take over. He's in the privy throwin' up.

I flip back the coverlet and sit on the edge of the bed long enough for my equilibrium to settle. *Good catch. Love you.*

Should we wake Kevin?

No. Get Nikon.

On it.

After turning up the flame on the bedside lantern, I grip the handle and head to the outhouse room. By the time I get there, Calum is sitting on the floor in the hall looking wrecked. Setting the lamp on the little stand, I reach into the washroom and dip the hand towel into the water pitcher.

"Decided we need more excitement in our life, did you?" I press the damp cloth against his forehead and kneel beside him. "How long have you been sick?"

"Half an hour."

I'd like to think that's not too bad, but I honestly don't know. "Do you want to get back to the bedroom or are you good here?"

"Here is good." A huge shiver racks through him. "Shit, I'm cold, Fi. I feel like shit."

"I know." I refresh the cloth, squeeze out the excess water, and fold it to stay on his head. Then I rush back to our room and grab the blanket off my bed.

"Fi?" Kevin says, his voice graveled with sleep. "What's wrong? Why are you rushing around?"

"It's Calum's leg. There was venom on the blade, and he's worse."

He scrambles to his feet and is half jogging, half staggering toward the door. "Where is he?"

"In the hall by the bathroom." The two of us get back to Calum, and I wrap the blanket around his shoulders. I'm glad he sleeps in his boxers so I have access to his wound. "I'm going to cut away the dressing and have a look, 'kay?"

Calling Birga forward, I grab the edge of the fabric wrapped around his leg and slice through it. The bottom layer sticks to his skin and objects to being picked free.

Where the hell is Nikon?

With a bit of fussing, I get the dressing off. Coagulated blood crusts off as fresh blood oozes into its place. The exposed gash smells rank, the poisoned flesh discolored and raw. As bad as all that is, it's the runnel of black tissue snaking up his leg toward his hip that has me panicking.

It's as if a poisonous serpent is wriggling its way toward his core organs.

Rushed footsteps bring my attention to the arrival of Nikon and Dionysus. "Hello again, *carissima*. With all these wee hour rendezvous, people are going to start talking."

"Thanks for coming. Do you two know what type of venom we're dealing with? Do we have an ancient anti-venom bank handy?"

"Even better." Dionysus holds up a leaf and taps my nose with it. "You have me. Open up, big guy. I need you to chew this up good and swallow it."

I wake groggy, my head filled with the cloud of fog and the weight of sand. My first thought is of Calum. I roll to my back and sit up on the floor pallet to check on him. "How is he?"

Kevin is lying on the guest bed looking tired but calm. "Sleeping peacefully."

I chuckle. "At least that makes one of us."

He smiles. "After the wizard coma, I hoped we were done with sleepless nights where he's hanging onto life by a thread."

"I don't think it was that bad yet, but I hear you."

"However bad it was, it would've been worse without Dionysus and his leaf of life."

"Agreed." I make a mental note to show him our unwavering devotion as soon as life returns to normal.

"Did you get any sleep? There's still one trial left."

I stretch my arms over my head and tilt my head back and forth. The soft *pop, pop, pop* in my neck releases the tension I've been carrying. "I had a dream about Sloan and me... Well, it was more a replay of a memory. He was presenting me with my Claddagh and telling me he loves me."

Kev smiles. "That was a great night."

It was. I want that again. As beaten down and tired as I am, having Sloan visit me in my sleep has refilled my faith and hope.

Today it ends.

I'll kill the trial, and I'll be back in his arms.

"What do you think today's trial will be?"

I honestly have no idea. "I hope it doesn't involve crushing my soul with the weight of death and destruction though. Been there, done that, not a fan."

Kevin chuckles. "You and me both."

I chuff. "Dionysus got the save on that one too."

"He definitely did," Nikon comments while leaning against the frame of the bedroom doorway. "Who's ready to end this bullshit throwback and go home?"

Kevin and I both raise our hands.

He nods. "I hate to say it, but it's time to get ready."

The glow of lantern light brightens the symposia, and Yaya and Papu are waiting to eat with us as they have each morning since we arrived.

"There she is." Papu rises to greet me as we enter. "How does the day greet you, Fiona?"

"I am well, thank you."

"Are you excited to see what Themis has in store today?"

"I am."

"Then," Nikon says, waiting until I sit before settling onto the couch beside me, "when it's over, to see Hecate's face when she's lost."

I believe that will happen—I honestly do—but I don't want to jinx it. Sorting through the selection of cold meats and cheeses, I nibble and try not to get too excited.

Sloan is still very much with me after my dream, and I'm anxious to get back to him.

"Where is Calum?" Yaya nibbles a little cheese. "Enjoying a few extra moments of rest before you leave?"

Nikon straightens. "Calum fell ill last night—an aftereffect from the injury he suffered during the first trial. He and Kevin will be staying here with you today."

Papu's smile fades. "You'll be alone on your task?"

I appreciate his protective concern but wave it away and

enjoy a sip of wine. "I'll have Bruin with me. He and I are quite a formidable team. We'll be fine."

"How ill is he, *agori mou*?" Yaya asks. "Should we send for the surgeon?"

Nikon shakes his head. "Dionysus gave him a medicinal leaf from a tree on Olympus. It seems to have staved off the poison for now. Once we get back home, we'll have one of our healers check him over again."

Yaya still looks worried.

I am too.

I dip my bread in the olive oil and herbs mixture and try not to think about it. Calum will be fine. He has to be.

Papu breaks off a chunk of bread. "I forgot to mention. Yesterday, while in town, Lysias noticed two local merchants weren't attending their stalls at the market. He inquired and learned that a tremendous plague of mold and moths had destroyed their entire yield."

"Imagine that." I hold up my fist to bump with Nikon. "How did the do unto others thing go again, Greek?"

He grins and meets my knuckles with his. "So, whatever others do to you, do also to them, for this is the Law and the Prophets."

I hold up my glass and grin. "Turn around is fair play. Couldn't have happened to a nicer—"

The barking of Atlas and Chaos has us all turning to the open wall leading out to the grounds. Papu is getting to his feet when the sharp yelp of one of the dogs sets my shield off.

"Papu and Yaya, get somewhere safe." I call Birga and my body armor forward and meet Nikon's confused gaze. "My shield is on high alert."

I'm the first out the door, and I release Bruin. "We have company, buddy. There are bad guys out here."

The moment I step onto the grass, I'm under attack.

Flaming jugs of hot oil hit me and explode, enveloping me in orange flame and black smoke. "Stay back, you two." I launch to smack down another lobbing bomb.

It's an ancient Greek Molotov cocktail.

"Bruin, find the supply of bombs and take that guy out. Get rid of their ammunition."

I shout into the darkness, hoping my bear heard me. I curse as a flaming jug arches well over my head and lands on the upper balcony. "Nikon. Second floor. Hurry."

Three loincloth-covered gladiators rush across the grounds, swinging swords and spiked clubs. I see the incoming firebomb and kick one of my attackers to take it in the back. His baleful scream emerges, and he drops out of the fight to writhe on the grass.

Two against one is even easier.

Normally, I enjoy facing off with thugs like these, but I don't have the time. The sun is peeking over the line of the horizon, and I have somewhere to be.

"Bruin, how you doin'?"

A roar comes back at me, so I take that as a signal that Killer Clawbearer has his hands full. I cast a backward glance to check on the upper balcony and grunt as one of my opponents takes advantage and clubs me in the chest.

Resetting my footing, I swing Birga over my head and come down hard on his dominant shoulder. "That was for cracking me in the boob, dickwad."

"Fi, I need sand. It's a tar fire." I hear Nikon's plea, and my attention returns to the upper balcony.

Shit on a stick. The fire is spreading.

"Help me hold these guys off."

"I have your back, sista." Arrows rain in from the other end of the second-floor balcony, and I blow my brother a kiss.

He might be down, but Cumhaills are never out.

When Nikon snaps down, he grabs the sword off the guy I

tar-broiled, and I shift my focus to the strip of beach at the base of the cliffs.

"Sand Storm." With my connection, I pull up a funnel of sand and direct it at the flames spreading across and up the villa's wall.

I have my back to the battle and am focused on the house when Nikon grapples me and takes me to the ground. We roll as one as a beast of a man barrels past. Before the juggernaut has time to turn and come back at us, Nikon is on his feet and taking him down with a sword.

Bruin races past me as I get back to my feet and regain control of the sand.

"Incoming," Nikon shouts. "Fi, twenty more coming up the grove path."

Fuckety-fuck. Twenty more?

Papu has rallied the house slaves and is leading the charge by taking people out with a crossbow. Right. Nikon's granda was a military man and knows his way around battles.

Not waging battles on his front lawn, but life is full of surprises.

There are too many coming at me to keep them at a good range for Birga, so I return my girl and grab the two discarded short swords. If Sloan were here, I'd kiss him on the mouth. He's such a stickler for me learning to handle all weapons.

Ye never know when ye might find yerself without yer spear. It's best to be prepared, aye?

"Aye, hotness. It's best to be prepared." I end the last of my three and run to join Papu and his men trying to hold off twenty men coming in from the grove.

That is until I see twenty more cresting the slope from the vineyard grounds. "Twenty more coming up the slope."

"Fuck me." Nikon snaps to my side. "I'm going to alert my uncles. Two minutes."

"Hurry back."

Papu and his men are fighting hard against the grove battalion and with Nikon gone for reinforcements, that leaves the vineyard twenty for me. I glance back to see if Calum can help. Nope. He's taken up the sand and is working on the fire.

"Bruin, where are you, buddy?"

When I get no answer, I figure I'm alone on this one.

Okay, twenty against one. I can manage. No biggie.

"Entangle." I cast the call for the vineyard to help me and command the vines to join the fight. "These are the assholes who tried to take you down. Now's your chance to get even."

It's easier to see what I'm dealing with now that the sun is up and they've lost the tactical advantage of darkness.

"Erupting Earth." I drop and place my palms flat on the dew-damp grass, asking for the earth to rise and swallow these assholes.

Sweat is dripping down my nose, and I try to shake it off. Four of the attackers make it through the heaving and caving ground and come straight at me.

"Whirlwind." I stand tall and reach for the heavens. The air is calm, but as I focus, a breeze gathers. Forcing the connection, I pull the current into a gale. Squinting through the hair whipping my face, I swing toward the edge of the cliff.

My gust of wind hits the men with hurricane force and drags them sideways and over the cliff.

Nikon returns with men who are very obviously Tsambikos family members. Nikon heads straight for the ones I've trapped in the caved-in ground while the men he brought run to help Papu and his slaves.

I jog over to back up Nikon, but he has things well in hand. After a survey of the land, I downgrade the situation to taking out the trash.

The battle is won.

I'm doubled over panting when Nikon runs back to me. "Fuck, Fi. We're really late."

Crud, the final trial.

I pinch my fingers under my tongue and let out a whistle. "Bruin, come on. We gotta book it. We're late."

"Shit." Nikon makes a face. "Don't tell the bear, but I almost left him behind again."

I chuckle. "Well, it's good you didn't. You would've been king of his shit list."

"No doubt."

Bruin races over, and I sag against his muscled frame. I raise my arm for Nikon to grab hold, and Calum appears and grabs my wrist. Kevin's there too. "You weren't thinking about leaving us behind, were you, baby girl?"

I shake my head. "No way. Never crossed my mind."

CHAPTER TWENTY-ONE

We arrive at Hecate's temple, and the witch bitch looks far too happy with herself. "You're late. Themis already left."

"Are you fucking kidding me?" Nikon shouts, shifting his gaze from her to Dionysus. "We were attacked. Fifty armed thugs just raided my family home. We were putting out the fire."

"Literally," I say, still a little breathy. "Big tar fire on the second floor. Look, Calum didn't even stop to get pants or shoes."

Dionysus raises his hand and Calum is dressed. "Yes, Themis left, but I know her. She believes in fairness. She's not going to forfeit the challenge over you not arriving on time as expected."

"That's what you think," Hecate spits. "They're late. The last challenge is forfeit."

A peal of female laughter fills the temple a moment before Themis returns with her daughters at her side. "I shall decide the outcome of the Challenge of Trials, thank you. This is, after all, my domain of power."

Snap. Take that.

Suppressing the urge to fist-pump and gloat, I retain an heir of maturity and lift my chin. "We are sincerely sorry to keep you all waiting. There was an attack on Nikon's home and family. We had to tend to that."

"You chose to defend others rather than secure your chance to get home to your family?"

I shrug. "Without question. It was the right thing to do. Nikon's family are good people and have been good to us. We couldn't just leave them."

Themis smiles. "I appreciate your moral code. Moral conviction and compassion are often lost in the pursuit of what is desired most."

I smile at Team Trouble and stand tall. "Getting to the finish line doesn't mean much if you lose yourself along the way. We believe in right and wrong and the love and bonds of family. We also believe that if you do your best, the rest will work out as it's meant."

Atropos grins. "You have faith in the Fates guiding you toward the intended end."

I've never really thought about it, but sure. "I believe everything happens how it's supposed to, so yeah. I have faith in you ladies."

Themis picks up a stone. "Today's trial was to be a trial of moral fortitude to test your convictions, but I find you have already faced that test today and won the battle."

She places the stone on the weigh scales, and when the two plates come to rest level with one another, she nods. "Congratulations. I declare you the victors of the Challenge of Trials. You have won your freedom."

"Seriously? We're done? It's over?"

I barely have a chance to turn before Nikon sweeps me up in a rib-crushing hug and Kevin and Calum join in.

"You did it." Nikon's voice cracks and I see the tide of emotion rising in his eyes. "I'll never be able to—"

Calum pulls Nikon in, and Kev wraps the two in his arms.

I leave them to hold Nikon together and look at Themis and

Dionysus. "Thank you both for all your help. It has truly been the honor of a lifetime to spend time with you."

Themis nods. "Your terms have been accepted and will be enforced. Hecate, you will release Nikon Tsambikos from your focus and set him free to live and love from this day forward. You will return them to their time, and you will make no effort to track them or punish them or interfere in their lives in any fashion."

Hecate glares. "I demand the final trial. That they were late should be enough to declare me the winner, but if you choose to overlook that, they at least need to finish the fourth challenge."

"The day is won," Themis says. "Fiona and Calum have proven themselves as strong in character and compassion as they are in strength and skill."

Hecate shakes her head. "Not good enough. Nikon is mine. He shall ever be mine."

Themis raises her hand, and a pair of golden shackles bind Hecate's hands. "If you force my hand, I will ensure you remain unable to interfere in their lives. An official ruling of a Challenge of Trials supersedes your powers, as you well know. Now, accept your loss, or it shall force me to investigate the attack on the Tsambikos family."

Hecate's glare narrows. "What do you imply, Themis?"

The Goddess of Justice chuckles. "I imply nothing. I state plainly I suspect you had a hand in the troubles that kept Calum and Fiona from our appointed time. You cannot possess the guile to incite violence against them and not anticipate I would hold you suspect, could you?"

The flare of fury in Hecate's eyes confirms that Themis has pegged her right. What an insufferable bitch.

"Now, remove the anti-aging spell you cast upon him to freeze him in time. He shall be free from your torment." She removes the shackles and waits expectantly.

Hecate glares at Themis with a promise of future vengeance,

but Themis doesn't care. With a flick of her hands and a sneer, Hecate casts—or uncasts—a spell.

I only hope she's doing what she's supposed to and not messing with Nikon again. With the level of hostility she's oozing, I'm not hopeful that's the case.

With an ear-piercing screech, Hecate flashes out and leaves us to ourselves. The bickering with Hecate seems to have given Nikon something to focus on, and he's pulled himself back together.

Good. I didn't want to rush away without them knowing how incredibly grateful we are for their support.

I open my mouth to say as much but Themis holds up her hand. "I know what is held in heart and mind, Fiona, and you are welcome. Giving me the right to take something precious from Hecate is as much a gift to me as it is to Nikon."

"In the spirit of giving gifts," Atropos says, "I present you with this tapestry."

I accept the folded cloth and study the intricate weave and beautiful colors. Unlike the tapestry we recovered for Theostratus that was heavy with dark colors, this one is bright and beautiful with scarlets and greens and golds and copper. "It's stunning, thank you...but I don't understand. Aren't the tapestries you work with the lives of men?"

She nods. "They are, but this life has ended. I did not cut your brother's thread, Fiona. That was a mortal conflict and beyond my dominion. Still, I thought you might like to have his tapestry."

I blink back tears, but it's no use, so I stop trying. "This is Brendan's tapestry?"

"It is. He was a beautiful soul. I am sorry for your loss."

I hug the bulky fabric to my chest and try to breathe. Turning, I fall against Calum's chest. Now his arms are holding me together. "Thank you so much," he says, his voice deep with emotion. "You can't even know... We will cherish it forever."

Atropos nods. "I know you will. That is why it belongs with you. Be well."

When the ladies disappear, Calum turns us toward Kevin, Nikon, and Dionysus. Their images are lost in the wavy wall of tears blurring my vision, but there's no helping it. "Okay, this was unexpected."

Dionysus swipes a hand under his eyes and blinks fast. "It was, wasn't it."

I close the distance and hug the god. "You're adorable. I'm proud to hold you as my patron god. Thank you for everything. You're a rock star."

He lifts my chin with a gentle finger and drops his mouth to kiss me. I chuckle, shift, and give him my cheek.

"You resist me now, but one day, Red. One day."

When he flashes out, it's only the four of us. "We did it, Greek. We won. You're free. And we're going home."

Nikon pulls me against his chest again and the other two pile in. We stay there, me hugging Brendan's tapestry, them hugging me, and I'm so thankful. Life is good.

We spend the rest of the day helping Yaya and Papu recover from the attack and saying our goodbyes. Papu wants us to stay and celebrate, but we're anxious to get back home. I miss Sloan, and I want Calum's leg looked at as soon as possible.

Nikon spends the afternoon with his mom, and I wonder about his relationship with his father. Maybe he hasn't reached out to him while we're here because he's immortal and hasn't missed him like his gran and mother. I feel like it's more than that.

Whatever the reason, he spends his time with the two women he'll lose when we leave, and he seems content.

"This is the letter I mentioned, Papu. I've written the dates and important facts about me meeting Kallista. Give it to me and make sure I read it. What happened to her is my greatest regret and knowing now that I'll be truly free of Hecate one day, I can wait. Let her live."

Papu takes it and nods. "I'll keep it safe and deliver it to you when the time comes."

We finish with our goodbyes, and Nikon snaps us to Hecate's temple for what I hope is the last time.

The Scales of Justice are gone, and everything appears as barren and stark as it did the first time she brought me here.

"Catey, we're ready to go home." Nikon doesn't seem surprised she doesn't answer right away, and after the past five days, I'm not either. "Catey, let's not make this a fight. Let's part on better footing than we've shared in the past."

Still nothing.

"Hecate, please. We want to go home, and Themis has ruled. Don't force us to call her back and make a big deal of things. You lost. I'm free. Let me go."

The surge of power drops the veil of privacy, and the temple is once again lavish and gold.

"Are you sure you won?" An arrogant smirk curls Hecate's lips.

Nikon nods. "You know we did. Our victory binds you to send us home."

She nods. "That's right...and I will. One day."

I shake my head and stiffen. "No. Not one day. Right now. Send us home as Themis ordered."

Hecate's grin is as bright as it is cold. "Your exact words were 'We fight for the four of us to return to our time without retaliation. We will continue living on our natural course with those we love.' Nothing in that statement says I need to snap to your demand and take you back this instant."

Nikon curses. "That's the part about 'our time.' Their life spans aren't like ours. They're mortal and have a finite amount of years to live and share with their family."

Hecate shrugs. "Then as long as their family lives, it is still their time. I'll take them back but not until the last moment. Maybe that will be in five years, maybe twenty, who knows?" she chuckles. "Oh, well, I do because I know how long it will be until the next Cumhaill dies. You can stay here and rot until that time."

When she flashes off, I stare at Nikon. "Can she do that? Is she serious?"

He looks as bewildered as I feel. "I have no idea. Fucking hell, when will she stop?"

"You're back." Yaya straightens from where she's sorting through debris on the lawn. "I thought you would be home by now."

"So did we, Yaya," Nikon says, steaming. "Hecate is still trying to control us. Now she says she will take us back to our time but when she's good and ready."

Yaya purses her lips. "I'm afraid my feelings for the goddess are not charitable in the least. Forgive me for saying so, but she needs a swift kick of a mule to the backside."

"At the very least," I agree, at the end of my patience. "When did you say that cousin of yours with time-shift powers will be born?"

Nikon grunts. "Not for a few centuries yet. Sorry, Fi." He opens his mouth to say something else but thinks better of it and bites his tongue. He probably doesn't want to say something uncharitable in front of his grandmother.

Putting some distance between me and everyone else, I wander over to the cliff and sit on the grass. Settling Brendan's tapestry on my lap, I examine the warp and weft of threads as my heart aches. "Damn it, hotness. Now how do I get home to you?"

"Och, ye don't need to do everythin' yerself, Cumhaill. Sometime ye gotta let yer man save the day."

I roll to my feet and—"Are you freaking kidding me?"

I race across the lawn to close the distance between us and leap into his arms. It's a good thing he's ready to catch me because there's no holding back.

I wrap my legs and arms around him like a horny koala and his laughter hints that he doesn't mind a bit.

"Missed me, did ye, *a ghra*?"

I'm crying into his neck, clinging to him to make sure he's real. "I love you, Sloan Mackenzie, but damn, it took you long enough."

His chest bounces beneath me. "I'm sorry about that. With yer ring, I could track ye to Greece in a blink, but I couldn't figure out why I couldn't find ye. I called in Andromeda, and she took me to her granda's place, and he was the one who had the answers. My trackin' spell on ye was for place. I never thought to include time. Yer always testin' me."

I giggle and ease back to look at him. "You found me. That's the important part."

He sets me on my feet and makes sure I'm steady. "That I did, *a ghra*. Now, how about we go home? Ye have family and friends worried sick and waitin' on word."

I hug him once more and cup his face in both my hands. "I missed your face."

He winks at me and chuckles. "I missed yers too."

The flutter in my chest isn't a surprise. I let Bruin out, and he takes form next to Sloan. While I run back to collect Brendan's tapestry, my boy gives Sloan a bear hug. "Good to see ye, sham."

"Glad to find ye. I see ye took good care of our girl."

"It's a full-time job, but I try."

Sloan chuckles and curls me into his shoulder when I return. "Don't I know it."

Together we head back to where Calum and Kevin are standing with Nikon, and I introduce him to Yaya and Papu. Then, I turn to the guy in jeans and a black hoodie.

Nikon gestures at the new arrival. "Fi, this is my cousin, Alec."

"The time-shift cousin, I presume."

Alec bows his head. "At your service. I've heard great things about you and your family."

"Thanks for coming to get us."

"My pleasure. Papu called me months ago to give me a heads up. He wanted to make things right he wasn't able to fix at the time."

Right… The Papu standing before us now would know how long Hecate tortures us before returning us home. This way, the power is taken out of her hands. Time is a little mind-bendy.

"Much appreciated. Are you good to return or do you have a turnaround time you need to rest?"

He shakes his head. "The sooner, the better for me. I get a bit of a time hangover when I go back this far."

"Okay, then we won't dawdle." I hug Helene and Nikon senior. "Thank you for everything. It was so good to meet you. We couldn't have asked for kinder hosts during a difficult time."

Nikon hugs his gran and says goodbye, then raises one finger and snaps out.

Sloan looks at me, wondering.

"He's likely gone to say one last goodbye to his mom. He'll be right back."

The sad realization dawns in Sloan's eyes. Returning to our time means he'll never see his mom or his gran again.

I nod. Yeah, it's super sad for him to leave them.

When Nikon returns, he's not as sad as I expect. "Let's go home." He wraps his arm around the back of me to pat Sloan's shoulder. "Thanks for coming for us, Irish. It means a lot that you'd search the world and time to find us."

Sloan chuckles. "Fer her, yes. That yer here too…that's just a coincidence."

I burst out laughing because he's obviously joking. "Harsh."

Nikon laughs and pats his chest. "You wound me, man."

I pat my chest and Bruin joins me. With him in place, Brenny's tapestry in my arms, and Sloan, Nikon, Calum, and Kevin at my sides, I'm truly ready to go home.

"Take us home, Alec."

Alec connects with us, and in the span of two heartbeats, we move from standing with Papu and Yaya under the back portico of the Tsambikos villa to standing in the same place years later. Papu is still there, but the woman next to him isn't Yaya.

Logically, I understand no one can expect the man to hold a torch for his first wife for eternity, but it's hard not to feel a little betrayed on her behalf.

"Fiona." Papu steps in. "Did it work? Was the timing right? Nikon's free, and you were trying to figure out Hecate's intentions to bring you back?"

I nod and squeeze his hand. "The timing was perfect."

Nikon senior turns to his namesake and presses his hand over his heart. "Welcome to the first day of the rest of your life, *agori mou.*"

Nikon hugs his granda and slaps his back. "Thank you for everything, Papu. Did you always know?"

"Didn't I always tell you there would come a day when your situation would change, and you'd enjoy living again?"

"Yes, but I thought that was a pep talk, not you hinting about an outcome you knew was coming."

"What does it matter?" Andromeda rushes out of the house. She hugs her brother, then Calum and Kevin, and moves to me. "You're here, and you're safe and free from that bitch for good."

As she steps back, she looks at me in my warrior leathers. "Damn, girlfriend. You look sexy fierce in these."

I chuckle. "Nikon snapped to Rome after our first day of trials and got me dressed for the part. My yoga pants and cotton tank didn't fare well against stone gargoyle warriors and demented mole men."

"No. I suppose not."

"Are you guys good from here?" Alec asks. "I have a wicked travel aura bursting in my vision, and in about five minutes I'll be puking. If someone doesn't mind taking me home—"

"I have you." Nikon jogs over to his cousin. "Fi, show Sloan the view. I'll be back in five."

Nikon snaps out, and I slip my arm through Sloan's and tug him toward the cliff. "It's so beautiful, isn't it?"

When Sloan doesn't say anything in return, I turn to find him looking at me. "Stunning."

I roll my eyes. "You always do that."

"It's always true." He opens his arms, and I hug him again, this time without panic and excitement.

It's a simple exchange of affection, but it's exactly what I need to set my world right again. "Thank you for coming to get me."

"I've told ye before, Fi. There's nowhere I won't follow to see ye safe home."

"Thank the goddess for that."

We stay like that for a moment longer until Nikon whistles and waves us in. "Anyone want to get home to their beds?"

I ease back and send Sloan a lascivious look. "Yes, please."

His chuckle is sweet and sexy. "Ye'll have to fend off yer family before we get any alone time. We've all been ravin' mad, lookin' for ye."

"Right. Okay, I'll assure them I'm perfectly fine and promise them a play-by-play after I catch my breath. And by catch my breath, I mean—"

"Och, ye haven't been gone so long that I don't know what ye mean, *a ghra*. Consider me on board with whatever ye want whenever we can get a moment alone to do it."

"Good answer, hotness. I appreciate your dedication. Now, let's go home."

CHAPTER TWENTY-TWO

Nikon brings us home, and the moment we materialize in the living room of our house, it's obvious someone texted the fam jam and told them we were on the way. Manx stands on his hind paws, and I snuggle him in and scrub his fur. "Hey, Puss. I missed you."

"We missed ye right back."

Da cuts in and pulls me against his chest. Cupping the back of my head, he lets out a long breath I'm sure he's been holding for days. "Are ye all right, *mo chroi?* Ye had us in a state of worry once again."

I chuckle. "We're fine. I'd like to point out that this time the unexpected disappearance had nothing to do with me. This was all Hecate and her stalker fixation on Nikon. I was an innocent bystander swept away in the tide of crazy."

Dillan pulls back from bumping knuckles with the Greek and arches a dark brow. "You have a goddess stalking you?"

"Not anymore." Nikon is grinning like a fool. "Fi and Calum took her on and beat her down."

"Take no prisoners," Calum says.

"Damn straight." I meet his fist with a bump.

Kevin picks up Daisy and gives her some love. "It was a little nerve-racking taking it in from the sidelines though."

Nikon nods. "Still, it was something to see."

"I bet it was." Dillan grins. "I'm envisioning a slow-motion pillow fight. Am I close?"

I laugh. "No, nothing like that."

Andromeda chuffs and shakes her head. "That bitch has held him under her thumb since he was seventeen years old."

"But no more." Nikon reaches over, pulls me to his side, and kisses the side of my head. "Fi and Calum challenged her claim on me and won my freedom. They slew the beasts, took on the evil queen, and rescued me from a life of isolation in the tall tower."

"Noice." Emmet winks at me and smacks Calum's arm. "Well done, Team Cumhaill."

I slide my foot back and make a quick curtsy. "Thank you. In return, Nikon got me these badass leathers."

"You look fucking spank, baby girl," Calum says. "Congrats, Greek. We're happy for you."

Cue a round of celebratory hugs for Nikon from my brothers and Da.

When the excitement dies down, Da looks at his watch and points at Emmet. "We need to leave in ten. Get dressed and get to the car or ye'll miss yer ride."

Emmet gives me a parting hug and jogs for the stairs. "Work. Work. Work."

Calum is kissing Daisy and nods at something she says. "Daisy would like a little snuggle, Greek. She was worried about you."

I chuckle about that. Calum's animal companion skunk is more worried about Nikon than me? That's gratitude for you.

Nikon extends his hands and accepts the fuzzy lump of love into his arms. It's obvious the two of them have their own thing going on, and I'm glad. Nikon needs as many love connections as he can get. Keeping people at a distance over the entirety of his very long life has cost him.

My phone is *binging* with notifications every couple of minutes, so I take a sec and catch up.

I send a quick message to the "Fi is not dead" WhatsApp group my family and friends put together and hit send. Then I skim through and send a heart emoji to Myra, a smiley to Suede, and a swirly poop to answer Liam's question about how I enjoyed my latest adventure.

When I've sent those, the phone rings in my hand. The haunting African tones of the *Lion King* hit the airwaves, and I send an apologetic look to Sloan. At this rate, there's no telling when we'll get to be alone.

"Hey, Garnet. What's up?"

"Glad you're not dead, Lady Druid."

"Thanks. Me too. As much fun as it wasn't, I'm looking forward to getting out of gladiatorial leathers."

He chuckles. "Of course, you are. In a time when you could be swathed in flowing, sleeveless gowns, you're wearing gladiator leathers."

"Hey, I tried the flowing gown routine. Let's just say it didn't end well."

"For you or the gown?"

I snort. "For the gown. I kicked ass."

"Of course, you did." There's no missing the deep undertone of pride in his amusement. As much as Garnet plays me off as the thorn in the lion's paw, he secretly lurrrves me and enjoys being along on the wild ride that is my life.

"So, were you checking on me, or was there another reason you called?"

"Bit of both. I wanted to check in and tell you that despite there being a Guild Governor's meeting in the morning, I'm letting both you and Nikon off the hook. In fact, as your team leader on Team Trouble, I'm giving you both a week off."

"Sweet. Thanks. I will be spending the entire time lounging in my bed."

The deep chuckle on the other end of the line hints that he's not surprised. "I only ask that you take a moment to call Myra at some point. She worries."

"Cross my heart."

"All right. Don't let me keep you. Be well."

"Thanks. I'll try."

When I get back to the gathering, Calum has his pants off, and Sloan is frowning at the wound. "I'll text my father and see if he'll come to look at it. I could take you there in a few days, but I'd rather not wait."

"I'll get him if he's able to come," Nikon says.

"Text Tad too and see if he'll come. He should get a feel of where we are in case we need Order backup at a moment's notice."

Sloan nods. "Good idea. Are ye okay with that, Greek?"

"Sounds good. Text me the time and place, and I'll get them and deliver them here." I give him the good news about skipping the Guild meeting in the morning and the week off, and he takes Andromeda home to relax.

Kevin takes Calum up to their room. Dillan and Aiden head next door. As the living room clears out, I release Bruin and give him fair warning. "There will be sex, Bear. Flee if you must."

His deep chuckle makes me laugh. "Och, I must. Manx, Daisy, and Doc. How about we turn on the fireplace in the man cave and I tell ye about ancient Greece?"

The companions trot off as a furry little gang of compatriots, and I smile. "What's this? A quiet house? Privacy? Can it be?"

The moment his arms come around me, we materialize in our room. That's my guy.

Why waste time walking when you can *poof*?

I tilt my head back and give him access to my throat while I undo the button of his jeans and shove his pants down his thighs.

"I missed you, hotness. We didn't get to finish our romantic weekend."

"No time like the present." He nips my jaw. "Although, I'm not feelin' all that romantic at the moment."

"Fine by me. You do you, Mackenzie."

As an early riser, it's unheard of for Sloan to lay in bed past seven. He makes it to eight-thirty the next morning before he can't take it any longer. "We haven't gotten around to breakfast, or showers, or getting dressed, or checkin' on yer brother. Nikon will be here with Da within the hour, and I'd like his first visit to our home to shine a favorable light on the life we're makin' fer ourselves."

I laugh at how uptight he gets. He's a neat freak. The house is spotless, and he couldn't look disheveled if he didn't shave or shower for months.

"Fine, you go have your shower, and I'll get up and pull myself together." My words come out less convincing than I mean them to.

"Don't lie to the man who loves ye most."

"Adulting sucks."

Sloan chuckles and presses a kiss to the small of my back. "There now. That's better. Now, up ye get. We can't live on love alone."

"It would be fun to try though."

"It would at that." He grunts and rolls to his feet, holding his hand out to help me up.

I wave away the help and snuggle my face into my pillow. "You're first in the shower. That means I get five more minutes. I missed King Henry."

"King Henry will be right here when we're finished with my Da and yer brother's wound. He's not goin' anywhere. He hasn't gone anywhere in four hundred years." Sloan grabs my feet and tugs me toward the edge of the bed.

I squeal and flip over, grabbing for the blankets and mattress for a hold. I get nowhere. On the edge of the bed, I sit up and huff. "That was rude. Can't a girl laze about naked for a few hours after battling her way back to her beloved?"

Sloan chuckles. "While I love that I am the beloved in that scenario, no. Yer worried about the venom in Calum's wound, and Da will soon be here to examine him. I would appreciate a united front on his first home visit."

"You are so damned responsible." I roll my eyes as I head to the washroom to get cleaned up and ready to go.

After four days of salt air and heat, my hair is defying all styling products and embracing a wild disregard for the laws of gravity. There's no helping it. In the end, I clip it back and pull on the first jeans, sweatshirt, and lumberjack socks combo I come to.

"Good enough. Let's go."

Sloan blinks at me and chuckles. "If yer sure."

I hold my hands out to the side and look down at the *What Not To Wear* ensemble I've pulled together. "Yep, I'm sure. It's a take me or leave me kinda morning. Let's go."

Sloan laughs harder. "All right. I'll not argue."

"Good. If you're embarrassed to be seen with me, just say so, and I'll crawl back into bed."

He shakes his head. "Never in a million years. All righty then. If you have no regrets, I sure don't. Let's go."

"All hail the conquering heroine," Myra says when I arrive at the bookstore a week later. She rounds the counter to hug me at the same moment Imari runs in from the back.

"Auntie Fi!"

"Imari Rose!" She giggles as I call her name and swing her up into my arms. "I missed you, girlie."

"I missed you more."

I shake my head. "No. I missed *you* more."

"No. I missed *you* more."

Myra rolls her vertically-slit eyes and shakes her head. "No way. You two aren't going to start that again. I still have a headache from the last time."

I set Imari on her feet and ruffle her hair. "Fun police."

Myra smooths Imari's ruffled hair and chuckles. "Imari, baby, I have some work stuff I need help with from Auntie Fi. Can you read Leniya another story while we get that done?"

She nods. "He likes the one about the bunny with the floppy ears who hangs upside down in the tree to make his ears go straight."

"*Leo the Lop*. I like that one too. That's one of Jackson's favorites."

Imari blows me a kiss, and I catch it and put it in my pocket to save for later. When the little bear shifter is gone, I turn to her mom and smile. "So, what's up? Am I working?"

She shakes her head. "Not really, but you can help me shelve books while we chat if you don't mind?"

"I don't mind. I'm the one who left you running this place by yourself, yet again."

Myra chuckles. "I ran it by myself for the past fifty years. It's not an imposition. If you're kidnapped, there's not much to do about it."

"True story."

"So, tell me about Nikon and Hecate and everything you've been up to."

It takes a half-hour to fill Myra in on everything, and when I finish, she looks like she has something to say. "Go ahead. Spill it. What are you trying not to say?"

She lifts one shoulder and slides one of the new goblin texts into place. "Maybe it's not my place to say."

"*Buuut* that's never stopped you before, so go for it. What's on your mind?"

"I don't think Hecate was altogether wrong in thinking that Nikon is in love with you. He plays like he's teasing, but I see the way he looks at you when you're not aware."

I pick up the next book on the pile and sigh. "I adore Nikon, and I know him as well if not better than he knows himself. He might think he has a thing for me, but he doesn't. His feelings have been locked away so long that I'm the first person he's connected with in centuries. You watch, now that he's free to date and fall in love, his affections will shift to someone open to love him back."

Myra arches a brow and casts me a skeptical look. "If you say so."

"I do. Besides, I happen to know he's fooling around with other people behind closed doors. He was just lonely and trapped. He'll find his soul mate."

"I hope so. He's a good guy."

I find the spot on the shelf for the next book and insert it. "He is. Someone amazing will snatch him up, and I'll be the first one in line to congratulate them. His destiny is just beginning."

"Speaking of destiny, how goes it with you and Sloan's parents? His dad came to check on Calum, didn't he?"

I lean against the bookshelf and cross my arms. "Yeah. He's been good. He double-checked Calum's leg and says that while the skin and incision are pretty gnarly from the venom, the leaf Dionysus gave him to chew seems to have cleared up the poison."

"Excellent. That's great news. So, he's been good as a healer. How has he been to Sloan?"

"Supportive. Polite. There's obviously still some stiffness and sore feelings there, but he's trying."

"And his mother?"

"Janet's another story altogether. She can't see past her insecurities to realize Sloan doesn't need her or his father or me to make decisions. He's a big boy and knows what he wants."

"I don't know why they'd find that so surprising. He's one of the most intelligent people I know."

"Exactly. Now that he's piecing together his passion for antiquities and safeguarding magical items, he's really excited about putting together his shrine."

Myra laughs and shelves another book. "Well, of course, he is. What's a Keeper of the Shrine apprentice do without a shrine?"

"Fall in love and move across the ocean?" I laugh and check the time on my Fitbit. "Speaking of which...."

"Do you have to go?"

I nod. "Emmet, Kevin, and Calum are property-hunting with the Greek. Nikon's looking to rent a studio space to share with Kev. He's going to get back into the arts, and I suggested he could pass along some techniques to Kevin."

"That's a great idea. Oh, and here." She sets down the book she has in hand and jogs back to the counter. Pulling out a gift box wrapped with a blue ribbon, she hands it to me. "An engagement gift for the boys."

"You didn't have to do that."

She winks. "I know, but I wanted to. Take the time to celebrate love. It's not much, but I think they'll like it."

"I'm sure they will. Thank you." I raise one arm and hug her before I wave into the back room. "Bye, monkey. Love you."

Imari runs up to hug me. "Love you too. Will you come to my house and bring Jackson and Meggie to play with Contessa McSparkles?"

"I absolutely will. I'll talk to Kinu about it as soon as I see her and we'll set something up. Maybe for the weekend?" I check with Myra, and she nods. "Okay, leave it with me, and we'll see what we can do."

CHAPTER TWENTY-THREE

I set the gift box on my SUV's front seat and hit the ignition button. The engine rumbles to life, and I check my mirrors before pulling into traffic.

The address Nikon sent me is already programmed into my GPS, so I follow the instructions. After parking in the private lot behind the building, I meet the guys in the lobby.

Looking around, I frown. "Why does this building feel so familiar?"

Nikon grins. "Because the Team Trouble Batcave is on the tenth floor."

"Oh, I've never come in the front door. Hilarious." I text Sloan so he knows we're in the same building when he and Garnet finish with their meeting about a Toronto archive location.

"So, you're thinking about renting out part of one of the floors for a studio?" I ask Nikon.

He winks. "Something like that. Come. I'll show you the space, and you can tell me what you think."

Nikon takes us into the elevator and hits the button for the ninth floor. The power of the hydraulics pull us into motion with a whispered *hiss* and soon after the quiet whine of mechanics, the doors open.

"Ninth floor, art, sculpture, and divine muses being released," Emmet says.

"Sounds perfect." I step out to check out the space. Like the office entrance one floor up, the elevator core lets us out, and we face a frosted glass wall with an access door into the suite.

Nikon taps a keycard against the security pad and opens things up. Unlike upstairs, where there are offices along the outside walls and a conference room in the center, this floor is a wide-open, unfinished space.

"I'm not sure it's big enough." Emmet chuckles at the vast interior.

Kevin laughs, wandering inside. "Wow, with the windows on three sides, there's certainly enough light."

"It lacks the eau de feline urine ambiance of your other studio," Calum teases.

"I'm willing to overlook that as a drawback," Kevin retorts, his gaze alight. "Holy shit, Greek. What would our rent be?"

Nikon waggles his eyebrows. "I negotiated a great deal with the owner. The guy's not only a shrewd businessman. He's also a lover of art. It took some doing, but I whittled him down to get us the best deal evah."

"Which is what?" Kev asks.

I see the delight in Nikon's gaze and chuckle that they haven't clued in yet. "I'm sure a kiss would do it."

Kev looks at Nikon and me, then Calum and I laugh when they all catch up.

"You bought the floor for us?" Kevin's jaw drops.

Nikon chuckles and waves that away. "Nah, I bought the whole building. I figured with Andromeda and Fi involved upstairs, us needing a space for art and Sloan needing a space for archiving, and us each having gym memberships to have a place to train…why not put everything in one place?"

"Why not, indeed?" I kiss his cheek. "What's a couple of million among friends? Very thoughtful, Greek, but I've told you before, you do too much."

He shakes his head. "And I've told you before, Fi. After everything you and yours have done for me, I'm just getting started."

There's no convincing him that he's done enough, so I accept the gesture as he meant. "You're a great man, Nikon Tsambikos. I consider myself lucky to call you family."

It takes a couple of weeks to get set up on the floors of the Acropolis, which is what Nikon and I decide to call his newest piece of real estate. In ancient Greek, the term acropolis means "high city" and is a stronghold built on elevated ground. We thought the name made perfect sense.

The tenth floor is home to the Batcave, and we've pretty much settled in there.

The ninth is the Studio of Art, Sculpture, and Sexiness, which they reverse-engineered to call their space SASS. No surprise there.

The eighth will be our training center, which we currently refer to as Badass Bootcamp, and once the springy floor is in, we'll start moving in training equipment.

Sloan picked lucky number seven for the Shrine of Toronto's Objects and Antiquities, or STOA. Technically a stoa was a covered porch in ancient Greece, so not a slam dunk, but it's a Greek word so we went with it.

We're focused on the seventh today. Sloan has been working with a private security firm all week, installing metal shielding sheets to cover the windows, ceiling, and floors. The entire floor is essentially a huge, metal vault.

It seems a shame to block out all the sunlight, but Sloan insists the shields will protect the objects from sunlight as well as anyone thinking about coming in through the glass to gain access. He also had them lined in lead to eliminate magical fae access as well as heat vision.

I'm not sure who he thinks will use heat vision to steal old brooches and pottery, but it's his thing, and he's happy, so I'm happy.

"Thanks so much fer all yer help." He ushers the last of the workmen out the door. "I'll be sure to call yer boss and express my thanks fer a job well done."

When the door closes, he winks at me and rubs his hands together. "Now the fun part. Everybody ready?"

Emmet, Dillan, Da, and I nod. "Dora wanted to help too. Nikon's picking her up now."

The words are still hanging in the air as the outer door *beeps* and Nikon and Dora stride in. "Are we late?"

Sloan shakes his head, picking up a prybar from on top of a wooden crate. After forcing the lid free from its fastenings, he and Nikon shift it off and set it aside. Emmet and I peer into the container and select a couple of pieces of raw stone.

"This is really pretty." I admire the gray striations and rose deposits in the rock, running my finger over the natural surface.

"It's a strong metamorphic gneiss," Sloan says.

"Uh-huh." How cute is it that my boyfriend gets excited about the strength and makeup of rocks? "And pretty too."

It takes ten minutes with all of us toting rock from the crate to line the walls, and when that's finished, we're ready.

Sloan kneels on the floor. I do the same beside him a few feet away with Emmet on my other side, then Da, and so on.

"Wall of Stone." Sloan expands the stones on the floor to rise and cover the wall in a sheet of glistening rock.

"Wall of Stone." I do the same, smoothing my rocks up the wall to join his.

It takes us a solid hour of working the room and casting our druid abilities before we finish the job. Dora casts an impenetrability spell on the floor and ceiling, and we're ready to start bolting in the shelving.

"There isn't much to store on shelves yet," Sloan says.

"But boy are we ready for an influx of ancient antiquities." Emmet grins.

Calum and Kevin join the fun. "Wow, it's hard to believe it's the same building as SASS and Bootcamp."

I know exactly what they mean. With the stone walls and sconce lighting, it's more like Ali Baba's cave than a Toronto low-rise. Still, it suits Sloan and his calling perfectly, and that's all that matters.

As Dora adds her magical touches, Da keeps her company and shoots the shit. Nikon and Emmet head up one floor to work on the training center and I take advantage of the lull in activity.

I wrap my arms around Sloan's waist and hug him from behind. "I'm proud of you, hotness. You're going to rock this Toronto shrine stuff."

He turns in my arms. "I've been training for it with yer granda my entire life. I always knew I loved shrine keepin'. I just never expected to be able to have that anywhere else."

"Well, I'm glad you can because I wouldn't want you to be anywhere else."

He kisses my forehead and smiles. "Neither would I. Here is exactly where I was meant to be."

I might be biased, but I couldn't agree more.

CHAPTER TWENTY-FOUR

"I can't believe you hung out with Dionysus for five days and never once got drunk or naked."

I burst out laughing and hand two bags of ice to Emmet. "You realize we were fighting for our lives back here, right? It wasn't fun, although Dionysus was a fun guy. Everything we faced was a necessary step to free Nikon and get back home to you dumbasses."

Dillan and Aiden are both on ladders with drills in their hands, so I try to focus. "An inch higher on your side, Aiden. Yeah, that's perfect."

The two of them set the wooden frame in place and drill in the brackets. When they finish, they climb down and step over to stand with me and check things out.

"It's fucking awesome," Dillan says.

"Aye, it is at that, my boy." Da rests his arm across Auntie Shannon's shoulder and stares up at Brendan's tapestry. "Ye did a fine job, Kev. It's perfect."

Calum grabs Kevin's jaw and plants one on his cheek. The first SASS project for Kevin and Nikon was to design a frame for

Brendan's tapestry. They drew up plans, checked with us, and built it in their new studio space.

Nikon is taking me up on the idea to teach Kev some of the ancient art techniques of the times he lived through, and I can't wait to see what they create together.

"I think that calls for a toast." Liam smiles up at the woven representation of my brother's life.

"Absolutely," Calum agrees from behind the bar set up on the kitchen island. "Everyone, grab your shot glass."

Jägermeister was Brendan's favorite, so there's no option of what we're drinking. Calum and Kev pour them out and pass them around, and we're ready.

When everyone settles, Da lifts his shot glass. "To Brendan. Ye may not be with us in body, but ye'll always be with us in spirit and soul."

"Hells yeah," Aiden affirms.

With that in mind, I stride across the open concept front room and open Mam's curio. Inside the family photo album Da gifted me with when I moved here, I pull out Brendan's New Year's Eve predictions for last year.

The room falls quiet, and I look around to see if everyone's on the same page. The reassuring nods spur my courage.

I open the envelope and pull out the piece of paper I wasn't ready to read two months ago. "I, Brendan Cumhaill, being of polluted and slightly perverted mind—"

"That sounds about right," Liam interjects.

We all chuckle.

"—wager that in the year to come, I shall finally kick Jackson's ass in Hungry Hungry Hippos, expose a ring of corruption in a takedown that will be talked about for all time, take a trip to lands unknown and inspire all you sorry sacks to worship me for the god of groove I am. Shakira forevah!"

I smile. "Good one, bro."

Da nods and smiles up at the tapestry. "To Brendan."

When the emotion of toasting Brendan's permanent place in our home dies down, the party gears up. Garnet and Myra arrive first, followed by Anyx and Zuzanna. About fifteen minutes after that, Andromeda and John Maxwell come in. Then Suede, Zxata, and Dora. Finally, Tad *poofs* in with the heirs of the Nine Families.

The gang's all here.

Aiden introduces Kinu to everyone. Then she takes Imari next door to have a sleepover with Jackson and Meggie. I assured them that Mrs. Graham across the road could babysit, but Garnet insisted on providing the sitters for the night. Apparently, tactical military training and mastery of three martial art disciplines is a must for entertaining three crazy kids.

"I'm so glad you're home safe." Suede hugs me. "I know we should be getting used to this sort of thing, but still, we worry."

I take a long drink of my whiskey and smile. "This is fantastic, Greek. Thank you."

Nikon blows me a kiss from behind the bar, his bottle of aged whiskey a housewarming gift that has lain in wait for the actual housewarming party. With everything going on, I figured the drunken festivities I promised Dionysus would count.

With that in mind, I rub the pendant hanging around my neck. "Hey, god of pleasure and festivities. If you're not too drunk and busy with hedonistic ecstasy, come join the fun."

"I thought you'd never ask."

I giggle as he appears beside me. He's dressed in stylish ripped jeans, a white button-down that's tucked in but unbuttoned, and a kickass belt buckle. "Damn, dude. You're smokin' hot in modern clothes."

He grins and bites his lip. "Any chance you're finished with your druid lover and have tossed Nikky to the curb?"

I roll my eyes. "No and no."

"And you're still a monogamy girl, I suppose."

"She is." Sloan slides in to join us. "Nice to meet you. I'm the druid lover, Sloan Mackenzie."

Dionysus arches a brow. "Yes, you are. Nicely done, Red." He waggles his chestnut brows and grins. "What's our stance on polyamory?"

Nikon joins the fun, chuckling. "Forget it. I've been whistling that tune to crickets for months. They're a closed door, those two."

"More's the pity," Dionysus says. "Have we any open doors in this group?"

Nikon reaches around the guy's shoulder and grins. "Come with me. I'll introduce you around."

When the two of them leave, I chuckle and get back to Myra. She's shaking her head at me.

"What's that look for?" I ask.

She tips her glass to her lips and shakes her head again. "Oh, nothing. We'll talk later."

Sloan arches a brow and turns to meet my undivided gaze. "What was that about?"

"I haven't the foggiest."

He chuckles. "So, you and Nikon and Dionysus in ancient Greece for five full days and nights…and you weren't tempted to taste the forbidden fruit?"

I shake my head. "Not even a little. Are they sexy? Sure. Did I want anything other than what I have with you? Nope. Not a bit." Easing back, I pull my Claddagh band off my right hand and move it to my left. "I figure we may not be engaged, but there's no reason to leave any doors open. You're it for me, broody man. You're my one."

Sloan grins and moves his ring too. "Yer my one, too."

I kiss him and smile out at the gathering of friends and family. "Life is good."

"That it is, *a ghra*. That it is."

Thank you for reading – ***An Immortal's Pain.***

While the story is fresh in your mind, and as a favor to Michael and me, click HERE and tell other readers what you thought.

A star rating and/or even one sentence can mean so much to readers deciding whether or not to try out a book or new author.

And if you loved it, continue with the Chronicles of an Urban Druid and claim your copy of book seven:

A Shaman's Power

DICTIONARY

Slán leat – health/safety be with you
Agape mou – my love
Agori mou – my boy
Paidi mou – my child
Gliko mou – my sweet
Carissima – sweetness/honey (female)

NEXT IN SERIES

The story continues with A Shaman's Power, available at Amazon and through Kindle Unlimited.

Claim your copy today!

AUTHOR NOTES - AUBURN TEMPEST

WRITTEN APRIL 10, 2021

Taking Fi and Nikon on an adventure to ancient Greece was amazeballs.

The historic reality, as well as the mythology of Ancient Greece and Rome, have always been passions of mine.

I'm not sure how many art projects, essays, and book reports I did on Pompeii, the eruption of Vesuvius, the life of Caesar, the pottery and architecture of Roman civilization, etc. This is a painting I did for Art History class many, many years ago.

I even took years of Latin in high school and can still say important things like, 'The dog is in the street,' and 'Mother is in the garden singing,' and 'Father is in the study writing.'

That's one of the beautiful things about this career. As an author, we can steer the lives of our characters in directions that interest us. I hope you enjoyed the adventure.

Next up is A Shaman's Power. You'll meet a couple of new characters as well as spend time with many of the usual suspects as Fi learns more about Fionn and her destiny as the chosen leader of the modern-day Fianna warrior.

Blessed be,
Auburn Tempest

AUTHOR NOTES - MICHAEL ANDERLE

WRITTEN APRIL 13, 2021

Thank you for not only reading these author notes, but you know, the whole story before them, too!

IMPORTANT NEWS…

Which I will mention at the bottom of these author notes somewhere. Probably in a riddle…if I can think of one by that time.

AROUND THE WORLD

As many of you know, I run (now) an entertainment company that has a publishing company as a part of it.

Actually, I'm not sure many of you knew that.

Here is the Cliffs Notes version:

2015 – I started writing and publishing a series called *The Kurtherian Gambit* in November. I released four books in November and December.

2016 – I built a company focused on publishing one author—me—with aspirations to publish others AND become an entertainment company. This was a very large, bodacious, hairy goal since I was only publishing one author, and as such, my knowledge was pretty minimal.

2016 - December – I release other authors (2) and their stories in my Kurtherian Universe.

2017 - MORE AUTHORS! MORE STORIES! LMBPN Audio is born with the first release of the Kurtherian Gambit series in audio via LMBPN Audio.

2018 – More stories! Other genres, and now we have published other authors for the first time (I think it was 2018.) We are talking with a German company about translations.

2019 – LMBPN focuses on growing massively by putting out between twenty-two and thirty-five books a month in English. In January, we release our first German translation of *Death Becomes Her.*

2020 – We look at all the broken pieces in the company and start fixing what we broke in 2019. We now have approximately nine hundred titles in our company, we have published over fifty authors, LMBPN has published over 230 audiobooks, and over 350 other audio titles have been licensed. We are one of the fastest-growing Sci-Fi / Fantasy imprints in Germany.

2021 – I hire a President to take over LMBPN Publishing, Worldwide. I change my title to Chief Creative Officer of LMBPN Publishing, and now we have fifteen series in production in German. Further, we announce the LMBPN International group includes Dutch, French, Italian, and Portuguese.

Ok, now you are caught up.

Because of the work above, I now talk to people around the world. As a matter of fact, Auburn Tempest (Jenny Madore) lives in Canada.

No bonus points for guessing why we decided to use Canada as the home base for Fi's amazing and fun family.

Anyway, the point of this is, I speak to people around the world and find out what is going on with the COVID situation in their area. For instance, my Canadian friend is still in a really tight lockdown in Canada right now.

I don't know how she deals with it, frankly. I am considering going stark raving mad in sympathy with her plight.

That's a thing collaborators do, right? We look at the situation our partner is dealing with and lose it?

Perhaps it isn't a thing, but it most likely should be. I'll wear the t-shirt.

SHUT UP MIKE AND TELL US THE IMPORTANT NEWS!

So, I'm lying down on my daybed in my office, reading the latest 20,000 words from Jenny and laughing my ass off. The family is <redacted> while Fi is <redacted>, and then our favorite Greek says "<redacted>."

Then, I realize I'm reading book 08, and frankly, knowing it's supposed to be the last book is not making me a happy reader.

It makes me a sad reader. Sad enough (as a fan of the story) that I go virtually knocking on Auburn's door and slide out the idea that maybe she might consider doing…four more?

Would that be ok?

So, unofficially (unless you are reading these notes way late and you already know the outcome), we are working with Auburn Tempest (Jenny Madore) to expand this series one more time out to twelve books.

Which pleases me.

Now, if YOU would be so kind as to send her a note, encourage her on Facebook, or leave a review where you mention your support for another four books…

I'm not above emotional twisting whatsoever, just saying.

Feel free to encourage Jenny to live a wonderful life…and write more FI. Perhaps not in that order;-)

I'm joking. Joking! I'm well aware that passionate readers occasionally push us writers when we are already pushing hard ourselves.

But…as a reader, would you enjoy a chance to put something

like this into the back of a series to encourage a series to go further?

I mean, if John Ringo would let me, I'd bug the ever-loving @#%!#% out of him to push for more books in one of his series.

And don't get me started on a few other series I'd love more books in.

Maybe as a publisher, my super-power will be to ring those writers up and see if they have any interest in "Just one more book…or maybe four?"

Ad Aeternitatem,

Michael Anderle

ABOUT AUBURN TEMPEST

Auburn Tempest is a multi-genre novelist giving life to Urban Fantasy, Paranormal, and Sci-Fi adventures. Under the pen name, JL Madore, she writes in the same genres but in full romance, sexy-steamy novels. Whether Romance or not, she loves to twist Alpha heroes and kick-ass heroines into chaotic, hilarious, fast-paced, magical situations and make them really work for their happy endings.

Auburn Tempest lives in the Greater Toronto Area, Canada with her dear, wonderful hubby of 30 years and a menagerie of family, friends, and animals.

BOOKS BY AUBURN TEMPEST

Auburn Tempest - Urban Fantasy Action/Adventure

Chronicles of an Urban Druid

Book 1 – A Gilded Cage

Book 2 – A Sacred Grove

Book 3 – A Family Oath

Book 4 – A Witch's Revenge

Book 5 – A Broken Vow

Book 6 – A Druid Hexed

Book 7 – An Immortal's Pain

Misty's Magick and Mayhem Series – Written by Carolina Mac/Contributed to by Auburn Tempest

Book 1 – School for Reluctant Witches

Book 2 – School for Saucy Sorceresses

Book 3 – School for Unwitting Wiccans

Book 4 – Nine St. Gillian Street

Book 5 – The Ghost of Pirate's Alley

Book 6 – Jinxing Jackson Square

Book 7 – Flame

Book 8 – Frost

Book 9 – Nocturne

Book 10 – Luna

Book 11 – Swamp Magic

Exemplar Hall – Co-written with Ruby Night

Prequel – Death of a Magi Knight

Book 1 – Drafted by the Magi

Book 2 – Jesse and the Magi Vault

Book 3 – The Makings of a Magi

If you enjoy my writing and read sexy/steamy romance, my pen name for the books I write Paranormal and Fantasy Romance is JL Madore. You can find me on Amazon HERE.

CONNECT WITH THE AUTHORS

Connect with Auburn

Amazon, Facebook, Newsletter

Web page – www.jlmadore.com

Email – AuburnTempestWrites@gmail.com

Connect with Michael Anderle and sign up for his email list here:

Website: http://lmbpn.com

Email List: http://lmbpn.com/email/

Social Media:

https://www.facebook.com/LMBPNPublishing

https://twitter.com/MichaelAnderle

https://www.instagram.com/lmbpn_publishing/

https://www.bookbub.com/authors/michael-anderle

OTHER LMBPN PUBLISHING BOOKS

CPSIA information can be obtained
at www.ICGtesting.com
Printed in the USA
LVHW091118120723
752274LV00020B/280